ROGUE HUNT

&

ENCHANTED HUNT

Applause for L.L. Raand's Midnight Hunters Series

The Midnight Hunt
RWA 2012 VCRW Laurel Wreath winner *Blood Hunt*
Night Hunt
The Lone Hunt

"Raand has built a complex world inhabited by werewolves, vampires, and other paranormal beings…Raand has given her readers a complex plot filled with wonderful characters as well as insight into the hierarchy of Sylvan's pack and vampire clans. There are many plot twists and turns, as well as erotic sex scenes in this riveting novel that keep the pages flying until its satisfying conclusion."—*Just About Write*

"Once again, I am amazed at the storytelling ability of L.L. Raand aka Radclyffe. In *Blood Hunt*, she mixes high levels of sheer eroticism that will leave you squirming in your seat with an impeccable multi-character storyline all streaming together to form one great read."
—*Queer Magazine Online*

"*The Midnight Hunt* has a gripping story to tell, and while there are also some truly erotic sex scenes, the story always takes precedence. This is a great read which is not easily put down nor easily forgotten."—*Just About Write*

"Are you sick of the same old hetero vampire/werewolf story plastered in every bookstore and at every movie theater? Well, I've got the cure to your werewolf fever. *The Midnight Hunt* is first in, what I hope is, a long-running series of fantasy erotica for L.L. Raand (aka Radclyffe)."—*Queer Magazine Online*

"Any reader familiar with Radclyffe's writing will recognize the author's style within *The Midnight Hunt*, yet at the same time it is most definitely a new direction. The author delivers an excellent story here, one that is engrossing from the very beginning. Raand has pieced together an intricate world, and provided just enough details for the reader to become enmeshed in the new world. The action moves quickly throughout the book and it's hard to put down."—*Three Dollar Bill Reviews*

Acclaim for Radclyffe's Fiction

"*Dangerous Waters* is a bumpy ride through a devastating time with powerful events and resolute characters. Radclyffe gives us the strong, dedicated women we love to read in a story that keeps us turning pages until the end."—*Lambda Literary Review*

"Radclyffe's *Dangerous Waters* has the feel of a tense television drama, as the narrative interchanges between hurricane trackers and first responders. Sawyer and Dara butt heads in the beginning as each moves for some level of control during the storm's approach, and the interference of a lovely television reporter adds an engaging love triangle threat to the sexual tension brewing between them."—*RT Book Reviews*

"*Love After Hours*, the fourth in Radclyffe's Rivers Community series, evokes the sense of a continuing drama as Gina and Carrie's slow-burning romance intertwines with details of other Rivers residents. They become part of a greater picture where friends and family support each other in personal and recreational endeavors. Vivid settings and characters draw in the reader…"—*RT Book Reviews*

Secret Hearts "delivers exactly what it says on the tin: poignant story, sweet romance, great characters, chemistry and hot sex scenes. Radclyffe knows how to pen a good lesbian romance."—*LezReviewBooks Blog*

Wild Shores "will hook you early. Radclyffe weaves a chance encounter into all-out steamy romance. These strong, dynamic women have great conversations, and fantastic chemistry."—*The Romantic Reader Blog*

In **2016 RWA/OCC Book Buyers Best award winner for suspense and mystery with romantic elements** *Price of Honor* "Radclyffe is master of the action-thriller series…The old familiar characters are there, but enough new blood is introduced to give it a fresh feel and open new avenues for intrigue."—*Curve Magazine*

In *Prescription for Love* "Radclyffe populates her small town with colorful characters, among the most memorable being Flann's little sister, Margie, and Abby's 15-year-old trans son, Blake…This romantic drama has plenty of heart and soul."—*Publishers Weekly*

2013 RWA/New England Bean Pot award winner for contemporary romance *Crossroads* "will draw the reader in and make her heart ache, willing the two main characters to find love and a life together. It's a story that lingers long after coming to 'the end.'"—*Lambda Literary Review*

In 2012 RWA/FTHRW Lories and RWA HODRW Aspen Gold award winner *Firestorm* "Radclyffe brings another hot lesbian romance for her readers."—*The Lesbrary*

Foreword Review Book of the Year finalist and IPPY silver medalist *Trauma Alert* "is hard to put down and it will sizzle in the reader's hands. The characters are hot, the sex scenes explicit and explosive, and the book is moved along by an interesting plot with well drawn secondary characters. The real star of this show is the attraction between the two characters, both of whom resist and then fall head over heels."—*Lambda Literary Reviews*

Lambda Literary Award Finalist *Best Lesbian Romance 2010* features "stories [that] are diverse in tone, style, and subject, making for more variety than in many, similar anthologies...well written, each containing a satisfying, surprising twist. Best Lesbian Romance series editor Radclyffe has assembled a respectable crop of 17 authors for this year's offering."—*Curve Magazine*

2010 Prism award winner and ForeWord Review Book of the Year Award finalist *Secrets in the Stone* is "so powerfully [written] that the worlds of these three women shimmer between reality and dreams...A strong, must read novel that will linger in the minds of readers long after the last page is turned."—*Just About Write*

In Benjamin Franklin Award finalist *Desire by Starlight* "Radclyffe writes romance with such heart and her down-to-earth characters not only come to life but leap off the page until you feel like you know them. What Jenna and Gard feel for each other is not only a spark but an inferno and, as a reader, you will be washed away in this tumultuous romance until you can do nothing but succumb to it."—*Queer Magazine Online*

Lambda Literary Award winner *Stolen Moments* "is a collection of steamy stories about women who just couldn't wait. It's sex when desire overrides reason, and it's incredibly hot!"—*On Our Backs*

Lambda Literary Award winner *Distant Shores, Silent Thunder* "weaves an intricate tapestry about passion and commitment between lovers. The story explores the fragile nature of trust and the sanctuary provided by loving relationships."—*Sapphic Reader*

Lambda Literary Award Finalist *Justice Served* delivers a "crisply written, fast-paced story with twists and turns and keeps us guessing until the final explosive ending."—*Independent Gay Writer*

Lambda Literary Award finalist *Turn Back Time* "is filled with wonderful love scenes, which are both tender and hot."—*MegaScene*

By L.L. Raand

Midnight Hunters

The Midnight Hunt

Blood Hunt

Night Hunt

The Lone Hunt

The Magic Hunt

Shadow Hunt

By Radclyffe

The Provincetown Tales

Safe Harbor

Beyond the Breakwater

Distant Shores, Silent Thunder

Storms of Change

Winds of Fortune

Returning Tides

Sheltering Dunes

PMC Hospitals Romances

Passion's Bright Fury (prequel)

Fated Love

Night Call

Crossroads

Passionate Rivals

Rivers Community Romances

Against Doctor's Orders

Prescription for Love

Love on Call

Love After Hours

Love to the Rescue

Love on the Night Shift

Honor Series

Above All, Honor

Honor Bound

Love & Honor

Honor Guards

Honor Reclaimed

Honor Under Siege

Word of Honor

Oath of Honor
(First Responders)

Code of Honor

Price of Honor

Cost of Honor

Justice Series

A Matter of Trust (prequel)
Shield of Justice
In Pursuit of Justice

Justice in the Shadows
Justice Served
Justice for All

First Responders Novels

Trauma Alert
Firestorm
Taking Fire

Wild Shores
Heart Stop
Dangerous Waters

Romances

Innocent Hearts
Promising Hearts
Love's Melody Lost
Love's Tender Warriors
Tomorrow's Promise
Love's Masquerade
shadowland
Turn Back Time

When Dreams Tremble
The Lonely Hearts Club
Secrets in the Stone
Desire by Starlight
Homestead
The Color of Love
Secret Hearts

Short Fiction

Collected Stories by Radclyffe
Erotic Interludes: *Change Of Pace*
Radical Encounters

Stacia Seaman and Radclyffe, eds.:
Erotic Interludes Vol. 2–5
Romantic Interludes Vol. 1–2
Breathless: *Tales of Celebration*
Women of the Dark Streets
Amor and More: Love Everafter
Myth & Magic: Queer Fairy Tales

Visit us at www.boldstrokesbooks.com

ROGUE HUNT
&
ENCHANTED HUNT

by

L.L. Raand

2020

ISBN 13: 978-1-63555-946-0

THIS TRADE PAPERBACK ORIGINAL IS PUBLISHED BY
BOLD STROKES BOOKS, INC.
P.O. BOX 249
VALLEY FALLS, NY 12185

FIRST EDITION: SEPTEMBER 2020

CREDITS
EDITOR: RUTH STERNGLANTZ
PRODUCTION DESIGN: STACIA SEAMAN
COVER DESIGN BY SHERI (HINDSIGHTGRAPHICS@GMAIL.COM)

Acknowledgments

Thanks to everyone who pitched in at the last minute to put this story together in one place, two self-contained romantic adventures with Sylvan and Drake, the Timberwolves, and a brand new Pack with its own new Alpha—and new enemies: senior editor Sandy Lowe for rearranging schedules, putting together a great cover, and generally putting up with my midnight hour brainstorms; editors Ruth Sternglantz and Stacia Seaman for somehow fitting this in; and Toni Whitaker for compiling the eBooks in such stellar form to make this paperback possible.

For Lee

Contents

ROGUE HUNT

Chapter One

The silver shadows of predawn gave way to glimmers of gold breaking through the canopy of evergreens, slashing across the forest path. Drake's chest burned with the rush of cold morning air scouring her lungs with every breath. Her heart thundered, shoulders and forelegs pistoning with every stride, paws barely disturbing the soft pine needles and damp soil underfoot as she raced along the narrow trail. Her prey, a small herd of deer that had strayed close to the Compound, bounded out just ahead, an occasional patch of white betraying their location as they tried to outrun her. One trailed behind the others, slowing even more as the chase drew on.

Drake sensed her guards running in the forest, close on either side of her, ready to join in the hunt or protect her from unexpected danger. No matter they were still well within range of the Compound and far from Pack land borders and the risk to her was small—they would not leave her even if ordered. The Alpha had commanded them to guard her, and they would, unto death.

Drake's senses—scent, sight, hearing—her instincts, everything that made her a dominant wolf and a deadly predator focused on her prey, but the nagging uneasiness coiled in her belly never relented. The persistent drumbeat of wrongness pulsed in her blood. With a low growl and a swift shake of her head, she crested a rocky shoulder overlooking a rock-strewn creek with frothing water overflowing its banks. Spring rains had turned the rivers and streams into seething waterfalls. The herd, a small one with several adult does, one herding two fawns ahead of her, was set to cross the stream. The deep water and swirling currents signaled a dangerous creek crossing. The oldest, and the obvious prey, lagged well behind.

Drake raced along the precipice, her footing sure and swift despite the mossy ground and loose shale, and deliberately turned upwind. The deer had known they were hunted, had sensed her chase just as she had sensed their flight, and now they would catch her scent.

Go, flee. And remember to forage at a safe distance next time.

She hunted, but she did not hunger, and she passed up the kill with just a warning to be wary on trails that crossed Pack land. The mother doe hesitated at the water's edge and searched the ridge, her ears flicking. Her gaze met Drake's and held a moment before she nudged her young away from the creek and into the adjacent forest. The rest of the herd followed her and, in an instant, were gone.

Drake settled on her haunches, raised her muzzle to the sky, and howled her joy in the hunt and the fierce, primal claim to all that was hers—this land and the Pack that roamed it. Turning, she trotted back the way she'd come, and at the bottom of the escarpment, three wolves broke from the woods and fell in beside her.

You're slow, she announced across their Pack link.

Jace, the young female dominant recently appointed captain of her personal guard, rumbled unhappily but did not object.

Drake chuckled to herself at the sleek silver and black wolf's discomfort at being a few strides behind her on the run. Sylvan had insisted Drake not run unescorted, and as much as she would have liked to run off her agitation alone, she accepted that as Prima, she had an obligation to the Pack to be safe. That morning she'd needed to run, even though she hadn't needed to hunt. Until Sylvan returned, she could not settle, she could not sleep. Even visiting their young in the nursery had not helped calm her. If she'd stayed in the Compound, her agitation would have spread to every wolf there, and she didn't need half their young warriors squabbling with each other and mated pairs too anxious to carry out their duties. As it was, even with her calming influence, none of them would be completely comfortable until the Alpha returned.

When she'd caught the deer herd's scent, she'd let her wolf ascend and gave chase. Jace and her two lieutenants had barely managed to shift and keep pace with her.

You were close enough. Any closer and I would have turned my teeth on you. Drake needed Jace to respect her boundaries while still feeling confident she was carrying out the Alpha's orders. Jace would find the balance soon enough.

Yes, Prima. The furrow between Jace's expressive eyes relaxed some, and her tongue lolled out in a happy grin. The other guards, an unmated male and female, raced in easy circles around them, still alert but blissfully carefree at being within sight of the Compound.

Drake's sex clenched as a surge of pheromones pulsed through her loins. She'd been without her mate for days. Her need would awaken every wolf within range, and no doubt these two would be tangling as soon as Jace released them from duty.

The sky had morphed to clear blue by the time the Compound stockade came into view. Drake cut off the main trail and headed to the den she shared with Sylvan. Jace followed at a distance and settled at the edge of the cleared space around the one-story log cabin. Drake shed pelt as she reached the front porch and emerged after her shower in black pants, a sleeveless white T-shirt, and boots. As she strode down the trail toward the main Compound, she said, "You're dismissed, Captain. I'll be at headquarters until the Alpha returns."

Jace, in skin now, strode beside her. "I'll be on duty until then, Prima. Please let me know if you have need of me."

"I will. Go, have something to eat."

Jace saluted, fist at chest. "As you command."

Drake had gotten used to the formality at this point and accepted it as part of the necessary discipline required to keep several hundred wolves living in close quarters as free as possible from skirmishes, displays of dominance, and just general irritation. They might appear human when in skin, but they were all wolf Weres, driven by primal instincts to sort themselves into a hierarchy ruled by tooth and claw and blood. The drives to hunt and mate ruled their bodies and their psyches. Without strong leadership and unyielding discipline, their society would deteriorate into chaos. As she strode through the Compound toward the two-story log building at its center which served as their headquarters, wolves dipped their heads, Weres young and old called a greeting, and warriors saluted. All celebrated the Pack leader's arrival as a wave of calm swept through them.

Suppressing her own distress before it spread to them, Drake bounded up the wooden stairs, entered the vaulted main meeting hall bracketed with huge stone fireplaces, and took the stairs to the second floor two at a time. Her run had helped, but the gnawing in her center persisted. Sylvan's absence was like a missing limb, a phantom pain that never went away. Their mate bond was strong, unaffected by the miles between them, and that sensation of union—body, mind, and soul—kept her sane. If it were to break, she would as well. Before she'd turned, when she'd been only human, she would've rejected the very idea of being so connected to another living being she couldn't survive without them. Now she couldn't imagine being without it. Sylvan was more than her love, more than her passion—she was her life.

Niki, Sylvan's second, stood guard by the door to Sylvan's office in a sleeveless shirt that hugged her torso and left her rippled abdomen bare and tight leather pants that outlined every cut in her muscled thighs. Drake suspected she'd been there for hours, waiting for Sylvan's return as was everyone else.

"Everything on schedule, *Imperator*?" Drake asked.

"Yes, Prima," Niki replied, her low alto gravelly with edges of her wolf bleeding through. "On-time arrival at Albany. The motorcade is en route."

Drake let out a long sigh. "Then she should be here soon."

"Yes. She should." Niki glowered, her powerful body vibrating with tension. A sheen of pheromones and aggressive hormones gleamed on her bare skin. She hadn't been happy that Sylvan had insisted she stay behind. Sylvan had taken an honor guard for the meeting with the new head of Urban and Praetern Affairs in Washington, DC, as would have been expected anytime she traveled, but she'd left her general behind to secure the Compound.

Drake hadn't been happy either. She slid an arm around Niki's tense shoulders and pulled her against her side. Some of Niki's tension seeped away, and she rested for an instant against Drake's body. As dominant as she was, Niki was still a Were, and she needed the strength and support of her Pack leaders just as did every other Were in the Pack. Drake never forgot that part of her responsibility as Sylvan's mate was to maintain the well-being of all that followed them. She rubbed her cheek against Niki's lush auburn hair, scenting the unique bond Niki shared with Sophia, and Niki whined softly in her throat. After a moment Niki pulled away, her tremors quieted for the moment.

"How are the pups?" Drake asked, knowing the slightest mention of the two young orphan pups Niki and Sophia had adopted would ease Niki's unhappiness.

Niki's forest-green eyes sparkled. "Growing quickly and already challenging the other pups in the nursery."

Drake laughed. "Why am I not surprised?"

"Sophia is convinced that Fiona is already showing signs of being a maternal, but Brax clearly has the makings of a warrior."

"I'm sure they'll let you know in time. How are they adjusting to the nursery?"

Niki shrugged. "Better than we are. It's necessary, I know, but it's hard not to have them in the den at night."

"I know. Our two are growing so quickly..." She pushed one of the paired carved oak doors, and Niki followed her into the office. "It's time for them to hunt."

"It's been a long time since we've had this many young," Niki said. "The Pack rejoices."

"Yes," Drake said softly. In the midst of so much uncertainty and danger, the ten young in their nursery held the promise of their future. She dropped into the chair behind the broad desk. "Let's hope this meeting with the new administration has been a positive one."

"The humans say one thing and do another," Niki said, gold ringing the green in her eyes.

"We have been betrayed by our supposed allies, that's true," Drake said. "But despite our strengths, our numbers are small, and not all our Pack choose to live in the wild. Many Packmates are at risk while living in close proximity to humans. We owe a responsibility to them too."

Niki paced, a sheen of faint red pelt covering her arms and etching down the center of her abdomen. Her wolf was uneasy, unhappy, and surging close to the surface. Rather than try to rein her in, Drake let her work off her anger. Niki had good control of her wolf, and she wasn't worried about her. Not as long as Sylvan returned soon. Niki's bond to Sylvan was nearly as strong as that to Sophia. Niki and Sylvan had been together since childhood, and if Niki had been less dominant, they might've been lovers.

"We can't trust anyone to take care of ours except another wolf," Niki said darkly.

"I agree, and that's why so many of our Pack go into law enforcement, even though most keep their true natures a secret. But still, we need peace with the humans."

Niki growled. She didn't necessarily agree, but she would follow Sylvan's lead, as would they all.

A shimmer of power coursed through Drake's body, stirring her blood, striking hard at her core. Her heart raced and her sex flushed. Her clitoris tensed and lengthened, her glands filling.

"The Alpha approaches."

She bounded to her feet, leapt across the desk, and was out the door in two long strides. Niki followed close behind her. Throughout the Compound, wolves howled, Weres shouted, and the air shimmered in celebration.

Sylvan had returned.

CHAPTER TWO

The stockade gates, twelve-foot-tall and ten-foot-wide slabs of ten-inch-thick hardwood, swung inward revealing the Compound's inner courtyard as the first Rover roared out of the forest. Invisible from the air, the approach road was the only vehicular access to the Timberwolf Pack's home. Guarded around the clock by *sentries* stationed at intervals on overlooks, the path snaked through terrain that discouraged even the most intrepid ground forces and prevented any armored assault.

Sylvan, riding in the front seat of the second vehicle, savored the scent of fertile earth and vital creatures and, most of all, her mate. Drake's scent swamped her senses, torching through blood and flesh to the marrow of her being. Her wolf clawed at her innards, demanding satisfaction.

Too long away.

Sylvan shuddered, bludgeoned by need. Too many restless days away from Pack, away from Drake. Too much worry and somewhere, deep inside, a dark kernel of fear she refused to acknowledge. Could not acknowledge. She was Alpha, and fear was a weakness she could not allow.

Soon. Soon we will be whole again.

The tailored shirt and trousers she'd worn for the flight among humans from DC tightened around her clenched muscles like chains. She could have ordered Max to drive the eight hours home, but the delay would have pushed her wolf into a rage, and a Were in wolf form made a poor chauffeur. Her rage would have forced him to turn, her call too powerful for any save her mate to absorb.

She was nearly mad now, wild for the connection to her mate and her Pack. Her muscles rippled, her wolf strained to ascend, and the sound of tearing fabric filled the vehicle. Sex-sheen burst from her skin, coating her body as silver fur erupted in a shimmering cascade down the center of her abdomen. Beside her, Max growled uneasily, his grip on the wheel tightening.

A chorus of uneasy whines emanated from the rear compartment. Sylvan glanced back. Her guest along with three guards occupied one long bench bolted to the sidewall, Sylvan's *centuri* opposite them. The foreign Weres snarled unhappily and her *centuri* grumbled and showed their teeth, too many dominants drenched in sex pheromones and battle hormones in a small space. Even the most submissive Weres would be likely to challenge a strange Were in the heart of the Compound. The added effect of Sylvan's absence and her wolf's near feral heat was a match to a powder keg.

"On your guard, *Centuri*," Sylvan warned, "we're entering the Compound."

The three saluted and replied in unison, "Yes, Alpha."

They would hold their urge to fight or tangle and prevent the newcomers from being challenged on sight. That would be long enough for the guests to be escorted to a safe place—for now.

"Just in time," Max murmured.

"Yes." Sylvan's fingertips tingled as a quarter inch of black claw burst through. Her sex throbbed, the ache for release maddening. Grumbling, Max dropped a hand between his thighs and straightened his legs, making room for the erection straining his black BDUs.

"Too long away," Sylvan murmured. She had no need to hide her urgency, even if she could. Any Were who absorbed her call, dominant and submissive alike, responded with similar need. "First homecoming since you were mated?" Sylvan asked casually.

Max floored the accelerator. "Yes."

Sylvan grinned. Max's human mate was in for a surprise. She glanced into the armored rear compartment. "The *centuri* and my *imperator* will see you to your quarters as soon as we disembark."

The young Alpha, her pale face, unlined, framed in chestnut waves and her dark eyes rimmed in gold, sat rigid on one side of the compartment flanked by her *centuri*. Sex-sheen streamed down her face. "Your hospitality is appreciated, Alpha Mir."

Her voice was cool, steady. Sylvan nodded, silently approving.

She'd been a new Alpha once and knew the pain of establishing control when every sinew burned for release.

Max pulled the Rover to a sharp halt behind the first vehicle, and the follow car carrying the rest of the entourage and that of her visitor drew up in the rear. The gates closed.

"Call a war council for an hour." She pushed open the door and glanced at Max. "That should be enough time for everyone to settle."

Max grinned. "Possibly."

Sylvan bounded out, leapt over the Rover's hood, and landed in the center of the Compound beside one of the great fire pits. A circle of wolves and Weres in skin awaited her. In seconds she was surrounded, wolves in pelt brushing against her legs, Weres drawing closer for a touch, a stroke on the cheek, a hand to a shoulder. She greeted them all as she walked through the throng toward headquarters, toward the one she desperately needed.

Drake waited on the top step, Niki beside her. Even from a distance, Sylvan felt Niki's tension and Drake's call overwhelming every other. Sylvan jumped to the porch, wrapped a hand around Drake's nape, and yanked her into a kiss. Teeth and tongue clashed, hunger unleashed at last.

The icy heat of Drake's mouth met the burning furnace of her own, and Sylvan growled, the dress trousers she'd worn rending along the seams as her flesh gave way to wolf. Drake's blunt, claw-tipped fingers scoured her back, shredding her shirt until the remnants dropped away and bared her torso. Drake raked her teeth down Sylvan's neck, challenging her, teasing her, blooding her. Sylvan's clitoris swelled and pulsed against the fabric of her pants.

Sylvan kept her grip on Drake's neck and eased away enough to swing an arm around Niki's shoulders. "All is well?"

"Yes, Alpha," Niki gasped, quivering against Sylvan's side.

"Good." Sylvan locked eyes with Drake. "We have guests, Niki. See to them."

Niki glanced past Sylvan into the yard and growled. "Dominants, all of them. Who are they?"

"You'll know," Sylvan murmured, tracing the curve of Drake's breast with a fingertip, "in about an hour. My *centuri* need time to recover from the trip and cannot stand guard."

Drake said, "Put Jace in charge of the guests, *Imperator*."

"Her control may not—" Niki began, protest in her tone.

"Her control is fine," Drake said, hooking a claw in the waistband of Sylvan's pants. "Do it, then go to your mate. She'll need you."

"Yes, Prima." Niki dipped her chin and jumped down.

Sylvan pulled Drake down the steps and through the gate to the wooded path to their den.

"I need you," Sylvan said.

"I know." Drake hooked her claws and sliced open Sylvan's fly, exposing the silver pelt streaming down the center of her abdomen between the tight columns of bulging muscles. "You should not have worn these pants."

"I didn't want to frighten the humans."

"Mm, they would have been lucky to see you in battle form." She tugged Sylvan to a halt at the foot of the steps to their cabin and kissed her, pushing her hand lower. Her fingers slipped on either side of Sylvan's clitoris and squeezed.

Sylvan's mind blazed into heat and fury. Her jaw lengthened, grew bold and heavy. The faint shimmer of silver over her torso thickened. "Drake...careful."

"Why?" Drake jumped onto the porch a step ahead of Sylvan, pushed open the door, and surged toward the bedroom, challenging Sylvan to keep pace.

Sylvan roared and leapt, catching Drake just as they reached the side of the bed. Tumbling down, Drake in her grasp, she ripped away the last of their clothing.

"Should I wait now?" Drake gasped and Sylvan rolled above her, her hips between Drake's splayed thighs.

When her sex met Drake's, a whine of want and need escaped her. She seized Drake's wrists in one hand and held them above her head, the other raking down Drake's torso, leaving thin lines of bright red. The mate bite on Drake's shoulder darkened and swelled, calling her. Her clitoris, extruded for joining, hardened painfully, and she threw back her head with a triumphant snarl.

Her mate. Hers.

Tilting her hips, she notched herself in the cleft below Drake's clitoris, locked to her, and readied to spill.

Panting, near blind with power, she met Drake's midnight-gold gaze. "I love you."

Drake anchored her legs around Sylvan's hips, bared her teeth. "Then give me what I want."

"Take it," Sylvan snarled, her glands burning to explode.

With a growl, Drake sank her teeth into the aching site of the mate bite above Sylvan's breast. The ecstatic pain and pulse of energy surged through Sylvan's sex, the glands buried at the base of her clitoris contracted, and her *victus* erupted. As her essence flooded and joined with her mate's, Sylvan howled, her very soul ripped from her being. Her hips pumped wildly, and she emptied over and over. Spent, she collapsed, her skin hot, feverish, streaming with sex-sheen.

Drake cradled Sylvan's head in the crook of her shoulder, her heart pounding beneath Sylvan's.

"I missed you," Drake whispered, stroking Sylvan's back with her free hand. "Just once will not take care of it."

Sylvan chuckled. "I think you drained me."

"Really, Alpha," Drake said dryly. "I seem to remember you were once more potent…"

Sylvan bit her neck and Drake chuckled. Her challenge caused Sylvan's clitoris to harden against her own again, as she expected. Drake smiled. "But if you need to rest…"

Drake bucked her hips and, although Sylvan was never taken by surprise, she rolled onto her back nevertheless. Drake knelt between her thighs as Sylvan watched her with wolf-gold eyes.

Sylvan tensed her thighs and lifted her hips, displaying her more than recovered distended clitoris. "Potent enough?"

"Always." Drake brushed her thumb over her and Sylvan's back arched. With a claw, Drake marked a thin line down the deep groove between Sylvan's abdominals, circled her once, twice, a third time until Sylvan gripped her nape again.

"Enough," Sylvan said, her wolf too hungry to be teased.

Drake leaned on an elbow and gazed up, lightly stroking over Sylvan's center. She loved nothing more than teasing Sylvan until her wolf nearly exploded. "Are you sure."

"Suck me, Prima," Sylvan ordered, her tone a guttural growl.

Smiling, Drake tipped her head and filled her mouth with Sylvan's flesh. She stroked Sylvan's chest and belly in time to the strokes of her tongue until the steel bands of Sylvan's thighs tightened around her. She sucked her to the core, and within seconds, Sylvan's essence filled her. Drake claimed her mate, giving Sylvan the release only she could provide.

When Sylvan finally emptied, Drake surged above her, pushed her center against Sylvan's still engorged sex, and rode her until she spent over Sylvan's abdomen and thighs.

Finally, the fire in Drake's belly ebbed and she settled in the curve of Sylvan's body, one hand still possessively cupped between Sylvan's thighs.

Sylvan kissed her. "Are you well, Prima?"

"I am now."

"The young?"

"Growing faster than I expected, even knowing Were young mature quickly." Drake was used to the human cycle of growth. Their pups developed on a far more aggressive schedule, and already their young in skin form were walking and talking. As wolves, they were not yet adolescents, but the boundary was nearing. "It's time for them to learn who they are."

"Yes," Sylvan said. "They'll need to hunt and understand the responsibility of the kill. I had hoped to begin already, but these political negotiations…"

"There is yet time." Drake stroked Sylvan's chest. "What of the meetings? Any progress?"

Sylvan sighed. "Words are not deeds, and I'm not sure who our friends are now. Torren has proved to be an excellent diplomat and, along with Katya, will act as our emissary."

"So we can expect no help from the humans if our enemies resurface," Drake said.

"We never could." Sylvan cupped Drake's cheek and kissed her again, a slow deep claiming. "We can only rely on Pack."

"I know." Drake ran her hand through Sylvan's golden hair. "You brought visitors. Who are they?"

"Weres who say they seek our aid," Sylvan said.

"Allies or enemies?" Drake murmured.

"We shall see."

CHAPTER THREE

"Jace"—Niki signaled as she landed in the courtyard—"with me. Bring Mags and Noa."

Jace, who'd been stationed at the door of headquarters while the Prima was inside, saluted. "Yes, *Imperator*."

The three warriors fell in behind her as Niki bounded across the Compound yard to confront the group of foreign Weres arrayed in front of the Rovers. The outsiders, in tailored black shirts, trousers, and boots, were wary, trying to hide their anxiety and failing. Their wide stances, folded arms, and subtly jutting canines betrayed their readiness to do battle. All, that is, except for the tall, slender, pale Were who stood slightly in front of the other four, her arms loose at her sides, the expression on her long, almost delicate face neutral, and her amber eyes taking in everything around her. The leader. The Alpha of that group, at least.

Niki landed a few feet in front of the leader, closer than she should have approached, but she didn't care if a stranger in her own territory considered her actions a challenge.

"I am the *imperator* of the Timberwolf Pack," she said crisply. "Alpha Mir has ordered you be provided secure accommodations."

"I am Alpha Zora Constantine of the Snowcrest Pack," the young dominant replied. She indicated a copper-skinned, black-haired female whose powerful shoulders strained the silk fabric of her tailored shirt. "Ash, the captain of my guard, and Ryan, Cybil, and Evan."

The Alpha met Niki's gaze as she spoke. Eye to eye, unblinking, unwavering. Calm, confident.

The challenge vibrated in the air and Constantine's guards tensed. Beside Niki, Jace growled softly and edged forward, her right shoulder an inch behind Niki's. Jace's scent vibrated with lust and battle fever. Niki's pelt shimmered beneath her skin and her wolf clamored for a tussle, but as Sylvan's second, she needed to walk a fragile line. On the one hand, Sylvan would be unhappy if she and the visiting Alpha tussled, but on the other, Niki commanded Sylvan's warriors, and she could not show submission to another wolf.

The visiting Alpha's eyes swiftly morphed from amber to wolf-gold and a golden sheen rolled beneath the skin left bare by her open-collared shirt. After a long moment, Niki lowered her gaze from the Alpha's eyes but did not dip her head. She could not challenge, but she would not submit. The Alpha rumbled softly, an acknowledgment of Niki withdrawing from the challenge, and a reminder that while she might be on foreign ground, she was indeed Alpha.

"The offer is accepted," Constantine said.

Niki swiveled on her heel and strode toward the barracks. After a moment, Jace fell in on her left and the other two warriors on her right. Constantine and her guard drew even with them at an acceptable distance, refusing to follow but carefully not preceding them. So that's how it was going to be. A constant demonstration from these newcomers that they would not be dominated. Niki smiled to herself.

If Constantine thought to challenge Sylvan in the same way, she would be sadly surprised. Sylvan would not expect another Alpha to submit, but she would not accept even a hint of challenge in her territory. She'd have the young Alpha's throat before the visitor could pull pelt. Constantine appeared to be confident in her position, and Niki expected Constantine's guard to come as close to challenging as they could as often as possible. She'd do the same in their place.

Any wolf who guarded an Alpha needed to be the most aggressive in the Pack. Here, in strange territory, surrounded by dominants and vastly outnumbered, Constantine's guards would be driven by the nearly visible cloud of potent battle hormones and pheromones to fight...or tangle. Niki had learned supreme control fighting at Sylvan's side for years, and even so, her need nearly drove her to give in to her wolf's demand to fight. She couldn't fight, but she could satisfy the agonizing gnawing in the pit of her stomach another way. Ever since Sylvan had returned, radiating power and sex to everyone within her range, Niki's lust for her mate scoured her nerves like fingers of cut glass. Sophia was in the infirmary, dealing with the usual minor injuries of a busy Pack. Niki could be there in less than a minute, could take her in less time than that, could finally ease the maddening pressure in her sex. But not until her duty was done.

Niki picked up her pace and jumped onto the wide plank porch fronting the long narrow barracks. Jace landed beside her and grumbled softly, half whine and half growl. Her face dripped with sex-sheen, gleaming, stark, wild. She'd been immersed in Drake's pheromones for hours, and now with Sylvan in the Compound, must be close to exploding. But she held, as the Prima said she would. Impressive.

Niki marched down the wide center hall of the two-story barracks, past the rooms on either side shared by soldiers and adolescent trainees, to a suite at the rear of the building. Three rooms, a large one in the center with two smaller on either side with connecting doors that allowed the Alpha's guards access for security reasons if they needed.

"Will you require anything else?" Niki asked after opening the doors to the rooms.

"Not as of this moment," Constantine said. "Are my wolves given leave to run? They've been traveling a long time."

Niki nodded, again taking care not to dip her head lower than the Alpha's, but not meeting her eyes. "There are trails that run inside the Compound perimeter—but they are likely to come upon our wolves if they go out without an escort. They may venture out, if they dare."

Ash strode past her Alpha into Niki's space. Her brown eyes were nearly black and ringed in silver-flecked gold. "We dare. And you should show some respect."

Nick's head jerked up and her canines punched down. "Remember where you are, Wolf."

"At your Alpha's invitation," Ash said. "Are all the Timberwolves so poorly trained as you?"

"Stand down, Ash," Constantine murmured. "The *imperator* is within her rights to demand we follow Pack protocol. You cannot traverse their territory without permission." She smiled. "I would not allow it at Cresthome."

Ash's eyes narrowed and she swept her heated gaze over Niki and the others. "Yes, Alpha."

"Jace," Niki said softly, her gaze fixed on the impertinent captain of Constantine's guard, "stand post outside and ensure our guests are not bothered."

"As you command, *Imperator*." Jace snapped a salute.

"We are perfectly capable of seeing to our Alpha's security," Ash snarled.

Niki ignored her. "Jace, Captain of our Prima's guard, will be certain of that." Insult delivered, Niki turned to Jace. "See to it."

"As you command," Jace said, canines gleaming as she regarded Ash. "Mags, Noa, you are dismissed. I'll be here should you require me."

The two *sentries* saluted. "Yes, Captain."

With obvious reluctance, Ash stepped back into formation on Constantine's left side.

"Alpha Constantine," Niki said, "when I receive further orders from the Alpha, I'll send word. Meals will be provided at the appropriate times."

Zora Constantine inclined her head a degree. "Extend our appreciation to Alpha Mir."

"It shall be done." Niki turned and bounded down the hall, off the porch, and across the Compound to the adjoining building before Jace had time to follow her outside. *Enough.* Her duty was done, and her mate awaited.

Sophia was in the office she used when she wasn't with an ill or injured wolf. She instantly rose from behind her desk when Niki strode in and slammed the door behind her.

"I wondered when you would come," Sophia said softly, her silver hair matching the silver of her wolf's eyes. "You've kept me waiting."

"Only by the Alpha's command," Niki snarled, stripping off her shirt and tossing it onto a chair as she reached over the desk, gripped Sophia's waist with both hands, and lifted her over the top. Sophia laughed as she slid down and settled against Niki, draping her arms around Niki's neck, her breasts pressed hard to Niki's chest. Sophia raked claws through the soft glimmer of red-brown pelt that lightly coated Niki's torso. "You have been waiting too, haven't you," she whispered.

Niki growled in answer and pushed Sophia back until Sophia's hips rested against the edge of her desk. Sophia braced her arms on the desktop and Niki dropped to her knees, the only Were in the world for whom she would kneel other than Sylvan. Sophia's scent, sunshine and saplings, cascaded around her like a fist to the gut and a hand to her heart. Everything that mattered. Her sex pulsed painfully and Niki growled.

Sophia gripped Niki's hair until Niki raised her eyes.

"These pants are brand new. Don't destroy them this time."

Carefully, deliberately, Niki unbuttoned Sophia's pants and lowered them. She could have shredded them, but her mate enjoyed tormenting her when she was this ready, and she enjoyed giving Sophia control.

"Very good." Sophia's white claws raked through Niki's hair as Niki bared her, one slow inch at a time.

Niki's vision wavered on the edge of wolf sight, her body on the edge of turning. She held back the flood of primal chemicals boiling through her but only because her mate demanded it.

"Open your pants," Sophia commanded.

Niki unzipped her pants and pushed them down as far as she could. She had no time to stand and shed them. She needed release or she would spill untouched.

"No more," Niki growled, and took Sophia fast and deep with her mouth.

"Niki!" Sophia's hips jerked and she pushed into Niki's mouth, tugging Niki's hair, riding her with chaotic thrusts and broken cries.

Niki stroked deep, pressing the tip of her tongue against the sensitive glands on either side of Sophia's opening, and Sophia's claws scored her shoulders.

"I've hungered for you," Sophia gasped, an urgent whine undercutting her words. "I need you to take me. Take me, I need to fill you."

Niki stroked the inside of Sophia's thigh and teased her with a blunt-tipped finger, working her clitoris until Sophia moaned and flooded her with her essence.

"Oh yes," Sophia said, shuddering as the last of the contractions rippled through her sex.

Snarling, Niki surged upward, wrapped an arm around Sophia's waist, and buried her canines in the mate bite on Sophia's neck. The bite she had longed for and feared for so long. But they were one now, and Sophia was hers. She trembled, the ecstasy in her heart matched by the pounding agony in her sex. Sophia spent against her thigh as the hormones burned through her, and then Sophia's hand was between Niki's thighs, massaging her, stroking lower to tease inside her. Niki threw her head back, the mate bite on her breast throbbing.

"Do it," Niki pleaded to the only Were she would ever beg. "Please. Please. I need…"

Niki trembled, whined, went blind with agony, and then Sophia bit, claiming her. Niki exploded, drenching Sophia's hand with all that she was. She dropped to her knees again, this time from weakness, her thighs trembling too hard to hold her upright. She pressed her cheek to Sophia's sex. "I love you."

Sophia stroked her head, brushed the sheen-soaked strands from her face. "I love you too. My mate."

"I can't stay."

"I know," Sophia said. "I sensed the newcomers. Powerful dominants."

Niki snarled, her canines lengthening. "They will not come near you."

Sophia laughed. "Really? You think they interest me?"

"You are Omega. They will be drawn to you." Niki tipped her head, met Sophia's gaze, letting her wolf ascend. "And you are mine."

Sophia's fingers rippled over the mate bite on Niki's chest, making her sex tingle and tense.

"You think I don't know that?" Sophia chided. "You think that's not what I've wanted all my life? To be your mate?"

Niki, grinned. "I like hearing it."

"I like saying it." Sophia kissed her.

When Niki rose, Sophia rubbed her cheek against Niki's shoulder. "Why are they here?"

"I don't know," Niki murmured, "but the Alpha has called a war council."

Sophia drew a sharp breath. "Again, so soon. Will there never be peace?"

"We're wolves," Niki said, and for her, no other explanation mattered. "Peace belongs to the strongest."

"Then go, *Imperator*," Sophia said, "and do your duty."

Chapter Four

Ash paced the length of the barracks and back, a hundred strides down the bare, wood-paneled hall to the broad double doors, a hundred strides back to the Alpha's chambers, though she could've covered the distance from a stationary position outside the Alpha's door in two leaps if necessary. In pelt, in seconds less. The windows in their rooms, high, long rectangles, opened onto gravel and dirt paths that disappeared into the forest three hundred yards away. Any attempt by assailants to breach their quarters could be easily defended. If they needed to retreat, the stockade fence was just visible beyond the tree line, and on the other side, freedom.

They'd still be in Timberwolf Pack land but Snowcrest wolves were fleet and crafty when running free. In the face of an overwhelming assault, she could create enough diversion for the Alpha to escape. She was the Alpha's last, best defense. Ryan, Cybil, and Evan were fearless, but not as seasoned as they needed to be given the new order in the Pack. The Alpha had withstood challenges to her assuming the mantle of leadership from half a dozen wolves, and some of those she'd defeated had refused to swear allegiance, leaving the Pack with their supporters. Snowcrest had never needed a large standing army and did not breed for warriors. Their dominants were as strong as any other dominant Weres, but their numbers were small and their battle training less formal. A weakness she intended to be sure this warrior Pack of Weres remained unaware of.

Ash had argued against coming to the Compound, reasoning neutral ground would be safer. The Alpha believed refusing to enter Mir's Pack land would show weakness. And she was Alpha. From the moment she'd met the Timberwolves in DC, Ash had been unaccountably uneasy. She had no basis to distrust them, and chalked her wolf's agitation up to being surrounded by the most dominant Weres she'd even met, aside from Alpha Constantine. The deeper they'd traveled into foreign territory, the more her wolf stormed and raged. She'd weathered the onslaught of tooth and claw so many times, she wasn't sure she had any intact intestines left.

And Mir's *imperator*, so brutally dominant and so obviously challenging Alpha Constantine, had only added to her unrest. Add on the arrogant captain—Jace—the *imperator* had left in charge, and Ash was stoked to tussle. Her wolf wanted blood, and she'd be happy to bleed in turn if it meant dousing the fires that seared her from the inside out.

Each time Ash neared the exit to the porch, her agitation grew. Something called to her on the other side of the door, some irresistible force that had dug claws into her underbelly and was slowly threatening to bring her to her knees, or drive her mad. As she caught the spicy scent of black currant and crushed pine, her abdominals tightened, heat flared down the inside of her thighs, and her clitoris twitched. Alpha Mir's call had struck her hard, not as deep as her Alpha's when the Alpha was in need, but enough to bring her wolf surging close to the skin. She'd contained the need, her battle hormones overcoming the urge to meet need with need and claim flesh, but now, something else, something as potent as the Alpha's call, filled her blood with the demand for release. She growled, her canines extruding, the tips of her fingers tingling as her claws punched out. She hadn't tangled since they'd left Cresthome. No time, no one she was willing to submit to. One or two of her fellow guards would have been willing to roll for her, but she declined. She'd spent her energy protecting the Alpha and guarding the tenuous status of their Pack from outsiders.

Alpha Constantine had not traveled beyond the confines of their territory since she had assumed Pack leadership, and with no heirs and none qualified to follow her, the survival of the Pack depended on her well-being.

Ash shuddered, felt pelt sweep beneath her skin, and growled. Slamming both hands against the closed doors, she fought down the pounding in her loins. Her spine bowed and her vision turned to sharp shades of black, grays, and stark whites. Her jaw grew heavy, her chest stretched the fabric of her shirt. The sweet call of her wolf rising filled her with excitement.

"Ash!" Zora's tone snapped down the hallway like a whip. "Leash your wolf."

Ash's claws gouged into the wood, leaving splinters jutting out along the long grooves, and she whined. Rivulets of shimmering moisture trailed down her neck and left her silk shirt plastered to her back. Not since adolescence, when the mere presence of another wolf radiating readiness to tangle would send her into sexual frenzy, had she felt so close to losing control.

"I…I'm trying."

"Obey your Alpha, Wolf," Zora commanded, the ice-cold tone cutting through the fever in Ash's brain.

Ash gasped, spun around, and her vision slid out of wolf range, returning color to the world. Her Alpha stood in the doorway at the end of the hall, hands on her narrow hips, fire burning in her eyes. Ash's stomach clenched and she went to her knees, head lowered. "My apologies, Alpha."

"Come, Captain." Zora spun on her heel and disappeared into her suite. The air vibrated with her fury.

Ash staggered to her feet, struggling to find her balance. Her Alpha's command tore at her core like barbs pulled through her flesh, and still she fought to pull away from the door to the outside, to resist whatever power called for her to leap outside, to rend and tear and howl. By sheer force of will, she pushed down the length of a hallway she should have been able to cover in a blink. In the time it took to reach the Alpha's room, her wolf had calmed enough for her to square her shoulders and steady her voice.

"I am deeply embarrassed, Alpha," she said, coming to attention, her hands behind her back. "I can't explain why I had such trouble controlling my wolf."

"Can't you?" Zora narrowed her eyes and shook her head. "How old are you, Captain? I don't think I've ever asked."

Ash stiffened. Did the Alpha think her too unseasoned for her position? "I'm twenty-five, Alpha. I was a lieutenant in your father's— the previous Alpha's guard."

"Not a *centuri*, then."

Ash flushed. "No, Alpha. We had only four Weres of *centuri* rank."

"Yes," Zora said dryly, "two I killed in challenge, one defected, and one now commands as *imperator*."

"*Imperator* Loris appointed me to head your guard. If you wish another—"

"Stand down, Captain," Zora said. "I need you in charge and I need you in control. Can I expect that?"

Ash slammed her fist to her chest. "On my life, Alpha."

"Good. Then give me your assessment of the situation."

Ash took a long steadying breath, her focus restored along with her sense of duty. "The Timberwolves are a warrior Pack, Alpha. They vastly outpower us, not just in number, but in battle experience. We cannot accept Pack challenge from them and expect to win."

"Alpha Mir could have moved on our territory at any time but has never shown any inclination to do so. We've had no border skirmishes, no raids, no ambushes." She snarled. "Until recently."

"With respect, Alpha, you've never been as personally vulnerable as you are here. If you were to be challenged and defeated, our Pack would be at the mercy of several neighboring Packs."

Zora smiled wryly. "I do not plan to be challenged, and if challenged, I do not plan on losing."

"Yes, Alpha."

"Our immediate position here?"

"Defensible, but only for a brief time. If we don't remain on guard, a surprise attack would overwhelm us."

"Keep a guard front and rear at all times, but I don't believe Alpha Mir has any reason to seek to weaken or destroy us. We're no threat, and her word would be dishonored if she attacked invited guests."

"If she is honorable." Ash had witnessed just how quickly allegiances and loyalties could turn after the battle for leadership that followed the death of the previous Alpha. It would take a long time for many of the Snowcrest Weres to trust their leaders again. Only the Alpha's strength and certainty had kept the Pack together during the transition.

Zora smiled thinly. "Alpha Mir has battled humans, Vampires, rogue Weres, and countless others to protect her Pack, and by extension, the integrity of us all. Her honor, her dedication to preserving our independence, cannot be denied."

"I will not argue that, Alpha." Ash struggled to offer wise counsel when she trusted no one outside her Pack. "Perhaps you should send for the *imperator*, Alpha. I may not be the best—"

Zora moved so quickly Ash next felt Zora's arm around her shoulders, pulling her closer. They were of a height, but Zora's mouth brushed over her cheek, her strength as supple and unyielding as a honed steel blade. The Alpha's body pressed against Ash's, offering safety and courage in equal measure. Ash closed her eyes and dropped her forehead to the Alpha's shoulder, unable to suppress the whine that rose deep in her core.

Zora's breath whispered against her ear.

"You are the captain of my guard, and you are not replaceable." Zora stroked the damp curls at Ash's nape. "You must learn to listen to your wolf. She will sense the true nature of things before any other awareness. Control her, yes, but do not silence her. We've been in strange territory for two weeks, away from Pack, away from our land. You've been on guard the entire time, surrounded by foreign dominants and an all-powerful Alpha."

"She is not my Alpha," Ash grumbled.

"No, she is not." Zora stroked her nape. "But her very presence affects us all. You know what you need now and denying it will only cloud your judgment."

"I'm sorry," Ash murmured.

Zora laughed. "Why? Because your wolf is young and healthy and demands satisfaction? We are safe for now. Find one of the others—let your wolf have what she needs."

"I cannot leave you now."

"You will do as I say," Zora said softly.

Ash trembled. "Yes, Alpha."

Zora kissed her forehead, let her go. "Alpha Mir's *imperator* has given you leave to depart the barracks. See to your wolf, then take advantage of the invitation to tell me what you discover of our new friends while we wait for their decision."

Ash tipped her head. "As you will, Alpha."

Ash pivoted, left the room, and quietly closed the door behind her. Zora let out a long breath. The room, while not spacious, was large for a barracks and more than adequate for a short stay. This was a martial compound, not a hotel, and she understood the need for them to remain isolated from the dozens of dominant Weres who would not appreciate their presence in their territory. Still, she couldn't help but feel imprisoned. She would have done the same with foreign Weres at Cresthome, but the knowledge did not ease the discomfort. Her wolf bludgeoned her with unhappiness, and she clamped an iron hand on her need. With a sigh, she settled on her back on the simple cot and closed her eyes. In her mind, she ran through the snowcapped forests, and as she ran, her wolf lifted her head and howled joyfully.

CHAPTER FIVE

Jace snarled as Anya, a petite redhead, raced around the fire pit in front of the barracks with a pair of barely out of adolescence trainees giving chase. The young male and female Weres, clearly fevered by Anya's powerful pheromones, laughed and howled in the throes of scarcely contained sexual frenzy. Anya toyed with them, slowing long enough for them to catch her, rub against her, fondle her, and her them. When they would have shed the rest of their disheveled clothes and presented themselves in readiness, she pushed them away and ran off again.

All over the Compound, wolves in pelt and Weres taunted and teased and tangled in the shade of tall pines, on the rich mahogany earth of the training yard, against walls, and in stairways. The fever would pass soon enough, now that the Alpha had returned and the long days of anxiety and uneasiness subsided. And the Alpha pair had dispelled their need.

Jace set her jaw against the pounding in her loins, ignoring the pressure in her chest as her wolf battled for dominance. Her wolf paced and growled and bit and snapped. Jace ignored her demands too, as she had been doing for days. She'd gone too long without release, even when the opportunity'd been there. Unusual for her. Her eyes narrowed as Anya raced onto the porch, her flushed breasts exposed where the buttons on her shirt had torn away. She slowed opposite Jace, a hand on the door.

"Come on. We've room for more." Anya's eyes sparked with gold flecks, her scent rich and ready. The young Weres pressed in behind her, the male rubbing against her side, the female wrapping an arm around her waist and nuzzling her neck. Anya laughed, a deep sensuous taunt, her gaze still on Jace. "They won't last long, and there'll be plenty for you."

"I'm on duty."

"Since when has that stopped you from a quick tangle?" Anya snapped. "I can have you spilling in my mouth in less time than it would take for anyone to cross the yard."

Anya was right. She'd done it before. Anya was a potent female in her prime, and every unmated dominant and quite a few submissives sought her out when their needs arose. And Anya reveled in the constant coupling. Ever since Niki had chosen a mate, Anya had been relentless in her pursuit of any unmated Were, tangling as often as possible.

But Jace had no trouble saying no, and duty was only part of the excuse. As much as she wanted release, she wanted...*something*. Something she couldn't identify, but whatever it was, her wolf was half crazed as a result. None of that made sense, so she used the excuse that was mostly true.

"We have visitors in the barracks. I can't leave my post."

"I know. I saw them come in." Anya pushed open the door and stared down the hall, her pheromones thickening. "He's one of them, isn't he?"

Jace spun around, her wolf instantly on guard, aggression and an unexpected prickling along her spine—possessiveness. The male at the end of the hall stood with legs spread, his hands behind his back, his expression flat and stony. Jace let out a breath. Not the captain, as she'd thought.

"Yes. And not to be approached."

Anya's eyebrow arched. "And if he should decide otherwise? He looks more than ready."

Jace shook her head. "Let them be, Anya."

Anya sniffed, strode across the hall, and kicked open a door to one of the rooms. The trainees crowded behind her, and they all disappeared inside. The sounds of their tangling carried through the walls, even if Jace hadn't been able to scent their sex or hear the howls the moment the younger Weres succumbed to Anya's power.

Jace glanced through the still-open main door and met the unyielding gaze of the Snowcrest guard. He gave no sign that his straining erection gave him any discomfort. She nodded briefly, spun around, and closed the door. They both had their duties.

❖

Ash left the Alpha's suite and glanced down the hall as the Timberwolf captain of the guard pulled the door closed. A rush of heat flamed deep in her belly. "Problems?"

"No, Captain," Evan grated. His chest heaved and sweat and sex-sheen coated his rocky jaw. "Just some of the Timberwolves came in to tangle."

Ash growled. Had the captain invited him to tangle? Her wolf clamped down on her spine sending agonizing shafts of pain into her loins. Her claws extruded, her canines punched down. "She is not for you."

He glanced at her quickly, surprise registering in his eyes, then quickly away. He lowered his head and stared down at the floor some distance away. "No, Captain. No invitation was given."

She brushed past him and shoved into the adjoining room. The air was murky with pheromones and the scent of sex. Cybil and Ryan, naked, tangled against the wall just inside the door, Cybil's back to the wall, her thighs clasped around Ryan's waist as he pumped frantically. *Victus* coated their bodies, and her claws raked his back, leaving dark streaks that gleamed like black oil in the slanted sunlight. His canines scored her breast, and her swollen nipples stood taut against her flushed skin. Cybil rolled her head in Ash's direction, her canines extruded, her eyes glazed. Grimacing as another wave of release rippled through her, she reached for Ash, grasped between her thighs, and squeezed her sex.

"Just in time." Cybil fumbled with Ash's fly, yanked the zipper down, and pushed her hand inside. Ryan groaned and shuddered.

Cybil gripped Ash's clitoris and milked her. Ash's canines shot out, and her head snapped back, a red haze clouding her vision. Cybil massaged her glands at the end of every stroke, teasing, working her with merciless skill. Ash's hips bucked and her belly burned. Cybil squeezed her as she released again, howling as she spilled. Ash's thighs trembled and she thrust into Cybil's hand, the press of blunt claws against her flesh inflaming her. She choked on need, her body slick with pheromones, and still, her wolf snarled and bit and clawed. Unsatisfied, unrelenting.

Icy cold shuddered down her spine, and Ash staggered back, the fever turned to fury. Denied the release she craved, she burst out into the hall and leapt the distance to the far end in a single bound. She slammed down, shoved the door open, and surged onto the porch.

Jace spun around with a snarl, already clawed, canines exposed. *Challenge!*

Ash's wolf gloried as battle lust tore through her. Ash shouldered Jace in the chest hard enough to take them both down into the courtyard, landing astride her hips, canines bared and ready to claim. Reason fled. She would have this wolf. She would feel her yield beneath her belly and taste her wild musk—almonds and black licorice—potent, powerful, exotic.

"Submit," Ash growled.

"Never." Jace rolled her, claws shredding her shirt and canines scouring her neck.

Ash roared at the surge of pain that almost drove her to release and shoved a hand between them. She caught the top of Jace's pants with her claws and tore them open. Her skin, soaked with sex-sheen, slid over Jace's bared abdominals as her hand closed around Jace's sex. Jace's clitoris, extended and hard, filled her palm and she squeezed.

Jace howled and thrashed.

Claws dug into Ash's flanks and rent flesh. Ash managed to gain the top again and ripped away the rest of Jace's shirt. Her own hung in tatters. Jace's breasts rose, pink tinged and swollen and inviting her bite. She would take her. Her wolf would be unchained at last. Skin shimmering with sex fever and battle lust, Ash surrendered control and her jaw lengthened. Her glands tensed and readied to spill. She cupped Jace's breast and squeezed.

Jace struggled beneath her, golden pelt bursting to the surface, on the verge of turning. Her sex pulsed in Ash's hand, hot and full. Jace's claws dug into her shoulders.

"Bite me and you die," Jace growled.

"You will not win." Ash rode Jace's thigh. So close now. So ready. Her wolf howled in victory and, *victus* exploding over Jace's sex, she struck. Silver blurred her vision and her jaws snapped shut on empty air. She roared, wild at the denial, and she surged to her knees, ready to challenge whoever had sought to come between her and her—

A sable wolf took her by the throat and threw her to the ground. The weight of her Alpha bore down on her and Ash trembled. A wave of fury enshrouded her, her Alpha's canines snapped inches from her throat, and Ash released in submission, her *victus* spilling down her thighs and coating her Alpha's belly.

You disobeyed me.

"I'm sorry," Ash whispered, drained and helpless. "I...I could not stop."

You are confined to your quarters.

Ash closed her eyes. "As you will, Alpha."

Get up.

The weight on her chest disappeared. Ash shuddered, opened her eyes, and struggled to her knees. A great silver beast circled a few feet away, snarling, terrifying in her power. Jace knelt, panting as if she had just run for miles, her hot gaze fixed on Ash. Ash stared back, and another wave of flame scorched her sex. She grumbled and Jace snarled.

The Timberwolf Alpha swung her head in Ash's direction, her gaze as piercing as a spear to the heart. *Enough!*

Ash ducked her head. Jace whined.

Jace, headquarters, now.

"Yes, Alpha." Jace jumped to her feet and strode past Ash without a glance.

Ash's Alpha faced Sylvan, her muzzle a fraction lower than Sylvan's.

The Snowcrest Pack apologizes for our captain, Alpha Mir. I would ask that you allow us to send her back to Cresthome, but if you desire retribution for the insult to your hospitality, the fault is mine.

Sylvan shook her head. *Your captain was not alone in this. My captain appears unable to contain her wolf as well. Let us call it even.*

Your generosity is appreciated, Alpha. Evan, Zora ordered, *escort Ash to our suite.*

"Yes, Alpha," Evan said, jumping down from the barracks porch.

"Vehicles approach, Alpha," a guard on the wall announced.

Hold, Zora ordered.

Ash stiffened. She might be disgraced, but she was still a Snowcrest warrior, duty bound to defend her Alpha. She stepped to her Alpha's side as Evan did the same.

Sylvan and Zora faced the closed gates.

The *imperator* bounded down from headquarters and strode into the center of the yard. "Identify?"

The guard on the barricade called down, "Jonathan reports he is with Liege Gates in the first car. Katya and the others are in the Rover."

"Open the gates," the *imperator* said.

The gates swung open and a gleaming black limo with blackout windows and subtle heavy armor pulled in, followed by a Rover. The limo swung around and halted in front of the steps to the two-story log and stone building. Guards in sleek black uniforms carrying automatic rifles and holstered sidearms exited the limo and formed a gauntlet leading from the rear door to the entrance. Humans—but not. More. Ash glanced at her Alpha, whose expression had not changed, but whose scent had grown thick with aggression. A thin figure in a black trench coat, leather gloves, and broad-brimmed fedora completely shading their face stepped out and was swiftly surrounded by the guards and escorted rapidly inside the building. Vampire, and a very powerful one to not only be awake during the daylight but risking the sun as well. The guards in black were their human servants.

The Rover's doors opened and Were soldiers emerged. And then someone else—*something* else. A tall ethereal being with jet-black hair and nearly translucent ivory skin, bedecked in a severely tailored cream-colored suit and copper silk shirt, stepped out with a young female Were at her side. The air around them shimmered as if a thousand rainbows did battle.

Ash blinked and the illusion disappeared. She sucked in a breath. She recognized the Fae, now. Torren, the one who had been in Washington. The one who was something other than even Fae. She was an old being, ancient and terrible. Ash growled.

Stand down, Captain. But be alert. Zora brushed against Ash's leg, subtly telegraphing her support.

Sylvan addressed Zora. *The rest of the council has arrived. I'll send an escort to take you to the dining hall while we convene.*

Sylvan bounded away, and the new arrivals followed. Ash remained with her Alpha and Evan, powerless to do anything save await the decision that might determine the fate of their Pack.

CHAPTER SIX

"Prima," Zahn, the first of Jody Gates's human servants, said with a nod as the group from the limo entered headquarters. Jody's second, lithe and nearly as lethally beautiful as her Vampire Liege, showed just the right amount of respect in her greeting—appropriate for Drake's station but with a hint of the Vampire arrogance that said they knew they were the apex predators. Sylvan would disagree, of course, but neither Weres nor Vampires wanted to disrupt their alliance over who could kill the other the quickest.

Or so Drake hoped.

"Hello, Zahn." Drake stepped into the shadows beyond the reach of the shafts of sunlight sneaking beneath the broad porch roof and stealing just inside the door as Jody broke from the protective scrum and kissed her cheek. "Jody. Is there anything the Timberwolves can provide for your comfort?"

Jody's obsidian eyes, permanently slashed with scarlet now that she was Risen, glittered with suppressed hunger, a reminder that the truly powerful Vampires were always a danger. Even when they were friends.

"Your company is sufficient, Prima."

Drake laughed. "Your consort would not agree."

Jody smiled. "Ah, you are correct. Nor would your mate, I fear."

"How is Becca?"

A flicker of emotion eclipsed the cold dispassion in Jody's gaze, reminding Drake just why her best friend Becca loved her. Jody might be remote and possessed of terrible power, but she had not completely lost her ability to care. Drake did not fear power—Sylvan was in every way as fearsome as any Vampire. Only Sylvan was ruled by instinct and passion, not the insatiable hunger of blood lust.

"She is well." Jody touched her pale, slender hand to her chest, over the spot where her heart once beat. "And she never ceases to remind me of all I should be."

"Tell her I miss her."

Jody nodded. "I shall."

Through the open door, Drake saw Jace storm across the Compound yard toward her quarters. A second later Sylvan's wolf bounded into the antechamber with Niki right behind her. Shoulders bunched, ears up, and golden eyes gleaming, the great silver wolf swung her head around and took in the group. Her gaze settled on Drake.

Join me?

Sylvan padded away toward a narrow hallway curving around behind the main staircase.

"If you'll excuse me," Drake said to Jody, "the *imperator* will escort you to the main hall."

"Of course," Jody said in a velvet tone that skimmed over Drake's skin like a warm breeze. If she'd not been mated, that tone might have stirred hunger of quite a different nature.

Drake followed Sylvan's scent down the hall and leaned in the open door of one of the many equipment rooms scattered throughout the Compound, filled with weapons, food caches, and uniforms. The silver wolf shimmered and turned almost faster than she could perceive it.

Drake smiled as Sylvan stood naked before her. "You enjoyed that little show in the courtyard, didn't you?"

Sylvan grinned, the last of the gold slowly bleeding from her eyes. "You know me too well, mate. Breaking up a tussle between two young wolves is always fun, and this gave me a chance to remind the Snowcrest wolves who ruled this territory."

"As if they could forget." Drake tossed Sylvan a T-shirt. She wouldn't ordinarily have bothered, as Sylvan often went shirtless, and she always enjoyed the sight of her mate's body, but considering they were about to enter the council meeting, Sylvan probably wouldn't mind a little more formality. Besides, once the meeting adjourned, Sylvan would be out among the Pack. The Snowcrest females were young and impressionable, and Sylvan was hers, even for viewing. "You should keep that on while we've got visitors."

Sylvan zipped her pants and raised an eyebrow. "Any specific reason?"

"At least one of those Snowcrest females is not so dominant she wouldn't mind being on her back for a big powerful Alpha like you."

Sylvan laughed. "You really just said that without smirking."

"It was an effort. But seriously, there's no need to torment them."

Sylvan laughed again. "I can tell when you're flattering me, you know. If you want more, all you need to do is ask."

Drake tapped Sylvan's chin. "Believe me, mate, when I want more, you'll know it."

"And what of the thrall hanging in the air I scented when I came in? Jody was broadcasting all over, and you were directly in her path." Sylvan's tone was light but her canines showed, and a growl rolled beneath her words.

"Ah, yes. Her hunger runs close to the surface this morning—but you did call a meeting when she'd ordinarily be feeding."

"You felt it, then?" Sylvan's question was casual but her jaw had grown heavy and a cascade of silver pelt rolled beneath her skin.

Drake grasped Sylvan's T-shirt and yanked her close. She kissed her, deep and hard. "You are my mate. Jody Gates cannot call me, no matter how powerful she is or will become. You are foolish to think otherwise."

Grumbling, Sylvan grazed her canines down Drake's neck. "I would have you now if they weren't waiting."

"I'm ready." Drake slid a hand beneath Sylvan's shirt and caressed her stomach. "And I'll be waiting."

Sylvan rubbed her cheek against Drake's, letting out a sigh that spelled contentment, one of the sounds Drake loved to hear from her, almost as much as she loved to hear the growl of satisfaction that came when she brought Sylvan to the edge and pushed her over. "Then we should go."

"Yes," Drake said.

Sylvan loosely clasped Drake's nape as they walked into the main hall. The meeting area occupied the center of the building with windows on one side, a twenty-foot-tall stone fireplace at the end opposite the enormous paired doors, and a balcony running around the second level where Sylvan's office and several other rooms were located. The ceiling soared fifty feet overhead. Oversized leather couches and chairs faced the hearth, although the bulk of those present were standing. A line of Jody's personal guards stood with shouldered weapons, their backs to the shuttered windows. Per routine whenever a Vampire was present during daylight hours, the *centuri*, overseen by Niki, would have double-checked all the locks on the light-blocking shutters before Jody's arrival. Her guards, however, would never rely on anyone else to ensure their Liege's safety.

Jody lounged against the stone column that bordered the fireplace, a crystal goblet of smoky brandy in her hand. She caught Sylvan's eye and lifted the glass in salute. "Alpha. Very nice."

Sylvan grinned with the slightest show of canines. Predator to predator. "Breakfast?"

Jody grinned back, a flash of incisors showing for a second above her pale lips. Her color was high, pink tingeing her translucent skin. She must've fed moments before arriving.

"Late dinner," Jody said. "I hadn't yet retired when I got your call."

"I realize this is inconvenient for you, Liege Gates."

Jody shrugged. "Another excuse to savor my consort. I have no complaints."

"Then, my thanks for being here." Sylvan turned from Jody, and nodded to Torren and her mate. "Lord Torren, I know it's been a long journey and you're anxious to be home, but something unexpected has arisen."

Torren sat in an oversized leather chair to Sylvan's left, with Misha, her young Were mate, draped across her lap. She swept a hand down Misha's mahogany hair and rested her long, elegant hand on Misha's shoulder. A large square sapphire gleamed on her left ring finger. "My lady and I are at your disposal, Alpha Mir, Prima."

Formalities disposed of, Sylvan and Drake sat on the large sofa. Jody remained standing by the mantel. "As we were embarking at the airport," Sylvan said, "the Snowcrest Alpha, Zora Constantine, approached me in private to request aid."

Jody frowned. "Snowcrest. They're Canadian, aren't they?"

"Actually, no," Sylvan said. "Their Pack descends from French-Canadian roots, but the bulk of their territory borders ours to the far north. They're our buffer zone with the Canadian Razorbacks."

"Who are mostly feral wolf Weres," Misha put in.

Sylvan nodded to her former lieutenant. "Correct. The Razorback territory is vast, their numbers are small, and their society consists largely of lone wolves."

Torren asked, "And these Snowcrest wolves? Who are they?"

"A small Pack that also occupies a large territory, spread out, as I said, adjoining our northern border on the southern side, the St. Lawrence River to their north, and the Great Lakes to the west. Most of the population occupies a mountain stronghold along the eastern border with Vermont, Cresthome."

"I take it that young Alpha in the Compound yard is their leader?" Jody asked.

"A recent occurrence," Sylvan said. "Constantine assumed the mantle less than a year ago after surviving a number of challenges that divided the more senior members of the Pack."

Drake frowned. "Isn't ascension to Alpha usually determined by heredity or, if not, by proclaiming the heir while the ruling Alpha is still in power? Why wasn't she challenged before she took the mantle?"

"Zora's father, the previous Alpha, was not her father by blood, but he had declared her his heir." Sylvan shook her head. "Not everyone in the Pack accepted that. Zora was found in the wild, having been raised by a pack of wolves, when she was three. After the Alpha's death, some of the Weres declared her *mutia* and gave challenge."

Misha gasped. "Abandoned? How could that have happened?"

"No one knows. The assumption is her mother might've lost her mate and possibly died in childbirth. Whatever, Zora was not entitled to lead based on blood, but she earned the right by sustaining the challenge."

"So it's not a question of rebellion that brings her here," Drake said.

"No. In the last month, multiple raids along Snowcrest's perimeter have resulted in the deaths of a number of their sentries and disruption of their trade routes to Canada. The Snowcrest wolves are traders. The deer, elk, and moose populations are without substantial predators throughout their territory. The Weres keep the numbers down to prevent starvation with frequent hunts and trade the pelts with merchants in Canada. Their economic losses have begun to mount up, but more importantly, the continued raids have brought Zora's leadership into question."

"Do they know who's behind the incursions?" Jody asked.

"That's part of the problem. They haven't been able to locate any evidence that would help them identify the raiders. Snowcrest wolves are excellent trackers, but they're not warriors. They've doubled their sentries, but they have no substantial army. Their lines of defense are thin and Constantine fears Cresthome is at risk."

"What is it that they've asked?" Drake said.

"Zora Constantine has offered allegiance, including conscription rights, should we go to war and need more warriors. In return, we provide protection, including ferreting out these raiders."

Niki, who'd remained silent until then, lounging against one wall, her arms folded across her chest, snorted. "As if the Snowcrest wolves would be of any use if it came to a fight."

Drake suppressed a smile. Their general considered their warriors without parallel, and she couldn't argue. The Timberwolf warriors had been bloodied enough to prove it. "A symbolic gesture, Niki, but one that solidifies an alliance for all concerned."

"We would come to their aid regardless," Niki grumbled.

"Indeed we would," Drake said.

Torren let out a breath. "Does anything about the timing strike you as odd?"

Sylvan grimaced. "More than odd. I sense a trap. Snowcrest has never been the object of aggression before. Now, when so much is in flux, when our negotiations with the humans are at their most uncertain, when the Vampire nation"—she glanced at Jody—"has undergone recent change of leadership, a situation almost guaranteed to draw us into potential conflict arises on our border."

"Not only that," Drake pointed out, "but another Pack asks us for aid, and we can hardly refuse."

"You distrust this Constantine?" Jody said flatly.

"I have no reason to," Sylvan said, "but it must be considered. If not her, one of those close to her could be working against her."

Niki stepped forward. "Then it's time that we take a squad north and take care of these raiders." Her eyes gleamed. "One way or the other, we'll have our answer about Snowcrest."

"There's something else that occurs," Torren said, "if I may theorize, Alpha."

"Of course," Sylvan said.

"I understand these Weres are trackers, and if they can't even find a trail, that might suggest there is none."

Misha stiffened. "A Gate? You think the raiders could be Fae?"

Torren stroked her arm. "Cecilia, Queen of Thorns and Ruler of Faerie, has been growing more powerful over the centuries—"

"And more unbalanced," Misha said. "And she wants to make an example of you, Torren. You can't—"

"I am not so easily ensnared, my lady love," Torren said, a swirling aura of power encompassing the pair for a moment. Misha shivered and curled closer in Torren's arms. "Except by you."

"Your Hound just wants to hunt," Misha said without heat.

"Always, my lady." A bemused smile on her face, Torren glanced at Sylvan. "My services are yours for this venture."

Sylvan nodded and turned to Jody. "While I hope this turns out to be purely a wolf matter, I will keep you informed."

"Vampires don't mind cold weather," Jody said mildly. "It thickens the blood. Should you need reinforcements, my Vampires stand ready to honor our allegiance."

"Then we are decided. I'll advise Zora we'll leave in the morning," Sylvan said. "I trust that gives everyone time to complete their homecoming celebrations."

Torren rose, her arm around Misha's waist. "We shall be ready. By your leave, we'll return home for now."

Sylvan nodded, and Torren and Misha glided out.

Jody strode over and clasped Sylvan's forearm in a firm, cool grip. "Be careful."

"Always."

Jody's human servants converged around her, and they moved en masse toward the entrance.

"I'll prepare our warriors, Alpha," Niki asked. "A squad of twenty will allow us to move quickly but field a substantial force."

"Agreed," Sylvan said. "Leave half the *centuri* here with the Prima, however."

Drake clasped Sylvan's hand. "Would you give us a moment before marshaling your warriors, *Imperator*."

Niki flicked a glance at Sylvan who said nothing. Nodding abruptly, she departed quickly.

Drake turned to Sylvan, her expression mildly quizzical. "You didn't think to tell me any of this before now?"

Sylvan almost managed to look innocent. "I was rather busy. Homecoming activities."

"Mm, I remember. There must've been a moment or two somewhere."

Sylvan let out a sigh. "What would you have me do, Prima. We can't leave the Pack leaderless."

"I am aware of how tenuous the political situation is," Drake said, "but we are deep in our own territory surrounded by the finest warriors, human or Praetern, in the world. How long do you expect this to take?"

Sylvan shrugged. "It's hard to tell. If we come upon a trail, or a traitor, quickly, it could be a matter of days. If we haven't made any progress in a week, I'll leave a squad behind to patrol with the Snowcrest sentries."

"A week then. And how long will it take us to return to the Compound? Hours?"

Sylvan's canines flared and her jaw tightened, a faint dusting of silver spreading down her bare forearms. "You seek to corner me, Prima."

Drake slid both arms around Sylvan's waist, kissed her neck, and bit her deep enough to rouse her wolf. "I don't need to corner you. You already know where I'm going."

Sylvan sighed. "We'll be five hours away by vehicle. Niki won't like both of us being absent from the Compound, and we can't field our forces without her."

"I know, but she'll just grumble a little louder."

"True." Sylvan slung an arm around Drake's shoulders. "We'll need to formalize a third."

"Agreed. Callan or Max?"

"Callan is a soldier and needed with our warriors. Max."

Drake nodded. "Agreed."

"I'll tell Niki," Sylvan said, "and we'll hold the ceremony tonight."

"I have a stop to make too, but after that," Drake said, sliding a hand under Sylvan's shirt and caressing her, "join me in the den?"

Sylvan gripped her neck, pulled her close, and kissed her. "With pleasure."

CHAPTER SEVEN

Drake followed the waves of distress she'd sensed while Sylvan was in the midst of the council meeting. Like Sylvan, she was psychically connected to every member of the Pack through her mate bond. The unique blending of hers and Sylvan's genetic and neurophysical chemicals connected them to each other and the Pack. While she wasn't as highly attuned as Sylvan to each member, especially at longer distances, she readily detected signals of pain, physical and emotional.

As much as every instinct drove her to protect and comfort her Pack member, she'd waited until Sylvan had completed the briefing. Hurrying now, Drake entered the auxiliary barracks where the *centuri* and upper level soldiers had their living quarters. Some mated Weres made their dens in the forest at the far extent of the Compound, as did she and Sylvan—far enough away for privacy, but an easy distance back to the fortified sections in case of attack. For the most part, however, the warriors who might be needed if an assault occurred lived in one of the barracks.

Like all the buildings within the Compound, this was an unadorned timber and stone rectangle with a center hallway, flanked by rooms with unmarked wooden doors and windows large enough for a wolf in pelt to use as an entrance—or quick exit.

Passing down the first-floor hall to the second-floor stairs, Drake identified Jace's location from the currents of anger, frustration, and, unexpectedly, confusion, emanating from her room, but Jace wasn't the Were who called to her. She bounded up to the second floor and knocked on the door to a suite overlooking the training area.

Andrea, a statuesque auburn-haired human, opened the door, her face registering surprise and embarrassment when she saw Drake. "Prima! Max isn't here. Is there something I can help you with?"

"I thought there might be something I could help *you* with," Drake said.

"Oh, of course." Andrea flushed, ducking her head as she opened the door wide. "Please come in. I should've known there was no way to keep anything from a Were. Especially not you." She shook her head. "Sylvan probably knows too, doesn't she?"

Drake said, "Sylvan is aware of your discomfort, almost certainly, but unlike me, she probably would wait for you to come to her."

Andrea smiled ruefully and gestured to the sofa in the small sitting area. "Can I get you anything?"

"No, I'm fine."

"So you can tell I am...upset," Andrea said, taking a bottle of water from the refrigerator, looking as if she needed something to occupy herself with while gathering the courage to talk about what was troubling her.

"That's hard to ignore. You're telegraphing much more strongly than I would've expected for a human," Drake mused. "It must be the mate bond, strengthening your chemical connection to Pack in some way."

Andrea sat down in an overstuffed chair opposite the sofa, put her water aside, and clasped her hands between her knees. She stared down at them for a moment, then met Drake's eyes. "There's no point in hiding it. I'm upset because Max refuses to accept there's anything different between our bond and if he were mated to a Were."

"Why do you think there is? You can feel your link to Max, can't you?"

"Yes, of course."

"And to the Pack?"

"Yes." Andrea smiled. "It's really quite amazing. I know Max can communicate with Packmates telepathically, and sometimes he can with me. That's new."

"So there's every indication your bond is growing stronger."

"That's not the problem."

"Does this have anything to do with Max being gone for a week? Other than when he was driven by mating frenzy, this might have been the first time you've been exposed to him under the influence of Sylvan's call."

Color slashed across Andrea's cheeks, and she grinned. "You mean his horns being so big he could barely get through the door without turning his head? That welcome home surprise?"

Drake laughed. "I don't think that metaphor really works for a wolf. Besides, that tends to be a natural state for most Weres, but yes, the thought had crossed my mind you might have been unprepared."

"The only thing that bothers me about Max and his needs is that sometimes he worries about me. That somehow I'll be overwhelmed."

"But you don't have any concerns."

"Believe me, I can handle him—anytime."

"Good," Drake said. "I'm sure you let him know that."

"Oh, in no uncertain terms."

"Then?"

Andrea let out a breath. "Max is my mate, my husband, in my way of thinking, and we're starting off with some challenges. Like I said, Max refuses to accept that any of them matter, but one does. One has to."

Drake nodded. "You're talking about young."

"Yes."

"Weres and humans have been interbreeding for generations. Probably longer. There's every reason to believe that you can conceive and carry Max's young."

"I know," Andrea said, "and our young will be healthy."

"That's right, and believe me, Elena and Sophia will probably be camping on your couch for most of your pregnancy. You have nothing to fear."

"Except I can't give Max a Were offspring."

Drake held Andrea's gaze. "As far as we know, no. The Were characteristics are transmitted through maternal mitochondrial genetic material, which is how dominant females can produce young with other females. Max cannot, as far as we know, impregnate you with the appropriate genetic material."

"He says it doesn't matter."

"Max is very honest, and he loves you." Drake kept her tone even. She'd suffered some of these same misgivings herself when she and

Sylvan mated. "You're his mate, and he deserves for you to believe him."

Andrea closed her eyes and rubbed her temples. "I know, I know. And I do." She opened her eyes, sadness swimming through the gold-flecked green. "I just want him to have everything he deserves."

"He already does. His wolf chose you, and so did he." Drake tilted her head. "Lean forward."

Andrea raised her brows but did as Drake asked.

"Your eye color is changing."

"Sorry?"

"You've got gold flecks in your irises."

"Really? Is that important…What does that mean?"

Drake shook her head. "Right now, I have no idea. But I can tell you this—genetic variants are not only naturally present in the natural Were population, they've been introduced experimentally. We don't know when those experiments began, or how many of us might be affected, or in what way. We don't even know how many humans have been exposed. For now, I would say the verdict is not in as to exactly what your mating Max will lead to when you become pregnant."

"How will we know?" Andrea asked quietly.

"You might not. I didn't. We weren't sure if I could bear Sylvan's young, and if I did, if they'd be Weres, or even healthy. It's terrifying, *but* our scientists and doctors are working on it. So my advice is to enjoy your mate as often as you like, and when the time comes, we'll know."

Andrea smiled. "I have to say that's the best prescription I've ever been given."

Drake rose. "Anytime you want to talk about it, come find me."

"Thank you, Prima, I will," Andrea said, her anxiety lessening.

Heading back to her den and Sylvan, Drake committed anew to protecting the well-being of the Pack. If that meant going to war for them, she was ready.

The Alpha was coming. Ash sat up on the cot where she'd been lying, staring at the ceiling, since Evan had escorted her to her room.

Evan had said nothing, but she sensed his sympathy. Cybil and Ryan hadn't emerged from the other room.

The Alpha entered alone and closed the door behind her. Ash dropped her head. "Alpha."

"Do you have an explanation, Captain?" Zora said.

"No, Alpha."

"No reason at all why you provoked one of Alpha Mir's *centuri*, the captain of the Prima's personal guard?"

"No, Alpha."

"Can you think of any reason why I shouldn't send you back to Cresthome immediately?"

"Yes, Alpha!" Ash's head snapped up but she kept her gaze below her Alpha's. "I wish to carry out my duty, Alpha, and that is to defend you with my life. I would ask you to allow me to continue to do that."

"And you can swear that there will not be a repeat of what happened."

"I…" Ash squared her shoulders. "I don't know, Alpha. I don't understand it, but every time I scent her, my wolf demands I tangle. The need strips me of all control."

"And you've never had this experience before," Zora said.

"No, Alpha. I've been driven to tangle when your call is strong, or when a female is in heat, but I've always been able to control my wolf. I wanted to…"

"You want to what?" Zora said softly.

"I wanted…"

"You attacked without challenge. Did you intend to hurt her?"

Ash frowned. "No…*no*."

"Well, she seemed to be intent on hurting you. Between the two of you, I couldn't tell which of you was winning that tussle out there."

"I wanted to bite her," Ash confessed.

"I'm sure she wouldn't be the first Were you've bitten in a frenzy," Zora said reasonably.

"This was different." Ash shuddered. "I wanted to leave a mark that everyone could see." Pelt flared down the center of her torso, streaked between her hardening abdominals, and dusted the surface of her thighs. Her wolf reared up, ferocious and demanding release. "I wanted everyone to see I had taken her."

"I thought so." Zora squeezed the bridge of her nose. "Ash, hasn't it occurred to you that what was happening was mating frenzy?"

"That's impossible," Ash said.

"Oh, why?" Zora asked.

"Because I don't...She's a Timberwolf, she's not Pack."

Zora smiled thinly. "She's an unmated female, and your wolf recognizes her."

"No. It's impossible," Ash said flatly. "It's just sex frenzy. Alpha Mir was broadcasting everywhere before we even reached the Compound. She was ready to take her mate as soon as we approached. That's all. I wasn't used to it. I'll know what to expect next time."

"Do you really think you can ignore the demands of your wolf and still function?"

Ash lifted her chin. "I will not have an out-Pack mating. Besides, she's too dominant to submit."

"Perhaps your wolf intends to submit to her," Zora said.

Ash snarled.

Zora sighed. "All right, Captain, assuming Alpha Mir's call caught you by surprise and that little display out there was just sex frenzy, we'll give you another chance to prove you can control yourself and carry out your duties."

Ash snapped to attention and saluted. "Thank you, Alpha."

"Your wolf needs to run. Go." Zora bounded across the room and swept Ash into a hard embrace. "Listen to your wolf, Ash. You can't fight what's part of you."

Ash breathed in her Alpha's scent, relaxed in the safety and security of Pack, felt the loneliness and confusion slip away. "Yes, Alpha."

Zora nuzzled her cheek, let her go, and disappeared.

Ash waited until she heard the Alpha return to her own quarters before starting down the hall. She'd sworn she could control her wolf, but if Jace waited outside, she wanted to be sure the Alpha wasn't around to witness her struggles if she was wrong.

Relief warred with disappointment when she stepped onto the porch and found a male standing post. Jace was gone.

"Can I help you?" he said.

"Is there a trail within the perimeter where I can run?"

"Follow the footpath between this building and the one on the right, and you'll reach the forest. The trail circles the Compound." He smiled. "It's a big Compound. If that doesn't work, maybe I can help."

She raised a brow. "Help what?"

"I can't leave my post yet, but I'll be relieved in an hour."

"I appreciate the offer, but no."

He shrugged good-naturedly. "If you change your mind, just ask for Darrell."

"I won't." Ash vaulted the rail and strode onto the path he'd pointed out to her. She shed her clothes in a stand of pines and left them in the cover of a rocky overhang next to some other hastily discarded shirts and pants, and let her wolf ascend. In seconds her paws struck warm earth and soft pine needles as her wolf howled with the joy of freedom.

Chapter Eight

"I know you're out there," Jace snapped. "You might as well come in."

The door to her single room, a privilege awarded the *centuri*, opened and her twin stepped in. He'd been among the cadre accompanying the Alpha to DC, and she hadn't seen him since his return. She'd sensed him among the crowd witnessing the aftermath of her tussle with Ash. Which meant he'd seen the Alpha discipline her in front of the whole yard. She tightened her jaw and glared. "What do you want?"

Jonathan, his golden hair and blue eyes matching hers, smirked. "I can't leave you alone for an entire morning without you causing trouble?"

"Being first in the birth order—by *seconds*—does not make you my keeper," Jace snarled. "And *I* wasn't causing trouble. *I* was performing my duty and a renegade wolf attacked me."

"Not exactly a renegade." Jonathan leaned back against the closed door, his smile widening, his wolf clearly enjoying the game of taunt and tease. "The way I heard it, the visiting Were is the Alpha's *guest*, and she challenged you."

"She never offered challenge. She just—" Jace frowned, still trying to make sense of everything that had happened. She'd anticipated Ash's approach from the moment Ash had left the room at the far end of the barracks and bounded down the hall. Ash had broadcast a potent mix of pheromones and aggression, and Jace's wolf had reacted strangely. She should have been in full battle mode, but her instincts had been clouded by a mixture of anticipation and a churning excitement in the pit of her stomach.

"So she provoked you into tussling." Jonathan shrugged. "Hardly a first for you."

Her brother was right again, and knowing it only added to Jace's frustrated confusion. She enjoyed a good tussle, and nothing pleased her more than a dominance match, especially when she always won. Well, almost always won. She had yet to best Callan, but he was a more experienced warrior. And she wouldn't even think of a tussle with the *imperator*. No Were would. The only wolf the *imperator* ever tussled with was the Alpha.

Jace tussled for the joy of physical contact and often ended her match with an offer to tangle. When the hormones subsided and her needs were met, she gave it little thought. But today had been different. She'd wanted to tussle with this stranger from the instant she'd scented her intoxicating blend of cedar and sun-drenched earth, wanted it so much the need still burned in her loins.

"We tussled," Jace said defensively. "What of it."

"And you let her get the best of you?"

"No!" Jace's wolf bristled, ready to challenge. "The Alpha intervened before I could defeat her."

"I heard she was about to bite you," Jonathan said, his tone halfway between provocative and questioning.

"No way was that happening," Jace said. But she wasn't really so sure. When Ash had straddled her, sex burning against Jace's thigh, her canines down, her eyes wolf-gold, her claws gouging Jace's flanks, Jace responded in a way she'd never experienced before. Her glands filled to bursting, her sex throbbed on the brink of release, and icy pain lanced through her muscles and deep into her spine. The pain, the need, was maddening. She'd known somehow that the piercing power of Ash's bite would have given her everything her wolf howled for—release, relief, paralyzing pleasure. Infuriated, she fought her instincts. She had never submitted to another's bite. Oh, she'd been bitten, and done the same to others, but a bite during tangling meant no more than spilling. But to burn for it, to verge on madness without it—to be ready to expose her throat? She stared mutely at her brother.

"You wanted it, didn't you," Jonathan said quietly. "Why are you afraid to admit it?"

"Never." Jace's wolf howled, savaging her with tooth and claw. Ash had released during their tussle, her *victus* hot and powerful, but

Jace had not. Pain scoured her nerve endings, her sex swollen and throbbing. Pelt rolled beneath her skin, her jaw lengthened, her limbs splintered and reformed, and her vision sharpened. Bunching her powerful shoulders, she bolted through the window, struck the ground running, and raced off into the forest.

Her wolf covered the ground in long fluid strides, the warm midday air pungent with aroma of prey—fox and rabbit, small ground animals, and mice. Deer bedded down in the shade of the thick undergrowth. But she hunted none. Her hunt was for something far different. She scented her, and the foreign scent of an out-Pack wolf Were should have stirred her battle lust, but the sweet-pungent trail Ash left in her wake inflamed her wolf with a flood of pheromones. Ash's trail was fresh, and Jace scented another wolf following her quarry, stalking what was *hers* to claim. She howled a warning, issuing challenge, and diverted from the narrow path snaking through the forest to cut over the crest of the ridge to her left and intercept her prey. She would finish what Ash had started.

Ash searched for a place to confront the two wolves who'd been trailing her almost since she'd left the barracks. They were fast, but so was she, and as soon as she'd realized they were tracking her, she'd run into a stream and followed it downwind, making it impossible for them to catch her scent. They'd found her again, of course, but she'd circled back to the trail and, if she stayed on the trail, could be back at the Compound before they caught her.

She could escape a fight, if she wanted. But she didn't. She would not relent now. She was ready, and she wasn't afraid of two wolves, or twenty. Her wolf had been frustrated over and over since they'd arrived in the Timberwolf territory, and then she'd been humiliated in front of the entire Timberwolf Pack, shamed in front of her Alpha, and, worst of all, denied what she had won by strength—she'd been denied the tantalizing satisfaction of claiming Jace in the instant of release. She had fought for it, fought *Jace* for it, and been denied. She would not be denied now—even if the satisfaction of winning a challenge with a pair of strange wolves would be a hollow victory. Her wolf wanted more.

Leaving the stream, she bounded up a steep embankment into a clearing ringed by fallen pines on three sides that formed a natural fighting arena. Sunlight filled the glade, and she put her back to the slanting rays. Her wolf lowered her back, shoulders bunched and muscles primed to leap. Facing the far edge of the clearing, she waited.

Two wolves, a brown and white streaked female and a larger, heavier silver-tipped black male, bounded from the forest and circled the grassy area, one breaking left, the other right. A simple tactic when the prey was outnumbered. They would strike at her from two directions in rapid succession, one seeking to take her down by the neck, the other to mount her and tear out her throat.

Ash growled, challenging them to try. She crouched, waiting for the first attack, her ruff standing up, her hindquarters quivering, her sex growing heavy and full. She wanted this. Needed it.

The male growled and eased farther to Ash's left, seeking to draw her attention. Ash kept him in her peripheral sight, but she watched the female. The pair expected her to anticipate the first attack from the male, but that would come from the smaller, swifter, more agile wolf. With no warning, the brown female launched herself at Ash, aiming to land on her back and sink canines into the back of her neck. The force of the blow would pull Ash to the ground where the male could take her belly and then her throat.

Ash pivoted to face the female head-on and counterattacked, leaping to meet her in midair where her greater weight threw the female off balance. Grabbing the wolf by the throat, Ash dragged her down, her canines piercing through pelt into flesh, drawing blood. Not a crushing bite—she had no need to kill her, not unless they took the attack that far. Shaking her head, Ash growled, flinging the female from side to side and threatening to clap her jaws tighter around the female's vulnerable windpipe. The female whined, her body going limp in submission.

Ash rolled her onto her back and mounted her then, seconds from riding her to release. A heavy blow struck her in the shoulder and broke her grip on the subdued female. Rolling away, Ash spun to meet the new assault.

The male attacked again, canines clamping onto her neck, claws raking her underside, scoring her belly. Ash thrashed, snapping and growling, trying to dislodge him. He pinned her with his larger, heavier body, and she caught a foreleg in her mouth. He howled, and canines raked her shoulder. The hard length of his sex pressed against her belly, and Ash slashed at his flanks with her claws. He howled again and she twisted her body into a tight curve, still holding his foreleg in her grip. His weight lifted from her back as he rolled to prevent her from snapping his leg.

The female snapped at Ash's haunches, but she ignored her. The male would submit, and then the female would give up the fight. Ash braced her rear and brought all her power to bear on the leg clamped in her jaws. The male whined and howled. The female raced in and out, biting and clawing. Ash was bloodied and tired, but she refused to loosen her grip. She could not hold off another assault.

The male closed his jaws on her ear, and Ash snarled. Then a silver wolf with gleaming blue eyes soared over Ash's shoulders and struck the smaller female in midleap. Jace's scent flooded Ash's senses, and her wolf howled in triumph. Whimpering, the female slunk away. With a surge of power bolstered by Jace's arrival, Ash flipped the male, straddled his belly, and set her canines into his throat. The hot flood of his *victus* streamed down her flanks as he submitted.

She held him down until he was completely motionless, his head tipped back, his throat exposed. With a final shake designed to remind him she could have torn out his throat, she loosened her grip. Their tussle had ended.

The black wolf, panting and shivering, turned his head away and crept off. Ash spun around and padded over to where Jace crouched, watching the forest for any sign of another assault. Her ears flicked as she cut her gaze to Ash.

Her whine was a question, even though Ash could not hear her in her head.

Are you hurt?

With a snort, Ash licked Jace's muzzle as if to say *From them? Ha.*

Grinning a pure wolf grin, Jace rubbed a shoulder against Ash's.

So close now, Jace's call was clear and sharp—laden with the promise of sex and power and pleasure. Ash's wolf rumbled, her ears rising in invitation as she backed away. Jace followed her with her piercing wolf-blue eyes. The air around her shimmered as she shed pelt.

Ash followed, and an instant later they faced each other, naked, flushed with triumph, Jace's eyes still glowing with the power of her wolf.

"What were you trying to do," Jace demanded, her tone rough with fury.

"Your wolves needed to be taught a lesson," Ash said offhandedly, watching Jace for signs she was about to attack. Jace's chest glistened with sex-sheen. Her breasts strained, tight-nippled and taut. Her stark abdominals rippled like granite. A mist of pheromones engulfed her, black currant and crushed pine, Jace's call.

Ash's claws punched out and her clitoris pulsed painfully. She ran a hand down her middle, watched Jace's eyes follow the path of her fingers as she traced the line of her pelt to the juncture of her thighs.

Jace growled, her gaze snapping to Ash's. "You had no call to challenge them."

"I answered challenge, as was my right," Ash said.

Jace circled her, a shimmer of snowy white pelt shimmering on her torso. Her wolf pressed close to the surface.

"As I will answer you, Captain."

Jace grinned. "You think you can?"

"I'm ready," Ash whispered. She wanted to tussle. She wanted the slick heat of Jace's sex rubbing over her skin as they rolled and thrashed. She wanted to put the arrogant dominant under her. She wanted Jace in her mouth. Pelt streaked her belly, lust raking her middle.

"I know," Jace growled. "You were about to spill all over Deirdre."

"Is that her name?" Ash taunted her, provoking her. "I'll have to find her later. She was willing and ready."

"No." Jace cleared the distance between them in a leap so swift Ash barely had time to brace herself. A claw-tipped hand grasped her nape. Fierce blue eyes bored into hers. Jace's breasts, hot and firm, crushed hers. "You won't."

Ash growled, her thighs hard as rocks, her glands so tense she was about to release against her will. "Why shouldn't I?"

"Because I'll have you first."

Jace snarled and took Ash's mouth in a crushing kiss. Canines caught at Ash's lip, and a velvet tongue—demanding as a blade—slid into her mouth. Jace's sex pressed to hers, the hard prominence of Jace's clitoris riding hers. Ash cupped Jace's breast, circled her nipple with a blunt claw.

Hips thrusting restlessly between Ash's thighs, Jace gasped. "Now. Now you are mine."

Jace bit her neck, and Ash howled. Jace locked her arms around Ash's waist, canted her hip, and threw her to the ground. Ash landed on her back and Jace rolled on top of her. Jace's thigh shot between Ash's legs, crushing her sex, and fire scorched her brain like wildfire cresting a mountaintop. Ash thrashed and twisted, got a hand between them, and squeezed Jace's sex. Hot firm flesh filled her palm and Jace's scent thickened in the air around them.

Jace reared back, a grimace of pain and pleasure etched in the sharp angles of her face. Ash pushed her away and, as Jace rolled, straddled her, ending up with her thighs clamped to Jace's midsection.

"Now I will have you," Ash panted, her glands ready to empty. Her heart pounded, her stomach clenched over and over, the muscles strained to force her essence over the wolf beneath her.

Jace bared her canines. "I will never submit to your bite."

The gleaming skin just above Jace's breast swelled with a rush of blood and hormones, and Ash fought her wolf's raging demand to bite her there, to claim her. Shuddering, Ash cupped Jace's sex and milked her with long, relentless strokes, working her thumb over the base of her clitoris. "I don't need you to submit."

Jace rode Ash's hand, wild and demanding. With a sudden thrust of her hips, she threw back her head and released into Ash's hand.

Ash gripped Jace's neck, pulled her upright, and kissed her. When Jace drove her claws into Ash's back, Ash spilled over her. Jace's howl of triumph was the last thing Ash heard before her strength deserted her.

CHAPTER NINE

Jace stretched, the bed of crushed pine needles beneath her body bathing her in their sweet aroma. Warm sunlight danced on her face, and heat of a different kind smoldered against her back. A body curled around her, firm chest and belly molded to the curve of her back and the swell of her hips. The unaccustomed weight of an arm draped across her middle. Jace's blood thrummed thick and heavy, a steady beat of arousal spreading down her thighs from her loins. Her wolf sighed and grumbled. Still needy. Pricking her inside with needle-sharp teeth and claws. Demanding she finish. Take. Claim.

Bite.

Jace's eyes snapped open. Still in the glade, the sun at half nadir. Late afternoon. She'd drifted, unaware of her surroundings, peaceful, her guard down, unprotected. Ash was still here—her arm encircling Jace's abdomen, her fingers still tapered to blunt claws, resting possessively on the underside of her breast. Jace's nipple tightened and her sex swelled. She'd never awakened this way before—she'd never slipped into such contentment after a tangle. Tangling was for the release of the pent-up tension and warring hormones that were a natural part of a Were's life—sex was as essential as breathing, and she took about as much notice of it. Or who she tangled with. Until now. Jace growled softly.

Ash nuzzled her neck, her breath a caress that tingled in Jace's clitoris. "You smell like the mountaintop after a spring melt—when the berry bushes break through the snow and the wind carries the first seeds of spring."

Ash's mouth moved slowly over Jace's neck, tasting her, skimming ever so lightly with her canines. Jace shuddered, her stomach twisting with need. Ash squeezed her breast and rubbed the hard peak of her nipple with her thumb. Jace's legs twitched and her glands pounded.

"Move away, Wolf," Jace warned.

"Why? You like it. So do I." Ash pressed her hips to Jace's ass, swept her palm down the middle of Jace's stomach, feathering the fine pelt line that dove between her thighs. Laughing lazily, Ash traced the cleft into the delta between her thighs and teased her sex.

Jace arched her back, lifting into Ash's palm and rubbing her sensitive flesh against Ash's fingers. She readied, the pressure in her belly an agony of desire. All she needed was for Ash to stroke her. The press-pull on her tense clitoris and bursting glands would empty her. She raked her claws down Ash's arm. "Massage me."

"Not yet," Ash murmured, her canines trailing down the side of Jace's neck to the curve of her shoulder. Ash bit down gently in the sensitive angle, not enough to puncture, just enough to incense Jace's wolf. Jace's wolf snapped and howled in a frenzy of sex and pheromones. Jace's pelt shimmered beneath her skin and her jaw tensed. Close—so close to releasing, so close to giving her wolf the power to take what she wanted.

"You presume too much," Jace snarled, yanking Ash's hand from her sex. The pain became a whirlwind of slashing claws and rending teeth. Her wolf set upon her in a fury. Jace shivered.

"Stubborn wolf," Ash chided and rolled onto her back, pulling Jace over with her. "You can't stop now. I can feel you about to explode."

"When *I'm* ready." Jace straddled her, her breath catching as she glanced down and saw Ash clearly for the first time since she'd burst into the clearing and driven off the wolves who'd attacked Ash. Then she'd seen only the fierce power of Ash's wolf in battle, quick and strong and fearless. Now Ash regarded her with an arrogant smile, the tips of her canines just brushing the edge of her full lower lip, sunlight casting her skin in bronze. Ash's eyes glittered, hungry and demanding. Jace traced the angle of her bold jaw with a claw. Her wolf rumbled in satisfaction, and Jace's sex quickened against Ash's belly.

"We should not have slept," Jace said, refusing her wolf's call.

Ash gripped Jace's hips in both hands and pulled her forward, arching beneath her, inviting, then pushed her away. "Our wolves would've wakened us."

"I need to return to the Compound, and you to the barracks."

"This won't take long. Stop fighting it." Ash kept up the back and forth push and pull, faster and harder, forcing Jace to ride her.

Fire shot through Jace's loins, and she curled forward when her abdominals clenched. She fought to break Ash's control of her, but every second she fought her need, the more her wolf fought her. The agony in her loins shredded her flesh from her bones. Jace gripped Ash's shoulders, leaned down, and snarled in her face. "You mistake a tangle for more. You will not bite me."

"No more than a tangle," Ash growled. "Just that."

Blood boiling with lust, Jace kissed her. Ash's eyes flashed gold and Jace caught her lip with her teeth and tugged. Ash jerked beneath her.

Yes. Now, yes. When you are mine.

Digging her claws in, holding Ash down where she belonged, Jace plunged her tongue into Ash's mouth, taunting and teasing, daring her to struggle. Ash bucked beneath her, dug her claws into her hips, forced her clitoris hard against her belly. The tussling stoked Jace's excitement, drove her wolf into a frenzy.

Ash jerked her head away, gasping. "You're ready to spill."

Jace snarled. "Are you ready to submit?"

Ash laughed, arrogant and possessive. She jerked Jace up onto her knees. "I'm ready to taste you."

Helpless with need, Jace thrust her hips forward, presenting her sex for Ash's mouth. Ash's lips closed around her, her eyes wolf-gold and mad with hunger. Flame exploded in Jace's sex and her glands burned. The pressure built, a fist in her midsection ready to tear her open. She arched her back, threw back her head, and howled.

Ash pressed her canines on either side of Jace's clitoris while she licked and sucked and pulled her deep into her mouth. Jace gripped her head and rode her mouth, guttural cries torn from her chest. She locked eyes with Ash, thrust in, pulled back, faster and faster. Ash's mouth slid up and down, her lips tugging and caressing.

Every muscle tense, Jace gripped her neck, claws possessive around her nape. "I'm going to fill you," Jace gasped and emptied in a hot flood that ripped her insides with breathless ecstasy. Jace's thighs trembled, her belly convulsed, and her sex beat in time with her raging heart. When the pulsations in her sex ended, she was drained, body and soul.

Jace slumped back, weak limbed and helpless.

Ash groaned, her chest heaving, her neck and chest gleaming with sex-sheen, her pelt shimmering close beneath the skin. The soft vulnerable juncture of flesh where her powerful shoulders, bunched and rippled, met her neck pulsed with the hot thick rush of her blood. She was a wolf in the fullness of her power, and Jace ached to sink her canines into her.

"Bite me." Ash writhed, frenzied with need.

Jace glowered, lust and fury choking her. Her wolf growled, demanding she take what was hers. Demanded she claim. "No."

Ash threw back her head, the delicate column of her throat bared. "Make me spill. Hurry. I can't—"

"Not yet." Jace clenched her jaws, refusing to take her. Not that way. She pushed her hips between Ash's thighs and notched her clitoris, hard again, below Ash's.

Ash bucked, her calves locked tight around Jace's. She panted, her abdominals rigid, her face a stark landscape of pain and pleasure.

Jace grabbed her hips, fitted her clit tightly into the cleft of Ash's sex, a joining, but not a mating. Jace gasped as pleasure impaled her. Ash was so beautiful in her wild need.

"Now—give it to me," Jace growled and bit the etched muscle of Ash's chest. Enough to make her release, but not a claiming.

Ash's neck arched, her jaw lengthened, and her sex pulsed against Jace as she spilled over her. Jace roared as she released again, catching herself on extended arms as she sagged down, her face inches from Ash's.

"Just a tangle," she gasped, "nothing more."

Ash bit her lip, drawing blood, and licked it away. "Nothing more."

Drake paced the broad porch of the den, eager for her mate. More than a week apart, a too-short homecoming, and already the threat of new dangers. She wanted her again before duty claimed her, and another battle awaited them.

Where are you?

On our way.

Sylvan's laughter reached her, and she scented their approach. Heart filling, her wolf ecstatic with anticipation, Drake watched the forest at the edge of the clearing for her family. Sylvan emerged with two cavorting young wolves at her heels, Kira silver pelted and blue eyed, Kendra midnight and gold. Kira chased Kendra, nipping at Kendra's rear, biting her haunches and forcing Kendra to spin around and snap at her muzzle. Kira yipped and feint-attacked, jumping agilely to one side as Kendra countered with a sharp lunge and snapping jaws.

Sylvan, hands on her hips, studied the maneuvers as if the young were already warriors in training. Drake shook her head fondly. "They're just playing."

"First step toward learning to hunt." Sylvan's gaze met Drake's, solemn and proud. "And to do battle."

"They were supposed to be with Roger, working on tracking with the other young today."

Sylvan grinned. "I just stopped by to see them. Haven't had a chance since I got back."

"And you liberated them." Drake sighed. "You couldn't wait, could you?"

"Roger said they were disrupting his lessons. Too much energy." Sylvan watched her young tussle. "Plus, every time they shift, all the other pups try and then Roger can't keep any of them on task. I was doing him a favor."

"They're getting better at turning at will, aren't they?" Drake braced herself as the twins loped around the clearing and launched themselves at her in a tornado of paws and wet tongues and joyful barks. Grabbing them by their ruffs, one in each hand, she shook them in playful welcome. Both had grown since the last time they'd shifted. "They're nearly as large as the adolescents now."

"They're young Alphas," Sylvan said proudly. "They should be the largest and the strongest."

"They're all that and more."

"Just a little sooner than we expected." Sylvan wrapped an arm around Drake's waist as the young tore off toward the forest. "Look at them—they're fine."

"I know." Drake tried not to worry, but as healthy and as strong as the twins appeared, she couldn't forget they were something entirely different than anyone had ever seen before. Kira and Kendra were born of the most dominant Were in the Northern Hemisphere and a human-turned Were who'd survived Were fever. Whatever genetic enhancement Drake's mating with Sylvan had produced was still being studied. By all rights, she should have died within days of being bitten by a fevered Were, and she almost had. Sylvan's mate bite and the fusion of their genetic and cellular chemicals had saved her. She'd not only survived, she had been able to bear young, and now Kira and Kendra were likely to be a new breed of Were. They might even be resistant to Were fever. If knowledge of that were to get out, they'd be in even more danger than being the Alpha's heirs already presented.

"Remember who we are," Sylvan said softly and rubbed her cheek over Drake's. "No harm will come to them."

As if to underscore her truth, the pups burst out of the undergrowth, a sleek white wolf in close pursuit. Sophia, the Pack Omega, the healer and calm center who maintained the balance between Were aggression and protectiveness for the entire Pack. She romped around the clearing, Kira and Kendra yipping and tumbling over their own paws in exuberance.

Drake pulled Sylvan's shirt loose and caressed her. "I know."

She and Sylvan—the whole Pack—would protect them with their lives. And for now, they were young who needed to learn the lessons all young needed to survive. "I suppose you had a plan once you helped these two escape their lessons?"

"I thought we'd run and wear them out." Sylvan stripped off her shirt and unzipped her pants.

"Be sure you save a little energy for me." Drake took in the long muscular lines of Sylvan's body, the power in her shoulders, the delicate dangerous contours of her abdomen, the beauty of her bold jaw and brilliant eyes.

"Always." The air around Sylvan shimmered and her wolf stood in the center of the clearing.

"I love you." Drake tossed her clothes onto the porch behind her and called her wolf. She padded to Sylvan's side and bumped shoulders.

Sylvan's wolf rested her muzzle atop Drake's. *I love you, mate. And don't worry, they'll tire long before me.*

Rumbling, Drake nudged her playfully. *Lead the way, Alpha.*

Join us? Sylvan called to Sophia, who crouched panting at the edge of the forest.

Sophia loped over and licked Sylvan's jaw. *With pleasure, Alpha.*

Sylvan barked a wolf command and the two young stiffened, their ears perking, eyes flashing. Sylvan raced across the clearing to the trail behind their den. Drake fell in beside her, Sophia and the young racing behind. Sylvan set a rapid pace, leaving the trail soon after they entered the denser forest, leaping over fallen trees, scampering up rocky escarpments, bounding across sun-drenched clearings. Drake and Sophia kept pace, while the young—loose limbed and heavy pawed—yipped and howled their excitement and made enough noise for an entire Pack on the hunt.

Their joy was infectious, and Drake raised her voice with theirs.

Sylvan leapt over a stream, and her ears perked, muzzle lifted to the wind.

Wolves nearby.

Drake caught the scent of sex, lust, and dominance all wrapped together. Not a simple tangle then. *We could leave them.*

Sylvan's ears flickered. *They do not have leave to challenge. In this I was clear.*

They have leave to run?

Yes.

Drake's wolf grumbled. *But this is more.*

Sylvan snorted and glanced at Sophia. *Omega?*

One of them is seeking a mate. And they both fight it.

Sylvan snarled. *One is out-Pack. My* centuri *should stand down.*

You may be too late to prevent that, Drake cautioned mildly.

We shall see. Sylvan growled and bounded up the slope.

CHAPTER TEN

Nothing more. Ash repeated the oath, even as Jace loomed over her, her eyes still ringed in gold, the tips of her canines still gleaming, still challenging. Ash ignored her wolf's primal urge to answer Jace's call, to demand more. To fight for everything—to give everything. Ash stared at the dusky invitation spread across Jace's chest, the flush of pheromones and roiling hormones an invitation for her to bite. To bite and join. The want in her stomach twisted into a barbed wire coil of need and urgency. She whined softly, a shudder of pleasure-pain rolling through her.

Jace leaned low and kissed her. Her kiss was hot and brutally gentle, a taunting, teasing promise of everything Ash feared—and longed for. She'd tangled with abandon since adolescence, tussling with her peers, challenging for her place in the Pack, venting her sexual need with those she called friends and those whose position she sought to usurp. Such was the way of Were society, where power and strength ruled. She would mate when her time came and her wolf recognized her match, when the unbreakable bond leapt into being and drove her to join with blood and body and soul. But not one she would never choose—not one who was not Pack. Pack was everything—Pack was life.

"Get off." Ash growled and rolled her hips.

"Why? I like you under me." Jace just laughed and steadied herself, thighs tight on either side of Ash's hips. She stroked Ash's chest and teased a finger down the center of her abdomen. "You only pretend you don't like it."

Ash's heartbeat filled her throat, and she swept her hands down the long curves of Jace's flanks, reveling in the steel muscles beneath the sun-kissed skin. Hiding her wolf's response took all her will. She ached too badly. She bled from a thousand slashes of claw and canine—her wolf's demand to yield. Panting to contain the pressure in her depths, she echoed Jace's earlier accusation, "You presume too much, Wolf."

Jace grinned. "Prove me wrong then. Show me you don't still want me."

"I don't..." Ash frowned. The air in the clearing vibrated with power. Her wolf snarled, every hair on her back standing at attention.

Jace stiffened, then bolted upright. "The Alpha comes."

Ash shuddered under the rush of dominant hormones flooding her senses. Even Alpha Constantine, whose wolf could force her to show her throat, did not affect her so strongly. If the Alpha opposed her tussling with Jace before, what would she do now? Attack her? Or Jace?

Growling, Ash leapt up and spun to face the edge of the clearing where the two Timberwolves who'd attacked her earlier had first emerged. She let her wolf rise, preparing to defend herself and her... *not mate.*

Not now, not ever.

Ash's pelt rippled and her bones screamed, jaw lengthening and limbs flexing.

"Ash, no!" Jace snarled and clamped on to her nape. "Stand *down.* If you challenge her, you'll die."

"I won't let her hurt you." Ash's words spewed like gravel, harsh and guttural. The change gripped her, a sweet rush of power and wild urges.

"She won't," Jace said. "She's my Alpha. Ash...*please!*"

The Alpha burst over the crest and landed in the center of the glade, easy striking distance from Ash. She could easily have torn out her throat before Ash finished changing. A black wolf, nearly the same size, landed beside her. The huge silver wolf swung her massive head from one to the other.

Jace lowered her head and saluted. "Alpha, Prima."

Ash edged slightly forward in front of Jace. Her wolf rode her hard, and she fought not to growl. Jace's claws dug into the back of her neck.

Silently, gaze fixed on Ash, Sylvan's wolf curled a lip. A warning. The only one she would be given.

Jace's iron grip turned briefly tender, stroking her neck and shoulder. "Show your respect, Wolf."

Trembling with the effort to hold her wolf at bay, Ash lowered her gaze to the Alpha's chest. "Alpha Mir, Prima. Greetings."

Sylvan *woofed* sharply and two pups came panting into view, corralled by a sleek white wolf with brilliant blue eyes shot through the gold. They raced across the clearing and crowded close to the Prima. The white wolf followed, resting her muzzle briefly atop each of the pups' heads before turning her gaze on Ash.

Ash's wolf raised her muzzle, her ears pricking in eager anticipation, an unfamiliar joy spreading through her chest. Her hackles settled, her fear and aggression calmed. The tension bled from Ash's shoulders, and beside her, Jace let out a long breath. What had just happened?

The Alpha's voice cut through Ash's pleasant confusion.

Was I not clear challenge was forbidden?

"No challenge, Alpha," Jace said.

And you, Captain? Are you sure?

"No challenge, Alpha," Ash said, keeping her eyes at a respectful distance below the Alpha pair's.

Then I can expect the two of you to perform your duties without incident.

"Yes, Alpha," Ash and Jace said simultaneously.

With a sharp snap of her massive jaws, Sylvan's wolf pivoted and bounded into the forest, her mate by her side, the young and their guard close behind.

"What did you think you were doing," Jace shouted. "She would have torn you to pieces."

"She put claws to you earlier," Ash said. "I don't know her."

"She's my Alpha. She won't hurt me." Jace grabbed her shoulders with both hands and yanked her close, kissing her fiercely. "Don't ever do that again."

Ash rested her forehead on Jace's shoulder, her wolf still oddly quiet. "That white wolf," Ash said, "who is she?"

"Why?" Jace's grip tightened, a sudden possessive rasp in her voice.

Ash raised a brow. "I felt...something from her...I don't know what it was."

"Did you try to call her to you?" Jace cupped Ash's face, swept her thumb along the line of her jaw, kissed her again, hard enough to bruise. "Why? Are you not yet satisfied?"

"I had no reason to call her." Ash laughed. "First, she's mated. That was clear. And...if I had called her, you would've felt it."

"Then why do you care?" Jace fought the urge to leave a mark on Ash's shoulder, to remind her, to remind *everyone*, that Ash was taken. For today at least. "She is our healer, and an Omega."

"Ah," Ash said, taking a long breath. "I wondered. I've never felt anything like that before. Sunlight, and calm, and unbendable strength."

Jace grumbled. "You felt a great deal."

Ash grinned. "She's beautiful. We have none like her at Cresthome."

Jace ran a claw tip down Ash's throat, repeating, "And she is mated. To the *imperator*."

Enjoying Jace's displeasure, Ash shrugged, although she would never challenge another's mate bond. She had no interest in mated wolves. But Jace didn't know that. "The *imperator* is impressive, true, but...any wolf can be defeated with the right motivation."

Jace snarled. "You're a fool to think that, and if you are still so ready you're imagining tangling with another wolf, I can change that right here."

Ash pulled away, tantalized by the possessive fury in Jace's eyes. Laughing, she shimmered into pelt, howled a challenge, and streaked off into the woods. Jace, teased and tormented and excited by the contest, shifted and chased after her.

Zora leaned against the railing of the barracks, driven outside by her wolf's restless unhappiness at being confined and a deeper, unsettling urge. An urge she had no intention of satisfying while among strangers, no matter how painful the claws raking her inside.

"Is there anything you need, Alpha Constantine?" the Timberwolf male assigned to guard her inquired. His breathing had quickened, and his scent deepened. His wolf reacting to the remnants of her call that could never be completely dampened.

Zora carefully muted her response—the question might be innocent, were it not for the timing and her own rising hunger. He hadn't moved. Wise of him. Had he encroached on her space, she would have seen that as an uninvited challenge, and protocol or not, she would have unleashed her wolf to put him under her. "No."

He was a senior soldier and held his place. As expected. Mir would never have sent an unseasoned Were, incapable of tolerating her wolf's presence, anywhere near her. Ignoring him, she studied the Timberwolf warriors who were training recruits in the vast arena in the Compound courtyard. So many warriors, so many young soldiers. Far more adolescents than she could ever expect in her Pack. An alliance with the Timberwolf Alpha would provide her Pack with protection, but at what cost? Her Alpha, her father, had avoided allegiances with other Packs, particularly those larger and more powerful, believing eventually Snowcrest would be absorbed and cease to exist. If her wolves were not slowly being bled away, victims of ambush and sneak attack by an enemy she could not find, she would not have considered it either. But the days when Snowcrest had existed in near isolation, with only a few members trading with similarly isolated merchants across the Canadian border, were gone. With the Exodus, all of them had been exposed, and all of them were now at risk. Her father had been opposed to intermingling with the human population. She could see his point, especially now, when the humans had chosen a different leader, one who outwardly voiced the opinion that humans were superior to all Praeterns and appeared to be sympathetic to the Humans First movement. She admired Sylvan Mir for her continued attempts to negotiate with humans, to push forward the agenda of Praetern recognition and Praetern solidarity, but she wondered if anything short of war would win those goals. And if war came, she would need allies with strong warriors.

One of the lieutenants, a female with a slash of white running through her midnight black hair, disarmed an adolescent with a swift series of movements Zora would not have been able to follow if she hadn't been watching her so carefully. She'd been watching the striking soldier far more than anyone else, admiring her sleek strength.

Admiring her just a little too much. Her wolf stalked her blood, alert and intensely focused on this female. Interested.

As if sensing the attention, the female turned and met Zora's gaze for an impertinent moment, then dipped her head, more in acknowledgment than a show of submission, and turned back to her maneuvers with a smile. Zora grumbled beneath her breath. Foolish wolf.

"Who is that?" she found herself asking the Timberwolf guard. Not that it mattered, but she wanted a name to put to the sculpted face and arrogant smile.

"That's Trent, Alpha," the male answered.

"A lieutenant in your army," she said.

"Yes, Alpha. A squadron commander."

Zora didn't need to ask if she was mated—she could tell she wasn't. She could scent the invitation of Trent's pheromones across the yard. So, she was certain, could every other Were in the vicinity. She turned away, ignoring her wolf's interest. She was a Were, after all, and she enjoyed a tangle as much as any other. But she was also Alpha. She ruled her pheromones, not the other way around. And while her Pack was in mortal danger, she could not afford to be distracted, especially not when surrounded by foreign Weres. Her wolf, and the constant thrum of want in her loins, would have to wait for a safer time and place. And a far safer Were to tangle with.

The guard stepped forward abruptly and Zora spun, growling a warning.

"Forgive me, Alpha," the guard said, dipping his head quickly. "The Alpha comes."

Power surged through the Compound, a blast of strength and primal aggression that brought Zora's wolf surging. Every Were in sight turned to face the same direction as a great silver wolf sailed over the stockade fence, accompanied by one of midnight black. A moment later, the smaller gates on that side opened and a white wolf, followed by two panting young, bounded inside.

A chorus of yips and howls and shouts welcomed the Alpha pair and their young. The *imperator* left the training group she'd been supervising and strode to intercept the striking white wolf. When the *imperator* ran a possessive hand though the wolf's sleek ruff, the white wolf brushed against the *imperator*'s thigh and rubbed her muzzle over the *imperator*'s hip.

The black wolf, Sylvan's Prima, herded the young toward the rear of the Compound in the direction where Zora suspected the nursery was located. That area was heavily guarded continuously. Had she more successful breedings in her Pack, she would do the same. Thinking once more of all the Weres in this Pack, and the strength of their line, she considered the constraints of isolation. As long as they remained limited in their association with other Packs, their matings would continue to produce few young. Snowcrest would always remain Snowcrest, but new blood born of new allegiances might only make them stronger.

Sylvan loped over to Zora. *All is well, Alpha?*

Zora hid her surprise at the silent communication. Considering she was not in pelt and she shared no Pack bond with Sylvan, she wouldn't have expected Sylvan could signal her so strongly. Zora wondered if anyone, Were or human, had any inkling of Sylvan Mir's true power. Zora lifted her chin, her gaze steady on Sylvan's. Despite her lack of experience, she could never let Sylvan think she considered herself anything less than an equal. "Other than my growing impatience to know your decision, I am satisfied."

Sylvan cocked her head and gave a wolfie grin, as if expecting nothing less than annoyance from an Alpha kept waiting. *Join me at headquarters now, and we'll talk.*

"With pleasure, Alpha."

Zora leapt into the yard as Sylvan streaked away and strode toward the central building. She'd sensed the female lieutenant approaching and, curious, slowed her steps just enough so their paths intersected. The Timberwolf Weres were very bold, or very foolish.

"Did you enjoy the training lesson, Alpha Constantine?" the female asked in a smooth sultry alto.

"Should I have?"

"Our recruits are very talented," the female said.

"I found them entertaining."

"Then I hope everything was to your liking." The female's gaze skimmed briefly over Zora's face.

"The instruction was…interesting. Your recruits are not afraid to attempt to overpower their trainers."

"We encourage them to *try* to win, and they're eager to please," the female replied with a subtle emphasis on eager. "As are their instructors."

Zora smiled to herself. An aggressive female, dominant. And very brave.

"I'm Trent," the female said.

"I know."

Trent's eyes glinted, a scattering of gold dancing in her dark gaze. Her breath quickened and her pheromones thickened. Zora enjoyed the answering heat in her depths—enjoyed, and contained. Her wolf deserved to play, but only that. A little teasing.

"I must return to my duties," Trent said. "Perhaps you'll return to observe more later."

"Perhaps." Zora walked on as Trent dropped back and disappeared. Rarely if ever had she been so boldly approached. Her Weres were far from submissive, although like any Pack, they couldn't survive without the special talents of their naturally less dominant wolves, but even the dominant Weres waited for her to call them, in the rare occasions when her need was greatest. The Timberwolf Weres were either very arrogant or very naïve. While she found their lack of respect vaguely annoying, her wolf was more than a little intrigued.

Grumbling, she bolted up on the broad deck just as Sylvan, dressed in casual combat clothes, walked out.

"Problems?" Sylvan asked.

"No."

If Sylvan heard the snarl in her tone, she didn't show it. She strode to the edge of the porch and announced to the yard, "A gathering at sundown."

Her voice carried effortlessly throughout the vast area. When the answering chorus died down, she turned to Zora. "We have Pack business to attend to tonight. I'd like you and your wolves to join us."

"We'll be honored." Zora crossed her arms. "Have you and the council made a decision about my petition, Alpha Mir?"

"We have," Sylvan said. "My Prima, *imperator*, and I will take a squadron of warriors to Cresthome to assist in apprehending your rogues."

The elite guard, Zora had no doubt. Small in number, but more than enough to overpower a non-warrior Pack. Zora stilled. "That's a very powerful force."

Sylvan regarded her steadily, one brow slightly raised. "Worried, Alpha?"

"Would you be?"

Sylvan smiled. "I would consider the possibility of a hostile takeover, if I were you—the Alpha of the smaller Pack, in such proximity to a much larger one. If I didn't know anything about that larger Pack."

"But I do," Zora said. "The Snowcrest and Timberwolf Packs have coexisted for a hundred years or more, and other than a few border skirmishes, we've lived peacefully."

"There's something else," Sylvan said, gold gleaming in her eyes. "The Timberwolf Pack does not make war on other Packs."

"I doubt that Bernardo's Pack agrees with that," Zora countered. She steeled herself for Sylvan's attack, but she could not cower before another Alpha. Not even Sylvan Mir.

Sylvan snarled, but her claws remained sheathed. "Bernardo was a renegade, an Alpha who abused his Pack and his duty. Had I known the extent of his exploitations, I would've interceded much earlier, when I could still offer a peaceful transfer of power. But he brought war upon himself when he attacked my wolves."

"If I did not trust you, Alpha Mir," Zora said quietly, "I would not have put my Pack at risk by petitioning for your aid. But all trust is calculated, is it not?"

"To a point, yes," Sylvan mused as she scanned her Compound, noting with satisfaction the calm, orderly activities. "But after a point, the test of trust must end, and allegiance given."

"Alliance first," Zora said, "then allegiance."

Sylvan nodded. "My approach as well."

"My wolves are loyal and brave and skillful," Zora said, "but they are not warriors. Some have the inherent skill, but we need instructors."

"I can provide you that, if your wolves are willing and truly as strong as you say."

"I can field fifty recruits immediately," Zora said. "And vouch for every one of them."

"Then I will send you ten of our lieutenants to test them."

Zora smiled. "The Snowcrest Weres stand ready to meet any challenge the Timberwolves may bring."

"No Alpha would offer less." Sylvan shook her head as Ash and the Timberwolf captain appeared out of the forest beyond the perimeter of the training yard, both disheveled and broadcasting sex. "Although we might see a challenge sooner than we expected. Your captain and one of my *centuri* are circling one another."

"I am aware." Zora sighed. "A complication I could do without."

Sylvan laughed. "Agreed. But nature is one thing we can only channel, but never control. I have never known a wolf who's chosen to be dissuaded."

"But this would be far from simple."

Sylvan shrugged. "Leading a Pack of Weres is never simple. The more your wolves interact with ours, the more of this we're likely to see. It's the nature of our beasts."

Zora watched the pair saunter closer. "There are times we must be more than our wolves to survive."

"It's been my experience our wolves are often far wiser than us."

Zora thought of Trent and the dangerous stirring of her wolf. "In this," she said, "I will have to disagree."

CHAPTER ELEVEN

"Jace," the blond-haired blue-eyed male called as he loped across the Compound toward them.

Ash stiffened and growled under her breath. Another dominant Timberwolf, come to challenge or claim? Her Alpha and Alpha Mir watched from the building across the yard. If she tussled with this one, she'd probably end up with her Alpha's teeth in her throat again. Her wolf bristled, uncaring. Too many Weres, too close to Jace.

Jace laughed. "You can stop grumbling. That's my brother."

"I remember him from Washington." Ash watched the male warily. The glint in his eyes as he took her in belied his easy smile. This one was dangerous, for all his casual manner. "I didn't know he was your brother."

"Twin," Jace said, her tone suddenly harsh. "And not for you."

Ash smiled. "Why not? He's unmated."

Jace clamped a claw-tipped hand on her shoulder and leaned close. "You're…"

"I'm what?" Ash murmured, her wolf still and waiting.

"Occupied," Jace snarled.

Jonathan fell into step beside them. "The Alpha has called a gathering for sundown."

"Do you know what it's about?" Jace asked, keeping a hand on Ash. *This one is not for you.*

Jonathan shook his head, taking in her hold on Ash. He took a half step ahead and focused on the dark-haired Were who regarded him with suspicious eyes. Her clothes were shredded in places, her skin still flushed with sex. The pheromones rushing off her muscled frame tasted wild and primal. He shuddered, his wolf perking up his ears and baring his teeth. He'd enjoy tussling with this one. "We haven't met. I am Jonathan, the dominant twin."

"Ash, Captain of Alpha Zora Constantine's guard."

"Yeah, I got that. I caught the tail end of your tussle with my sister earlier. Looked like she was winning." Jonathan grinned, testing how easily the female could be baited into a tussle. He hardened and let his wolf rise. Or a tangle.

Ash sidestepped and swung around to block Jonathan's path. She bared her canines. "Are you planning to challenge me next?"

"Do you want me to?" Jonathan smirked. "I don't usually share with my sister, but…"

Jace pushed between Ash and him, shouldering him back a step. "Jonathan, back off."

"It's not like you to leave a wolf wanting," Jonathan mused, "but I'm happy to help."

Jace snarled in his face and shoved him again. "You're not funny."

He met her gaze, smiled softly. "I don't know, I'm kind of enjoying it. You look…a little frenzied."

"Go away."

Jonathan narrowed his eyes. Jace vibrated with barely restrained fury—her wolf prowled so close to the edge her pelt dusted her throat. Jonathan shrugged. "If you're not done either, I suggest you do something about that before you start broadcasting to everyone in sight."

"I'm fine," Jace snapped.

"There are a dozen Weres waiting to answer your call."

Ash growled. "Her call has already been answered."

"Has it?" Jonathan shook his head. "Maybe not well enough."

"Enough," Ash snapped, grabbing him by the shirtfront. "I accept your chall—"

"Ash!" Zora Constantine landed a step away. Hands on her hips, she studied the three of them. Two nearly identical Weres, gorgeous in their youth and vigor, and her captain, strong and powerful. Pheromones poured from the trio, bombarding her with a mixture of sex and dominance. All three ready to tussle, and likely to leave wounds they could ill afford. She ignored the Timberwolf Weres and stared at her captain. "We are to attend a gathering tonight, and we leave in the morning for Cresthome. Get some food and then prepare the guard."

Ash saluted. "As you will, Alpha."

Zora pivoted and strode away.

Ash glanced at Jace. "I must go."

Jace nodded stiffly. She had her duty to attend to, but her wolf bristled at the idea of letting Ash go amid dozens of Weres. She watched Ash until she disappeared around the corner of the barracks.

"She's as dominant as any of our *centuri*. Too bad she's Snowcrest," Jonathan mused.

Jace growled. "She is not for you to tease."

"Oh?" His eyebrows rose innocently. "Why not."

Jace's jaw tightened. "As you said. She is Snowcrest."

❖

Ash ducked into one of the outdoor shower cubicles scattered around the Compound, stripped off her torn clothing, and pulled the chain to release the rainwater from the overhead cistern. Barely warmed by the day's sun, the cool water sluiced over her, doing nothing to temper the heat raging in her blood. She braced both arms against the wooden slats and dropped her head. Alpha Mir's warning had been clear—nothing more complicated than a brief tussle and an uncomplicated tangle, everyday occurrences in Were society, would be tolerated. No room for challenges for dominance or mating rights on the eve of a hunt. Ash agreed. She was here as a visitor. Her Alpha's captain. Her only job was to see that the guards were ready to do their duty. She couldn't afford to be distracted by need or anger or the other instincts Jace stirred in her.

Ash tilted her head back, eyes closed, sun glancing down through the open ceiling, bathing her face. Jace's face flickered beneath her closed lids, her golden eyes glowing, her face hungry and knowing. Ash's heart thrummed a drumbeat of desire and something unexpected. A gentle peace, unknown to her before this day. A feeling that only Pack had ever given her. Home.

Growling, she opened her eyes, shook her head clear of water and the unwanted imaginings that could never be. She would find no home with an out-Pack Were. Dizzy with the remnants of Jace's pheromones coating her, storming through her blood, she shook with the memory of Jace beneath her, above her, filling her. Her shoulder throbbed, pain lancing deep into her chest. The unbroken skin, bruised and swollen, pulsed with expectation. She freed the chain from the hook on the wall and the water stopped flowing. Rivulets ran over her chest, down her abdomen, between her thighs, cleansing her skin, but the tingle of Jace's essence remained. Snarling, she banged her way out of the cubicle, slamming the plank door closed behind her. A nearby shelf held clothes available to all, and she pulled on plain dark pants and a shirt. She stepped into her boots and strode toward the path leading to the barracks.

Jonathan slouched against the base of a tall pine near the rear corner of the building, his arms folded over his chest, his expression amused. "Feeling better?"

"I'm fine," she said.

"You didn't sound fine." Jonathan lowered his brows as if deep in thought. "You sounded…unsettled."

Ash closed the distance between them, her face close to his. "Do you intend to challenge me?"

He smiled, his smile so like Jace's, his eyes like hers too, but without the heat that spilled over to close Ash's throat and fill her belly with fire.

"I would," Jonathan whispered, "if I thought that's what it would take to get you to leave my sister alone."

Ash's canines punched out, pain tingling through her jaw as the bone grew heavier, longer. "You overstep, Wolf."

His smile remained, but gold streaks slashed through his blue irises. "I don't think so. A tangle"—he shrugged—"or two. Who cares? But it's more than that, isn't it? Your wolf wants her."

"You know nothing of my wolf."

"Really?"

He dropped his gaze down her body, then slowly climbed back to meet her eyes. Dominant to dominant. Wolf to wolf. "Your claws are showing. Your pelt is about to explode. Your wolf wants me by the throat. Why?"

"You're in my way."

"You'll be gone in the morning," he said.

"That's right," Ash said.

"So you won't mind when my sister satisfies her wolf elsewhere, will you."

Ash gripped him by the throat and shoved him against the tree, pinning him with her chest to his. Even though he was the larger, her fury fueled her strength. Her canines snapped millimeters from his neck. "She won't."

Jonathan drove his claws into her flanks, the pain nothing compared to her wolf's blind fury.

An iron bar of muscle clamped around her throat and dragged her back.

"What are you doing?" Jace growled in Ash's ear.

"He challenges," Ash growled, her wolf ascending, the change bursting over her.

"Ash, no," Jace snapped, pulling her back another few feet. "Stop. If you challenge, the Alpha will intercede. *Stop.*"

Ash shuddered, her wolf raging to be freed.

"Damn it, Jonathan," Jace said. "What did you do?"

Jonathan shook himself, the white glimmer of his pelt rolling beneath his skin and slowly subsiding. "Nothing. We were just talking about tangling."

Jace growled. "You tried to call her?"

Jonathan shook his head. "No. Just testing."

Ash shuddered, and Jace pulled her tight, her arm angled across Ash's chest. She pressed her body close to Ash's, brushed her mouth over her temple. "It's all right."

"I'm done now." Jonathan brushed by Ash. "You might actually be worthy."

Ash snarled and thrashed in Jace's grip. Jonathan's laughter followed him as he disappeared into the Compound. Jace spun Ash around and backed her against the tree, holding her there by the shoulders. "What did he say to you?"

"To stay away from you." Ash's chest heaved with the effort to contain her wolf.

Jace's arrogant grin returned, and she drew a finger along the edge of Ash's jaw and down the center of her throat. "Do you want to? Stay away?"

"I want a tangle, when there's time," Ash said.

Jace kissed her. "A tangle then. Nothing more."

Ash pressed her canines to Jace's throat, felt her tremble in response. She bit just hard enough to leave a faint mark. Not large enough, not deep enough, to send the message she wanted all to see.

Jace's breath hitched and her hips jerked. Her wolf called to Ash's—primal and fierce.

"Agreed." Ash summoned all her strength to pull away, to resist the call burning through her. "As you say. Nothing more."

❖

Drake perched on the end of the bed waiting for Sylvan to come out of the shower. When the door opened and Sylvan strode out naked, Drake took her time surveying the glory of her mate.

Sylvan stopped abruptly, her gaze narrowing. "You're not dressed yet."

"I noticed," Drake said in a throaty murmur.

"Are you waiting for something?" Sylvan asked.

"Not any longer." Drake leaned back. "I hope."

Sylvan pounced, covering her as she flew back onto the bed. With a growl, she nipped at Drake's throat, then her breast, then her belly. Drake pushed her fingers into Sylvan's hair, raked her claws down her scalp, and gripped her shoulders.

"We don't have much time," Drake gasped.

Sylvan pushed her legs apart, the tips of her claws leaving faint marks on her flesh as she settled between her thighs. She licked her, gazed up, eyes the color of sunlight. "Always time. Always yours."

"I love you," Drake said.

Sylvan rubbed her cheek over Drake's sex, kissed the prominence of her clitoris. "I love you. With my life."

Drake lifted her hips, offered herself to Sylvan's mouth. "I'm yours."

Hungry for her, Sylvan stroked and teased and took her quickly.

"Always...so...good." Drake arched and filled her, pulsing against Sylvan's mouth.

Incensed by pheromones released by their joining, Sylvan reared up and straddled Drake's thigh. Drake laughed and pushed her hand between them, cupping Sylvan's sex.

"In a hurry?"

Sylvan kissed her, rocking to her own sharp spasm of release. She shuddered, easing down on top of Drake. "Not anymore."

Lazily, Drake stroked her hair and traced the muscles in her shoulders. "It's almost sundown."

"I know. And dawn will come soon thereafter." Sylvan sighed and rolled over. "It is difficult to leave the young again so soon."

"They will be well protected."

Sylvan gripped her hand and met her gaze. "This might only be the first of many skirmishes. They will grow up in a Pack at war."

"They will grow up strong and unafraid. As long as we're together," Drake said softly, "we'll handle whatever comes. For however long it takes to keep our Pack safe."

"I could not do this without you."

Drake leaned over and kissed her. "You could, but you won't ever have to."

Zora emerged from her suite in a black silk shirt with sleeves rolled back to expose her forearms, sleek black trousers, and shining black boots. Formal attire for the gathering. Her power pressed into Ash's bones.

Ash, Evan, and the other guards were in uniform—deep charcoal shirts and battle fatigues, ankle high boots laced over their cuffs. They wore no weapons—they needed none. Their bodies were their strength. Ash saluted. "Alpha."

"Captain." Zora swept past and led the way outside. Ash fell in at her left side, Evan on her right, and the two other guards drawing up behind. They strode out into the Compound just as the sun set beyond the ridge of trees that encircled the stockade fences. A great fire roared in the center of the Compound, and several hundred Weres gathered on the far side in a huge semicircle.

Ash's wolf scented the air, her wolf eagerly seeking the one scent that pierced above all others. Jace was not present, and Ash clamped her jaws against the need to growl. She would find her soon.

Zora halted in an open space on the opposite side of the fire pit from where the Timberwolf Pack had gathered and stood with her hands clasped behind her back, gaze fixed straight ahead as the foreign

Weres jostled and covertly stared. None, not even the soldiers among them, met her eyes.

A rumble grew throughout the crowd. The Alpha pair approached. Beside her, Zora's wolf emanated controlled wariness. As Sylvan's cadre drew near, Zora pivoted to greet them.

Sylvan and the Prima, flanked by a dozen *centuri* in gray and black fatigues, strode across the Compound in a phalanx of power. Sylvan wore only dusky leather pants and boots, the Prima matching pants and a skin-tight collarless shirt. Sylvan's torso rippled with sleek muscle beneath shimmering skin.

Jace flanked the second row of *centuri* closest to Ash, and the wash of her pheromones made Ash's stomach twist. She met Jace's gaze for an instant and gold leapt into Jace's eyes.

"Alpha Constantine," Sylvan said, "welcome to the gathering."

"Alpha, Prima," Zora said, "we are honored to attend."

Sylvan faced the gathered Pack.

"Tonight we recognize a new alliance with the Snowcrest Pack," Sylvan said, her voice riding the air with a thrum of power. She turned to Zora and extended her forearm. Zora gripped it, palm to Sylvan's forearm as Sylvan took hers.

"Friends of the Pack," Sylvan said, her claws piercing Zora's flesh, drawing a thin rivulet of blood that gleamed crimson in the firelight.

"Friends of the Pack," Zora echoed unflinchingly as she in turn drew the ceremonial blood with her claws.

Sylvan and Zora drew apart, and Sylvan addressed her Pack. "Welcome our allies."

The Timberwolf Weres raised their voices in shouts and howls, a song to awaken the night. Ash met Jace's gaze across the short distance between them. Now there would be no need to challenge over territory or position when together. Allies, but not Pack.

"Now," Sylvan continued, drawing every eye to her, "we appoint a Pack third, Max Duvall. Award to him the loyalty and obedience you give to me, my Prima, and our second, *Imperator* Kroff."

Max came forward.

Sylvan said, "I entrust you with safeguarding my Pack, to the last Were, with your last breath."

"I pledge my life to you and the Pack and will stand for you in all things." Max offered his throat to Sylvan.

Sylvan glowed in the flickering firelight, and an instant later she loomed over Max's huge six-foot frame in half-form, her face a chimera of wolf and Were, her body hugely muscled and covered with silver pelt, her claws and canines extended. She clamped her jaws on his throat, and he shuddered. Blood ran down his chest, and his eyes closed.

Silence shrouded the vast yard until Sylvan released him, threw back her head, and howled. The gathered Weres trembled and howled, many of them pulled into the change by the force of Sylvan's wolf. Ash stood her ground as power rolled over her in golden waves. Beside her, Evan whined and his wolf burst free. An instant later, Cybil changed, her wolf dropping to all fours and shivering. Zora growled low in her throat, bearing witness to the supreme Alpha.

Ash's wolf alerted to the call of another, fierce and wild, and Ash met Jace's hot gaze. Jace's canines gleamed against her full lips. Her skin shimmered.

Mine, Ash heard above the roar of her blood, and let her wolf rise.

Chapter Twelve

The moon was at its zenith in a nearly cloudless sky when Ash walked out onto the barracks deck. The yard was bathed in silver light, and the moon's call for her wolf to run, to hunt, was stronger than she'd ever remembered. She knew why. Somewhere in the building twenty feet away, her quarry slept. Jace.

"Your shift doesn't start for two hours, Captain," Ryan said.

Ash scanned the dark narrow windows of the adjoining building, pinpointing the exact room on the first floor where Jace's signature scent was the strongest. Even from here, even without the ultimate melding of their chemistries that followed a mating, she knew her. The demand to shed skin and rush that flimsy barrier was so acute she fought not to double over in pain. Sleeping, eating were an impossibility. She hungered not for nourishment or rest. Only the sight of her, the taste of her, would ease the craving. "I'll take over. You're relieved."

He hesitated. Her agitation would have alerted his wolf.

Ash snarled. "That's an order."

"Yes, Captain." Ryan snapped out a salute and quickly retreated inside.

The door closed behind him, and Ash was alone save for a few Weres who still sat around the fire pits, mostly the young—teasing, tussling, inviting. She recognized the timeless explorations of young wolves, finding their place, finding their Pack within a Pack. She'd had friends like that as an adolescent—other Weres she tussled with to prove her strength, and tangled with to declare her status, and challenged to earn her rank. Friends then, Packmates now. As they'd all drifted into their places, the ties remained, and now and then, they still tangled when the need arose, friendly and unencumbered. Evan had been one such Packmate when they'd been adolescents, but her wolf had chosen a different path when she'd matured, and now it seemed her wolf had fixed on the unattainable.

Jace was everything she shouldn't want and couldn't have—a ranking warrior of another Pack. Both dominants—true, but so were Sylvan Mir and Drake McKinnon. Alpha and Prima, matched in power, stronger together. Ash's wolf feared no wolf, including Jace's. They would meet as equals, neither the weaker. But Jace was a Timberwolf, and she was Snowcrest. Allies now, perhaps, but allies sometimes became rivals. Where would her allegiance fall then? With Pack or mate? Ash gripped the wooden post, her claws digging trenches in the scarred upright. Pointless to wonder.

Her stomach clenched and her wolf jumped to attention with a sharp bark of anticipation. Ash couldn't smother the surge of triumph and self-satisfaction. Her prey had come to her.

"Couldn't sleep?" Jace said, her eyes gleaming in the shadows.

Ash shook her head. "Preoccupied."

"So am I." Jace leapt over the railing and crossed to stand beside her. Her shoulder brushed Ash's, just a whisper of contact, but the heat raced through her.

"We leave in a few hours," Ash murmured. "It's the hunt keeping us on edge."

"Which one?" Jace said, a gravelly rumble deep in her throat.

Ash readied, already full and hot. *No place, no time.*

"You know what I hunt." Ash turned, cupped Jace's jaw, ran her thumb over the arch of her stark cheekbone. "This more than any other."

Jace clasped her flank, pulled her tight until their hips met. Even in the darkness, her eyes glowed. "You're right. I know. I'm hunting too."

"You should go," Ash said, ignoring the claws that shredded her inside. The demand that weakened her resolve and burned along her spine. So easy just to turn her head, show her throat, invite the bite. To give and then take. "Go."

"In a minute." Jace kissed her, and the essence of black current and cedar surrounded her, soothing and exciting.

Ash clasped Jace's nape, held her in the kiss, probed and teased and stroked, wild to devour. She caught Jace's lip, tugged it hard enough to elicit a growl.

Jace backed her against the post. Kissed her while gripping her shirt and yanking it free of her pants. Ash snarled and caught her wrist, breaking the tantalizing caress. "No."

Jace pulled away, gasping. "We're not done."

"You presume, Wolf." Ash's breath came hard and fast. Her resolve fled with every beat of her heart. Jace tasted of truth.

"Do I? I know you want me." Jace grinned, her canines glittering in the moonlight. And then she leapt over the railing and disappeared into the dark again. Her voice floated back. "Remember what I said."

Ash rubbed her midsection, the knot of need a constant pain. *Not done.*

The rest of the night was quiet. Ash sensed Jace awake, as restless as her.

Others in the Compound awakened before dawn. Weres emerged from the barracks and out of the surrounding woods, changing form for a morning run in pelt, leaping from the stockade into the outer perimeter and racing toward the forested paths. Trainees burst out of the door behind her and stormed across the deck, laughing and cajoling, pushing and shoving, teasing and tussling, racing en masse toward the dining hall. Soldiers in fatigues carrying equipment bags and weapons congregated around the largest fire pit. The Timberwolf hunters.

Ash sensed her Alpha approaching and snapped to attention. Zora emerged, Evan, Ryan, and Cybil behind her. Cybil carried Ash's gear bag along with her own.

Ash saluted. "Alpha."

"Captain." Zora, in boots and a plain black shirt and pants, stepped up beside her, hands on her narrow hips, and surveyed the Compound. "All quiet?"

"Yes, Alpha."

"We have a few minutes," Zora said. "The guards should see to getting a meal. We won't have time when we reach Snowcrest territory. There's been another raid."

Ash stiffened. "Casualties?"

"Another sentry missing." Zora's jaw tightened.

"The tracks will be fresh," Ash said.

Zora stepped down onto the yard. "Yes, and this time we'll find them."

Sylvan and the Prima, surrounded by the *centuri,* entered the Compound. Zora went to meet them.

Ash said, "Ryan—make sure we have stowed enough rations for several days in the field. We won't be going to Cresthome first."

"Aye, Captain," he said and jogged away.

Ash followed Zora to meet the Timberwolves.

"Alpha, Captain," Sylvan said by way of greeting.

"Alpha Mir," Zora said. "I just received a message there's been another raid."

Sylvan's gaze narrowed. "Location?"

Zora gave her the coordinates. "Only two sentries were on post. One is missing. The other had little to offer but is remaining on site."

"Good." Sylvan turned to the Prima. "If we go overland through our own territory rather than on the highways, we can keep our arrival quiet."

Drake nodded. "The Rovers can make good time even off-road, and the route will be more direct. About the same time overall. I'll brief the drivers on the change of plans."

"Niki," Sylvan said, "assemble your warriors. We may be headed into an immediate engagement."

"Good news then." The *imperator* grinned, looking as close to feral as Ash had ever seen an uninfected Were. Ash's wolf bristled and bared her teeth. Sensing her wariness, Niki flashed her a smile, canines showing.

Sylvan faced Zora. "Will you have time to deploy any of your soldiers?"

"I've ordered my guards to remain at Cresthome. I don't anticipate an attack there, but I can't take the chance." Zora grimaced. "I'm afraid I have none to spare."

Sylvan shrugged. "We have enough. As soon as Lord Torren arrives, we'll leave."

Zora frowned. "When do you expect her?"

Sylvan glanced at the sky. The moon was reaching its nadir and the sun was about to cross its path on its ascent. "Any second."

Ash caught a glimmer of Sylvan's smile just as the air inside the gates glittered with a thin mist of iridescent fog. For a second the stockade fence seemed to melt away and then Torren and the female Were she'd been with earlier stepped into view.

"That was a Faerie Gate," Zora murmured. "I didn't realize there were any this far north."

"Torren makes her own Gates," Sylvan said mildly.

"Does she." Zora's tone was wary. "Powerful."

"Mm," Sylvan said, "for a Fae."

Zora laughed, Were to Were. "Of course."

Torren, one hand on Misha's back, drew close and nodded a greeting. "Alphas, Prima."

"It seems we'll have a fresh trail," Sylvan said and filled her in.

"Excellent," Torren said.

Five Rovers, heavily armored, pulled into the yard.

"You and your guards will ride in the first car, Alpha Constantine."

When Ash climbed into the rear of the Rover, stowed her equipment bag under the metal bench, and sat to her Alpha's left, she was directly across from Sylvan's senior *centuri*. Jace occupied the middle of the bench, her head tilted back as the Rover pulled out, her lids slightly lowered, her gaze fixed on Ash.

Trent pulled the Rover off-trail several miles from where the Snowcrest sentries had been attacked. Ash and the others disembarked and waited in the dense pine forest while Zora, Sylvan, the Prima, and Torren conferred. Jace slipped through the knot of warriors and moved in close behind Ash.

"It's a good morning for a run," Jace said.

Ash did not turn, but Jace sensed Ash's wolf alerting to her presence, eager and pushing to be closer. Jace smiled to herself.

"Good morning for a hunt," Ash murmured.

Jace rested a hand between them, low on Ash's back. Heat pushed its way through the fabric of Ash's shirt, seared her flesh. She needed to touch her before they headed into danger, when she could not shield her. She pressed her hips close against Ash's rear, a reminder of the claim she hadn't made but felt in her blood all the same. "See to your Alpha if we run into trouble, and let us do the fighting."

"I'll do what needs to be done," Ash said, but her voice held reassurance rather than challenge.

"Then do it carefully," Jace murmured. "I don't want you hurt."

Ash reached back, stroked the curve of Jace's thigh. "Nor I you, *centuri*."

"Remember," Jace said, "when the hunt is done, I'll want you."

Ash laughed, but inside her wolf huffed, pleased. "You presume again."

Jace leaned close, her mouth close to Ash's ear. "I do. And I will."

Zora motioned Ash to join her.

"Until after the hunt then," Ash said.

When Ash joined the Alpha, Zora said, "We'll take half of the Timberwolf warriors and circle around to the sentry's position from the southeast. Alpha Mir and the rest of her warriors will approach from the northwest, while Lord Torren and Brett, the Timberwolf lead tracker, take the center. We'll cover any potential trail that way, and if any intruders remain, we will encircle them at strength."

Ash saluted. "As you will, Alpha. I'll inform the others."

After Sylvan divided up her forces, the Prima joined Zora with Jace, Jonathan, and the remaining Timberwolves. Zora's wolf emerged and all the others followed. As the Weres shed skin and dropped to all fours, a glow surrounded Torren, and a huge Hound, as large as a pony with canines extending the length of a wolf's foreleg, appeared in her place. Leathery skin, dappled brown and gray, sheathed her sleek muscled shoulders. Her fathomless eyes, the irises eclipsed by inky pupils, promised an eternity of anguish. Shivering in the presence of such ancient and deadly force, Ash bit back a howl. The Hound shook herself and nudged playfully at the much smaller wolf who nipped at her muzzle with a peevish snap. Torren's Were mate. The Hound seemed pleased to have annoyed her wolf and set off into the trees at a casual lope. The wolf kept pace easily, and the pair melted into the forest.

Ash padded to the Alpha's side with Evan taking the opposite guard. The Timberwolves phalanxed their Prima. Zora and the Prima ran side by side, setting the pace for the wolf Pack that streamed into the forest, spreading out as it traveled. Finally free, Ash's wolf breathed deep. The morning air was crisp and cool and clear, and beneath the scent of the forest, Jace. The Timberwolf was out of sight now, but Ash's wolf knew exactly where she was in the wolf Pack. Not too far away to reach if Jace needed her. Close enough to protect.

Running at hunt pace, they covered the distance to the outpost in less than half an hour. Torren had already arrived and sat on her haunches in a swath of sunlight before a craggy rock face whiskered with pines clinging to the crevices, slanting over the deer trail and providing cover for the two Snowcrest sentries who'd been on guard. One remained, a young red-and-brown-pelted male. Ash knew him—he'd been a trainee not that long ago. Now he was a veteran of a war they couldn't even define. He crouched twenty feet away, hackles raised, teeth bared—growling at the Hound. Sylvan emerged, leading her warriors, and trotted over to join Zora.

Torren chuffed, an eerie amused sound, and stretched her long forelegs out in the direction of the sentry. The sentry growled and looked ready to spring.

Stand down, Zora broadcast and padded over to the sentry. She rubbed her muzzle against the top of his head, and he whined in greeting. Comforted by the Alpha's presence, he relaxed his defensive posture but kept a wary eye on the Hound.

The sound of an engine grew louder, and a Rover edged out of the undergrowth. The wolves shed pelt and grabbed clothes from the back. The air around the Hound wavered, and then Torren stood in her place, dressed as she had been that morning in a royal blue brocade shirt, tapered charcoal pants, and sleek black boots that came to her knees.

Sylvan, Drake, Zora, and their guards gathered around the two trackers.

"Anything?" Sylvan asked.

"The scents are mixed," Brett said. "Were but not Were. And something I can't identify."

Torren nodded. "Yes—either the raiders are masking their scent in some way, or we're dealing with more than just the usual border skirmishes between Packs. The scents are strongest here in this clearing, but no tracks lead in or out."

"This area is heavily forested." Sylvan frowned. "An airdrop would be difficult but there ought to be tracks from the approach once they landed."

Zora shook her head. "No, the sentry says he heard nothing before they were under fire, and they couldn't pinpoint a direction. He said it was as if they were suddenly surrounded in mist, and they couldn't see anything. He was struck unconscious, and when he awoke, the enemy was gone. So was the other sentry."

The Prima shook her head. "That makes no sense. Why leave him alive? And what was the point to begin with? Have there been any demands?"

"None," Zora said. "Thus far the attacks have been swift and focused on incapacitating our sentries, but perhaps they plan to interfere with our trade routes or our hunting grounds next."

Ash understood what the Alpha would not admit openly—the continued raids created unrest in the Pack and could call the Alpha's abilities to protect the Pack into question. The Alpha had already withstood more challenges than most in her position.

"No," Torren said. "If that was the case, they would attack those directly. I think your sentries are bait."

"For what?" Zora growled.

"More importantly," Torren mused, "for who?"

Sylvan said, "Where's the next outpost closest to your perimeter?"

"Twenty miles north of here."

"Then that's where we should go."

Drake said, "We can't overlook the possibility that Cresthome is also a target. Whoever's behind this appears to be able to travel at will." She turned to Torren. "It's a Gate, isn't it?"

Torren nodded. "Yes, I think so. I can taste the remnants of power. Only a very few Fae can open a Gate so precisely. Cecilia, Queen of Thorns and All of Faerie, Ruler of Dark and Light, Mistress of All Seasons, appears to be tired of allowing the Praeterns of this realm to rule themselves."

"Niki," Sylvan said sharply, "take half the company to Cresthome and secure their perimeter."

"Yes, Alpha."

Sylvan stroked Drake's back. "The rest of us will head to the nearest outpost and set up camp. If they're looking for bait, we'll give them some."

CHAPTER THIRTEEN

Drake rejoined Sylvan for the run to the next outpost, leaving Jace, Jonathan, and half of the remaining soldiers with Zora Constantine. Sylvan shifted into pelt and Drake followed, setting off beside her mate, the way it should be.

Sylvan bumped shoulders as they ran, her breathing easy and relaxed, her powerful body covering the ground effortlessly. *This has the feel of something more than a border skirmish.*

Do you think Torren's right? Drake asked.

About the Gate? Yes.

And the bait?

Sylvan huffed. A possibility. *The Snowcrest wolves don't represent a threat to anyone. But their territory is valuable, running along a third of our border.*

Drake agreed with her mate's reasoning, but she wasn't so certain territory was the issue. If raiders were attacking a Pack without soldiers, they must know eventually that Pack would reach out for aid. And where would they go? To the strongest Pack, their neighbors. Snowcrest would reach out to the Timberwolves, and everyone, humans and Praeterns alike, knew that Sylvan would respond. Sylvan could not have overlooked that possibility, but Sylvan refused to acknowledge threats to herself. That's what made her the Alpha, and also what made her so frustrating. Drake grumbled.

What? Sylvan thought, slowing to a trot a quarter mile from the outpost.

You know what. Drake nipped her shoulder. *You can pretend this isn't aimed at you, but we must be prepared.*

Sylvan's lips drew back in a wolfie grin. *You worry too much, mate.*

And you don't worry enough.

Sylvan signaled to her wolves to set a perimeter and wait for Trent, who would be along in the Rover with their supplies as soon as she traversed the dry streambed she was using as a road. Sylvan settled down in the sun on a craggy outcropping over a ravine with a thin creek wending its way through its base. A stand of evergreens stretched from there to the Snowcrest outpost under a rocky overhang. Behind, the mountain rose in a sheer wall, providing a natural barrier to their rear.

Good defensive positioning, Sylvan signaled.

And difficult to access, Drake replied. *Unless they're using a Gate.*

Sylvan rested her muzzle on her paws and sighed. *This would be a complicated plan, if you're right.*

Drake stretched out beside her and snorted. *Since when have the Fae ever been simple?*

Good point. Sylvan rubbed her muzzle against Drake's. *If it's us they want, we should know soon.*

Jace and Jonathan remained with Alpha Constantine's force, making Ash the captain of their squad. Jonathan bristled at taking orders from an out-Pack Were, especially one who he considered less dominant than himself. Jace found that amusing. When they reached the second outpost, they helped themselves to clothes from the cache kept there for the sentries. The only shirt she could find was a size too small, but when she pulled it on and noticed Ash watching her, she didn't mind. She shot her a look and a raised eyebrow. Ash frowned and looked away.

Jace huffed. Ash could pretend she didn't like it, didn't want her. But she knew better. Ash's desire radiated like the moon on a cloudless night—bright and strong. Jace's wolf had stopped tormenting her too, content now to wait. For a little while.

"You should stop teasing her," Jonathan grumbled, yanking on a pair of khaki BDUs.

"Why do you care."

Jonathan bared his teeth. "You know why. If you keep tangling with her, she's going to bite you. Then you'll have to accept her or challenge."

Jace gripped her brother's T-shirt and loomed in his face. "When I'm bitten for real, I'll choose."

"And have you?" he murmured. "Chosen?"

Jace didn't answer, refusing to lie.

Dressed in the same khaki camo shirt and pants, Ash appeared beside them. "Problems here?"

Jonathan tugged away from Jace. "None at all. *Captain.*"

"Good. We need a perimeter north and east. Your Alpha's covering southwest."

"I'll see to it." Jonathan saluted and spun away.

Ash watched him go, then said, "Your brother is skirting the edge of insubordination."

"He'll stand," Jace said mildly. "He is too much of a soldier not to follow orders."

"His temper is not just about the command chain, though, is it?"

Jace scanned the immediate area, saw that the others were occupied, and moved closer, hooking her fingers under the waistband of Ash's pants. "He objects to me teasing you."

"Does he," Ash murmured, her eyes sparking. "Perhaps I should remind him our affairs are none of his business."

Jace took a quick nip of Ash's lower lip—a brief tug and a swifter sweep of her tongue over the same spot. "When we make camp tonight, where will you be?"

Ash licked the bite and smiled. "On duty, Wolf."

"Me too, but if we have a moment, I will find you."

Ash chuckled. "When the mission is done, we'll need more than a moment."

"Remember—I *will* find you. See that you're careful then."

Ash ran a hand quickly down the center of Jace's chest, pressed her palm flat to Jace's midsection, igniting her body, inflaming her blood. "And you."

Jace felt the wolf leap into her eyes, recognized the same flash in Ash's, and then Ash pivoted abruptly and strode away. She let out a long breath. Jonathan was right. She couldn't tease her, not any longer, not without giving in to what her wolf demanded. To what she wanted. She shoved her hands into her pockets and walked to the edge of the rough camp they'd made among the pines. The sun was on its way down and shadows cloaked the ground beneath the tall evergreens. The distance she put between herself and Ash didn't diminish the connection. Nor did she want it to. Whenever Ash was out of sight, she sought her— sought the scent of fresh fallen snow and morning mist, sought the heat and power of her. Until she was filled with her presence, she was snappish and ready to snarl.

Frustrated, uncertain, she grumbled and paced until a press of power washed over her and she stiffened to attention. "Prima."

"Jace," Drake said, joining her on the edge of the stony escarpment above the creek. "Satisfied with our position?"

"Yes, Prima." Jace hesitated. "If we were expecting a standard assault."

Drake laughed wryly. "True enough. What are the odds of that?"

"From everything we've found so far—or *not* found—I don't think it likely," Jace said.

"I agree. Are Alpha Constantine's guards battle ready?"

"They're strong, skilled, and loyal. Not warriors, but I'm not worried about them in a fight."

"Aren't you?"

Jace stiffened. "No, Prima."

"Your wolf is restless. Anxious." Drake squeezed Jace's shoulder. "About someone."

"I..." Jace faced her Prima. "My wolf seems to have made a choice I'm not sure how to handle."

"The Snowcrest captain."

Jace nodded. "Ash."

"And her? Has her wolf chosen too?"

"She has not said." Jace shivered. "But she threatens the mate bite."

"How do you feel about it?"

Jace clenched her jaws, shook her head. "She is...not Pack."

"Not my question."

Jace scanned the surrounding forest—like Ash, strange, but still familiar. "I want her."

"We're more than our wolves, and mating is not just physical."

"I know. I want her." Jace squared her shoulders, met the Prima's eyes for an instant. "All of her."

"Then I suggest you stop fighting it."

"But she is Snowcrest. And I am Timberwolf."

Drake raised a shoulder. "I was human when I met the Alpha."

Jace smiled. "Yes, but you are…Prima."

Drake laughed. "Now, perhaps, but I wasn't always. I wasn't even Were."

"Did you…" Jace flushed and looked away.

"Did I what?" Drake asked gently.

"Did you want her—even when you were so…different?"

"Always."

Jace sighed, a weight lifting from her heart. "The Alpha would not have let you deny it."

Drake laughed again. "No. I couldn't deny her."

"Neither can I," Jace whispered.

"We can't know the future, but you must know your heart." Drake looped an arm around Jace's shoulders, pulled her close, and rubbed her cheek against Jace's hair. "All else will follow."

Jace closed her eyes, breathed the comfort of Pack and absorbed the strength that flowed from the power of the Alpha pair. "Thank you, Prima."

"Besides," Drake said casually, "I like her."

Ash completed her circuit of the sentries she'd posted in pairs overlooking the ravine and the most likely approach points. Jace and Jonathan took lookout above them on the rocky ledge. Even from out of sight, Jace's scent stirred her blood.

Zora sat on a log underneath the overhang where she'd established her command post. A small fire burned in front of her. If an attack came, this would be the focus, where the raiders would expect to find two lone inexperienced wolves. "The perimeters are secure?"

"Yes, Alpha." Ash crouched beside the fire, gazing across the flickering flames to the woods where the Timberwolves waited in darkness, camouflaged in case the raiders approached from the south.

"Alpha Mir has offered to post a cadre of soldiers at Cresthome to help train a warrior class from among our young."

"A good idea," Ash said. "We need to be able to protect ourselves, even with powerful allies."

"I want you to take charge of our trainees when we return."

"But…" Ash hesitated. "I have my duty as your guard."

"And you are valued. But I need someone experienced to deal with the Timberwolves. A senior dominant."

Ash chuckled. "Yes, I agree."

"Alpha Mir has offered to send senior warriors as instructors. We will need a liaison. I was thinking of Jace."

Ash sucked in a breath. "She is a *centuri*."

"I am aware. I am also aware that your wolf has chosen."

"I am Snowcrest, Alpha."

"A mating would not change that." Zora rose, her gaze traveling the darkened forest where friend, and possibly foe, awaited. "But the future holds change for us all."

Chapter Fourteen

Once full dark enclosed the camp, Ash took up a position to the left of the overhang, facing the guttering fire, with Evan on the right. The Alpha crouched on the ledge above them from where she could survey the entire outpost. The forest thinned for twenty yards beyond the ledge, creating a rocky semi-bare crescent of moss and low scrub. Beyond that, the tree growth thickened again and formed a barrier between their camp and the edge of the ravine. The midnight sky, inky black and cloudless, once again hosted a full moon. The silvery light courted the shadows at the edges of the clearing, forcing the wolves to take cover among the trees and rocky outcropping. Ash breathed deep, searching the pungent forest for signs of intruders, and found nothing beyond the expected night life and, cutting through the labyrinth of scents, Jace's unique signature. She couldn't see her across the clearing, hidden beneath the pines, but she didn't need to. The thrum of Jace's heartbeat in the dark echoed as strongly as her own heart pounding in her chest, the steady rhythms in perfect synchrony. Ash and her wolf were one in their certainty—Jace was hers. Ash's acceptance of their connection grew steadily with each passing hour. All that remained now was the ultimate union, when they would share the essence of their bodies and spirits. Mating fever burned in her depths, and only her Alpha's presence, formidable and demanding, kept her focused on the mission. Jace was near, and for now, that would have to be enough.

A crack like a whip rending flesh shattered the stillness, and Ash jerked to attention. The tapestry of stars above her head split with a gout of flaming red as if blood exploded from a mortal wound, leaving a yawning void—starless and wholly without form. An abyss with no beginning and no end.

Above her the Alpha howled a warning, and Ash's wolf leapt into battle mode, her pelt streaking down her chest and arms, her jaws instantly transforming, and her canines extending. Half a dozen monsters dropped out of the sky—boar-like beasts as large as oxen with tusks as thick around at the base as her thighs, gaping maws studded with dagger-length teeth as long as one of her limbs, and crimson eyes with slit pupils. Their leathery black hide was plated and armored, their stout legs ending in clawed feet. Upon touching the ground, the beasts spread out in a fighting circle, roaring a challenge, their shaggy heads with flattened snouts and stubby ears swinging from side to side.

The Alpha soared from the ledge and landed, facing the beasts from mere feet away. Their bulk dwarfed her, their wide lethal jaws capable of rending a wolf in two with a single snap. The Alpha bared her teeth, challenging the cordon of beasts. The sky above their heads roiled, swirling mists of flame and sulfur. Ash and Evan sprinted to protect her vulnerable flanks. Jonathan, Jace, and half a dozen Timberwolf warriors streaked from the surrounding woods. Across the clearing, Sylvan, the Prima, and the remaining wolves burst from the forest.

The boar-beasts charged.

Zora leapt to counter the attack, sinking her teeth into the throat of the nearest beast. Thick inky blood sizzled from the deep gouges Zora's canines dug in its flesh. Bellowing in rage, the beast shook its massive head and flung her to the far side of the clearing. Zora landed on her side and staggered upright. Ash darted at the nearest beast, aiming for its vulnerable underbelly and the weak areas around its legs. The circling wolves harried the others in the same way, gnashing and tearing with teeth and claws while trying to avoid the deadly tusks and cavernous maws. The larger number of faster wolves corralled the beasts in a tighter and tighter circle. where they could more easily be overpowered.

An eerie howl split the air, and Torren's Hound, twice the size of the boar-beasts, stormed into the clearing. She wove through the clustered beasts, rending and tearing, grasping them by the necks and flinging them through the air. Bodies crashed against the rock face at the far side of the clearing, and crumpled forms littered the ground at its base. Torren grew more powerful each time she vanquished one of the intruders.

Before the boar-beasts were completely overpowered, the sky belched another gout of flame and caustic sulfur. A dozen Weres dropped from the sky and spread out on the flanks of the boar-beasts. The Weres were wolflike in form, but more sinewy and skeletal, with longer limbs, double rows of canines, and golden eyes shattered with unnatural bands of crimson that wavered and sparked. Not natural Weres, or altered by some sorcerous force.

Ash closed ranks with a Were about her size, soaring toward its back to take its neck in a killing blow. The Were spun, faster than expected, and she barely managed to score its ropey shoulders with her claws. She hit the ground, dug in her claws, and twisted to make another strike. Weaving in and out, biting and slashing, she managed to avoid the Were's counterattacks with only minor wounds. Despite the wounds she inflicted, the Were continued its tireless attacks, seemingly impervious to her claws and canines. If they continued this back-and-forth dance, she might tire first.

Ash feinted a flank attack, pulling back at the last second. The Were spun to intercept her, and she dove low, under its snapping jaws, and clamped tight to its throat. The blood that filled her mouth burned like acid, but she held on, squeezing with all her strength. Emitting an unearthly scream, more human than wolf, the Were thrashed, trying to dislodge her. Ash locked her jaws, ignoring the claws raking at her sides. At last, the Were collapsed, and with a swift shake of her head, she tore through its throat. The dead Were's body crumpled into a foul pile of charred bone and flesh, searing the ground beneath it into a widening circle of death. As if it had never truly been alive.

Staggering upright, Ash took in the battle. Sylvan's wolves were surrounded by a few remaining Weres and the bodies of countless decimated others, all of them encircled with the same ring of charred remains. Zora battled two of the Weres, holding them off with swift feints as they circled her and alternated their attacks. A pair of shadow wraiths dropped from the tear in the sky, their flickering forms nearly transparent, but substantive enough to carry crossbows. One landed in the center of the clearing and took aim at the Alpha. Ash howled a warning.

Too far away.

She leapt at the nearest archer even as she saw the quarrel fly from its bow. The second archer fired, and another quarrel creased her flank. Fire streaked down her hindquarters. She struck the ground and lay panting, her rear leg flailing beneath her. Nearby, a wolf howled in pain.

Ash regained her legs as Torren's Hound streaked past, clamping the first of the apparitions in her great jaws. The wraith disintegrated along with whatever force empowered it. The Hound spun and pounced on the second. In an instant they were gone.

Ash struggled upright, battle lust coloring the world in blood. She'd heard that first quarrel find its mark.

The Alpha.

Ash swung around. Zora stood panting, unharmed, but a wolf lay before her, a quarrel embedded in her chest.

Jace!

Howling, raging, Ash raced to Jace's side. Jace's eyes were closed, the black-tipped silver pelt on her chest soaked with blood. But she lived. Ash straddled her, shielding her with her body, and showed her canines to warn everyone away. The battle receded into the background. How long it went on she didn't know. None of that mattered now. Her only need, her only purpose, was to protect Jace.

A wolf approached and Ash snarled and lunged.

Zora halted abruptly a foot away. *Ash, release her.*

Ash growled in challenge.

Another wolf raced toward her, silver and black like Jace. Jonathan growled, and Ash snapped at him.

Jonathan's Alpha appeared and shouldered him out of the way.

Ash, Sylvan commanded, *you must let us help her. She is mine to protect.*

No, mine. Ash feared none. She showed her teeth.

So be it, Sylvan said, *but I am her Alpha. Torren can help her. Back away.*

Zora stood shoulder to shoulder with Sylvan. Ash's Alpha. Jace's Alpha.

Ash shuddered under the force of their power. Whining with the pain of the assaulting instincts, she lay down with her side against Jace's still body, growling softly in her throat.

Zora ordered, *Stay there. She will need to feel your presence.*

The Hound loped over, the great beast Lord shimmering, and

Torren stepped forward. Crouching down, she placed her hand on Jace's chest. Ash snarled.

"Be calm, Wolf," Torren murmured, looking deep into Ash's eyes. "She's lost blood, but the quarrel missed her heart and lungs. She will live."

Ash shuddered as an ancient power beyond the realm of wolves or humans washed over her. Despite the fear tearing at her soul, she was comforted.

"I can stop the bleeding and a shift will repair the damage, but she will be weak," Torren said. "Sylvan, can you force her to shed pelt?"

Yes, Sylvan signaled.

Zora said, *Cresthome is an hour away by Rover. Our healers can tend to her until she's strong enough to travel.*

Very well, Sylvan said.

Power bloomed around Torren, a mist of glittering blue and crimson. She laid one hand on Jace's chest. Ash, pressed close against Jace, was bombarded by heat and a different kind of power than she'd ever experienced. A force spread through her, as light and unbreakable as tempered steel. Torren gripped the metal arrow shaft with her other hand and slowly withdrew it. The blood that had flowed around it ceased.

"Now, Sylvan," Torren said.

Sylvan transformed into half-form, an enormous looming Were whose call was like the summoning of the full moon. She growled, the sound like thunder emanating throughout the clearing, and everywhere, Weres shed pelt, shuddering with the abrupt change. Jace's pelt melted away and she lay still, curled on her side, a bright red scar marking the entrance of the quarrel into her chest. Ash followed her Alpha into the change and knelt beside Jace, one arm supporting herself on the ground, the other on Jace's flank. The sound of the Rovers filled the clearing, and an instant later Evan handed her shirt and pants.

"We're bringing a stretcher, Captain," he said.

Ash pulled on the clothes quickly, then stood over Jace's too still form. "Why isn't she waking up?"

Torren gazed at her with a gentle smile. Her mate had come to her side and had an arm looped around Torren's waist. "She is gathering her strength."

Jonathan and Ryan burst out of the forest carrying a stretcher. Jonathan bent to slide an arm under Jace's shoulders and Ash growled.

"Don't touch her."

He glared at her. "She's my sister."

"She's mine."

"Ash," Zora murmured. "Take her to Cresthome. Ryan and the others will not harm her."

Ash fought the crushing need to drive everyone away. To make sure no one hurt Jace again. "Yes, Alpha." She glared at Jonathan and Ryan. "Be careful."

In seconds, they approached the Rover. Trent stood by the open rear door. The engine was running.

Jonathan said gruffly, "She saved your Alpha."

"Yes."

"She made her choice."

"Yes."

Trent reached for the end of the stretcher and helped Ryan maneuver it inside. Ash jumped into the rear to be sure Jace was secured. Jonathan leapt in and settled opposite her. He gave her a long look.

"See that she recovers."

"I will."

He gripped the side of the stretcher but did not attempt to touch Jace again.

"You should hurry up with the mating. As soon as she is able." He glanced at her, a faint smile on his strained face. "Otherwise, you'll be fighting everyone, all the time."

She growled at him and he laughed, but his face was pale. His wolf, like hers, was frantic.

"I can sense you," Ash said.

"She's my twin."

"Then you know what I feel."

"I do." He let out a long sigh. "Just be sure she does."

CHAPTER FIFTEEN

"You and your wolves fought well," Sylvan said to Zora as she, Drake, Jonathan, and the Snowcrest Alpha clustered around the closed door to the treatment room.

Zora grimaced. "We would not have prevailed without your warriors."

Cresthome was a quarter the size of the Compound and not as heavily fortified. The century of isolation had left the Pack devoid of a warrior class and ill-prepared for hostilities like the ones they had just encountered. Zora glanced toward the closed door where the Snowcrest healer tended to Jace. "Your *centuri* put herself between me and a quarrel."

"As she should have," Sylvan said.

Jonathan growled. "If your captain had been faster—"

Zora's dark eyes glittered. "Would you challenge now, Wolf?"

Jonathan trembled and a steady grumble emanated from his chest. "I…"

"No, he would not." Drake swept an arm around Jonathan's shoulders and dragged him close to her side. "I apologize for our *centuri*, Alpha Constantine. His worry over his sister strains his control."

"I understand," Zora said stiffly. "Our healer is skilled, and Lord Torren made certain that the injury would be limited."

"Yes, and Jace is strong," Drake murmured to Jonathan.

"I should be with her."

"Ash is with her, and right now, the healer needs space to work without chaotic energy to block what she is doing."

He clenched his jaws, his blue eyes still slashed with gold.

"I can sense her," Drake said. "So can the Alpha, and so can you. Feel her strength. Trust her. Trust *us*. The Alpha and I will not let any harm come to one of ours."

Shakily, Jonathan nodded his head. "Yes, Prima."

The door opened at the far end of the building, and Torren entered with Misha at her side. In her first appearance since the battle in the forest, the royal Fae now wore narrow-legged black leather pants tucked into calf high gleaming black boots and a flowing sleeved blood-red shirt. Her naturally translucent complexion was a shade paler than normal, and her mate kept a subtle arm around her waist.

"Stay here," Drake ordered Jonathan, as if anything could move him from his sister's treatment room, and joined Sylvan and Zora with Torren and Misha.

"How is your wolf?" Torren asked.

"Improving," Sylvan said. "She won't be at full strength for a while, but I can sense her recovery is far faster than I would've expected." She raised an eyebrow. "Your influence?"

Torren smiled faintly. "I did little more than stop the spread of the damage. Your wolves are strong, and her bond with Ash and you is doing the rest."

Misha grimaced. "She would not admit the healing weakened her, Alpha. The quarrels were tainted."

"Poisoned?" Zora growled.

"A tincture known to cause the flesh to die beyond the direct area of injury," Torren said. "The process is subtle at first, and by the time it's recognized..." She shrugged. "Often too late."

"She pulled that into her own body," Misha snapped.

"My lady worries," Torren said, stroking Misha's hair. "The battle was unexpected, as were our adversaries and their...armamentarium. But I assure you, my powers remain unabated."

Sylvan laughed, appreciating the arrogance. Torren was a power she would not want as an enemy, and indeed, she was a formidable ally. She was also a friend, and Sylvan would not insult by thanking her again. "What were they? Those creatures out there? I've never seen them before."

"Some kind of abomination," Torren said darkly. "Those boar-beasts are not natural in the realm of Faerie. We have something like that, *burshee*, but they tend to be docile creatures, mainly herbivores who forage in the lowlands, and not used for battle. I think these were those gentle animals somehow transformed for war."

"The wolves were changed somehow too," Sylvan said. "Not just their appearance, but their aura. I can sense the spirit of wolf Weres even when they aren't mine, but I could glean no connection to them. All I found was darkness that reeked of some foul force."

Zora growled. "The wolves that came through that Gate—some were once mine. I recognized three of our missing sentries, but they were changed. I could no longer reach them."

"That's because they were dead," Torren said.

"Reanimated?" Sylvan said flatly, the rage that welled inside her carrying her wolf into her eyes.

"Ensorcelled, yes," Torren said. "And controlled by a necromancer. A powerful one, to control them between realms, and to keep them enslaved until the moment of their true death."

"Are they vampiric?" Zora asked.

Torren shook her head. "Not in the sense that Vampires have a life force—they can heal if provided blood, and some would argue even the Risen are capable of emotion, form loyalties, and, in the case of the very old or very powerful, are able to reproduce. These beings had no souls, no independent life force. They were puppets."

Sylvan said, "Is Cecilia capable of doing that? Creating and controlling the dead?"

"The Queen of Thorns is powerful indeed," Torren said matter-of-factly. "And it is not unheard of in the history of Faerie for our most powerful Queens to acquire greater and often darker powers as they age. Cecilia is still quite young, only centuries old, but necromancy is a power not natural to the Fae."

"A Mage then," Drake said, frowning at Sylvan. "Until now they have not concerned themselves with Praetern issues."

"New alliances abound," Sylvan muttered.

"If indeed a sorcerer is behind this," Torren said, "they are unknown to me."

Zora spoke up. "And the Gate that they used to access the Snowcrest territory? Will they return this night?"

Torren flashed a bright smile of lethal pleasure. "They will not employ that portal again. I have warded it, and any attempt to cross over will disable the travelers."

"What about its appearance in some other space," Drake asked. "Snowcrest, or Timberwolf?"

"It's possible," Torren said, "but divining a Gate that precise, capable of transmitting beings of such power, requires a tremendous gathering and expenditure of energy. I would not expect a recurrence anytime soon." She shrugged. "But at some point? Perhaps."

Sylvan rumbled. "Is there any way to anticipate when or where they might next break through?"

"I don't know," Torren mused, "and that makes me unhappy. This is something…new. You must understand that in a realm as ancient as Faerie, something new is often something to be feared."

Sylvan snarled. "We will not be daunted by enemies, alive or dead or otherwise."

"Then you must be prepared for battle at all times," Torren said.

Sylvan drew Drake to her side and pulled Zora's gaze. The Snowcrest Alpha bared her canines, and Sylvan smiled. "We will be."

Ash curled her arm tighter around Jace's middle and buried her face in Jace's hair. Jace had not yet awoken, but her heart thrummed steadily, and her blood pulsed full and strong. Deep in healing sleep, her back rested against Ash's front, her wolf curled deep in the shadows, watchful and protective. Ash covered as much of her as she could, sending her strength and comfort. She would have given her life and breath if she'd been able, but their bond was not yet complete enough for her to do that. Soon, it would be. With every passing heartbeat, their connection grew tighter, even without the final union.

When the door opened, soft light filtered in and partially illuminated the bed. Growling softly, Ash crowded closer to Jace.

"Rest easy," Sylvan said. "It's time to finish Jace's healing."

Sylvan bounded lightly over the two of them and stretched out on Jace's far side, facing Jace, and resting a hand on the crest of her hip. Jace twitched and rumbled as the Alpha's power enveloped her. Drake settled behind Ash with Ash's head against her chest. The Prima's healing strength rushed through Ash's body, and through her, to Jace.

"Close your eyes, Ash," Drake murmured. "You have done what needed to be done. You have given her the best of you, and now, the Pack will do the rest. You both have earned a rest."

Ash closed her eyes, knowing she wouldn't sleep, but trusting that she would be safe in the arms of the Alpha pair. The Pack would protect Jace now.

As Jace climbed to awareness, she knew Ash held her. Ash's scent, fresh snow and morning mist, unmistakable, her signature like none other. Jace came fully awake to the sensation of her body tightly coiled in the curve of Ash's. Warm breath coursed against the back of her neck, a possessive hand spread out across her abdomen, and one leg draped over hers. Jace stretched, yawned, registered the urge in her limbs to run, her heart pounding strong and steady. Deep inside, her wolf stood, shook, and sniffed the air—ready to hunt, and more. So much more, and soon. Jace turned on her side and opened her eyes. Ash's intent dark gaze met hers. Flashes of the battle returned with her burgeoning awareness.

Strange beasts, Weres that resembled wolves but were...other, and wraithlike creatures with unworldly substance, armed with crossbows and deadly quarrels. Aimed at the Snowcrest Alpha, aimed at *Ash.*

Jace snarled and pushed up on one arm, running her gaze over Ash's body. She was naked, her sleek form a canvas of beauty and deadly promise. "Were you hurt? I remember archers."

"I am fine," Ash said. "Minor wounds, gone now. And you, *centuri*? How are you?"

Jace chuckled and kissed her. "I have but one need."

Ash's breath drew in sharply. "And what would that be?"

"You know." Jace ran her fingers through Ash's hair, brushed her thumb over the arch of her cheek.

"In time," Ash murmured, struggling to mask the ravenous need unleashed by finding Jace awake and healthy and so close. Her body readied, her wolf surged, every instinct demanding release now that the rage and fear had subsided.

"Why must we wait," Jace asked, stroking Ash's breast. She lowered her head, grazed her canines across the hot, swollen flesh above Ash's breast. The flesh that was hers to claim. Her neck burned for Ash's mouth, for the moment they would join.

"You were seriously injured," Ash said. "And still healing."

Jace stilled. "I remember archers aiming at you, aiming at your Alpha. Was she hurt?"

"No," Ash said, "thanks to you. You risked your life to save our Alpha. Snowcrest will not forget that."

Jace lifted a shoulder. "I did my duty. But I am glad she is unharmed. Did we take losses?"

"None serious." Ash's grip on her shoulder tightened. Her hand was hot, her claws sharp against Jace's skin. "Other than you. The Fae Torren administered to you, and then the Snowcrest medic completed the healing."

"And you," Jace said. "I felt you with me, always."

"I would not leave you." Ash kissed her. "If you choose, I will never leave you."

"We will not have an easy road," Jace said, surprised at how calm and sure her wolf had become. Now that she knew, beyond all question, that Ash was her mate, she could be patient. She would hunt her mate, if her mate enjoyed being chased. She would lie in the shade of the great pines, her breath and body still, her heartbeat as slow and quiet as the new moon rising. She would chase and be chased, as long as Ash needed. "You are still Snowcrest, and I, Timberwolf."

Ash nodded. "And so it shall ever be. But if we are not united, our wolves will be forever seeking, and forever denied. I would not have you take another mate."

"Nor I you." Jace snarled. "You taunt me now."

"Do I?"

"You will not leave this room until you are mine for all to know."

"Will you accept Snowcrest as Pack, as I accept Timberwolf?" Ash asked.

"Your Pack is my Pack," Jace promised.

"Your Pack is my Pack," Ash echoed. She stretched out, pulled Jace on top of her. Her wolf rose in her body and her blood, certain and sure. "If you are not completely well—"

"You presume, Wolf." Jace braced herself on both hands, slid her thigh between Ash's, caught her lip between her canines. "I am better than well right now."

Ash chuckled. "I can tell. Your flesh is full and ready, as is mine."

"Will you take me now, as I take you?" Jace whispered.

Ash gripped her shoulders, dug her claws in deep enough to draw tiny pinpricks of blood. Jace growled and her canines lengthened. Ash's chest throbbed, waiting for the release she knew would come, for the overpowering agony of joining, on the crest of pleasure.

"I have always and ever been waiting for you."

"I will always and ever be yours," Jace growled. Sliding her hips between Ash's thighs, she fitted her clitoris against Ash's, linking them for the final exchange. Her sex readied for the explosion of hormones and neurochemicals that would fuse their flesh, unite their bond, and transform their essence.

Jace gasped. "I love you."

Ash took her deeper. "For you and only you."

Jace lowered her mouth to Ash's chest where her heart's blood flowed the strongest at the instant Ash's canines struck her exposed throat. Their bites were simultaneous and their release instant. Their roar of pleasure shattered the air. Heat scoured Jace's mind until her heart beat in time with Ash's. She rolled onto her back and pulled Ash above her.

"Again."

Ash took her as she had been taken, as equals, as mates, as they would ever remain.

ENCHANTED HUNT

CHAPTER ONE

Cresthome
Far reaches of the Appalachians on the Canadian border

Alpha Zora Constantine stalked the shadows that stretched in long fingers across Cresthome's central Compound as the moonlight shimmered and broke in the face of the distant dawn. The stark silhouettes of guards flanked the east and west gates, the only entrances through the eight-foot fences into the Clan sanctuary. Cresthome had never been breached in the centuries since her grandfather's father's father had led his Pack south from the Alaskan wilderness to settle along the US–Canadian border and the waterways linking the wilderness to the growing human settlements. Looking now at the modest security afforded by walls any Were could jump easily, she couldn't help but think of the stockade fences and battlements surrounding the Timberwolf Compound. Cresthome had not been constructed to withstand a siege, but to provide safety and security for the Pack in the far north woods where none but traders and trappers traveled.

Generations later, Zora had inherited a Pack of hunters, trappers, and merchants, not warriors. Her Weres would be completely vulnerable if another tear in the veil between realms should occur in the skies overhead, belching more monsters into their midst. In the wake of recent attacks on her outposts by enemies she still couldn't identify, warriors were what she needed. She growled, her dusky pelt rolling to cover her arms and lightly dust the center of her bare chest and abdomen. She'd awakened agitated and uneasy, sensing something amiss even though she knew nothing *could* be, without her wolf having alerted already. Still, she'd pulled on a pair of black jeans and bounded down from her second-floor quarters above the main dormitory in search of whatever had her wolf ready to burst free.

Enemies threatened from all sides.

Her Snowcrest Pack had been under subtle attack along their borders for weeks. She'd been present for the major assault her soldiers had managed to rebuff with the aid of the Timberwolf warriors and the Fae Master of the Hunt. She'd seen the abominations that had come through the rip in the veil. Reanimated wolf Weres, deformed and mindless, and mild-mannered herbivores, ensorcelled and transformed into beasts hungry for flesh and blood. Someone had unleashed these creatures of dark magic and malicious intent against her Pack. She still didn't know why.

The air within the Compound pulsed with the scent of foreign Weres—powerful, dominant, aggressive Timberwolves in the vulnerable heart of her territory. Her wolf bristled with the primal urge to drive out the threat to her supremacy, to erase the invaders in her territory. Fury rolled through her, and she growled again, her skin shimmering with battle lust she could not release. The Timberwolves were not her enemies—not yet—and her wolf would have to suffer their presence. If she hadn't seen the devastating power of her foes, she would never have considered inviting a cadre of out-Pack Were warriors into the heart of her Clan. She'd had no choice but to ask for an alliance along with combat support from Alpha Sylvan Mir and the Timberwolf Pack. Another attack could destroy everyone she'd sworn to protect.

Her rage at the attacks on her territory and the deaths of her sentries—Weres who were hers to keep safe—was a constant storm roiling within. She could not sleep, waiting for a faceless enemy to strike again. Instead, she prowled the Compound or vaulted the fence and ran in pelt until her limbs burned, scouring the forest for signs of intruders. Her personal guards and her *imperator* beseeched her not to put herself at risk, but if not her, if not the Alpha, then who? The hours she spent outside the security of Clan home did nothing to dampen the inferno consuming her body, or ease the ever-present gnawing hunger in her depths that grew more vicious every day.

She strode to the nearest gate, and the guards snapped to attention at her approach.

"Alpha," the young male guard exclaimed, briskly tapping his fist to his heart beneath his khaki uniform shirt. He carried no weapon. He was young and eager and not ready. Their guards were dominant by nature but not trained for battle.

Knowing that must change, and why, Zora snarled inwardly. She saluted the guard and his female partner. "Reas, Dinea. Stand easy."

The two young Weres maintained their rigid attention. Zora consciously tempered her power, knowing her unsettled energy transmitted to all her wolves and created anxiety and hair-trigger tempers. She needed her wolves alert and prepared for battle, not ready to explode into aggression with each other at the slightest provocation. A camp full of Weres seething with battle lust and dominance hormones was not what she wanted, and not what her wolves needed. She had to be strong enough to keep them secure and unafraid. She had to find a way to control her rage.

"All quiet?" Zora asked, knowing it was.

"Yes, Alpha," they replied in unison.

"Good." Zora passed on into the dark, putting distance between herself and the sleeping Weres in the dormitory. All the unmated Weres who were not assigned to the outposts or actively securing trade with their customers along the borders roomed there. And now there were the *others*—a dozen warriors seconded from the Timberwolf Weres to train her Snowcrest soldiers in the art of war. Twelve dominants whose foreign scents teased the air with new enticements and the promise of challenges to come. Her Snowcrest wolves might not be warrior class, but they would defend their territory and their potential mates from outsiders just as fiercely as any other wolves.

As must Zora, for as she led, so would they follow—unto death.

And so she stalked the night to put distance between her wolf and the tantalizing pull of sex and power radiating from the Timberwolves gathered in the rooms below her own. The pulse of random pheromones made her restless nights even more unsettled, but worse, her wolf continued to alert to the call of one particular black-haired lieutenant more powerfully than she'd responded to any other wolf, ever, with a tingling rush of excitement that danced over her skin and teased her wolf to come out and play.

She recognized the invitation and ignored it, just as she had since the first moment she'd seen Trent Maran on the training field in the Timberwolf Compound. That morning, as she'd watched Trent disarm a young trainee with lethal swiftness and then demonstrate to the awestruck cadet just how the move was done, her blood had heated and her sex tightened. She was an alpha, a dominant among dominants, and Trent was no match for her in pure power, but it wasn't power alone that had her wolf bristling with a painful cascade of hormones and erotostimulants. The unique mix of Trent's pheromones blended perfectly with her own. Their chemistries, their innate biological signatures, effortlessly connected. That involuntary pull of wolf to wolf was as natural as breathing, and just as hard to stop, but she was not just any wolf. She would not—could not—risk a bonding with *any* Were while her Pack was in danger. And Trent Maran was not just any Were—she was a Timberwolf warrior, an elite soldier from a larger, stronger Pack, and despite their temporary alliance, a potential threat to Snowcrest sovereignty.

Some of her wolves would answer the call of the Timberwolves to tangle, as was their right. She did not intend to be one of them. What her wolves needed now was a strong, unassailable Snowcrest Alpha whose only priority was their security. They needed her, all of her.

❖

Trent shifted restlessly on the narrow cot, drawn from sleep as the moon waned. Her wolf prowled close to the surface most of the night, alert and wary. Her skin tingled with the surge of pelt just below the surface, a sure sign of the need for release. She needed to run or hunt or tangle. If she'd been two hundred miles south in the Timberwolf Compound, she would have slipped out into the night and spent her lust with a Were who responded to her call, but here she was surrounded by Weres who were as likely to challenge her as tangle with her.

Agitated and edgy, she sat up in the unfamiliar cubicle adjoining the larger group dormitory room where her warriors were quartered. She led a cadre of midlevel soldiers, out of adolescence only a short time but all battle hardened in a recent confrontation between the Timberwolf Pack and the renegade Blackpaw Pack. None were truly veterans, which was just as well given the tension of so many dominant out-Pack Weres suddenly thrust into the midst of the Snowcrest Clan home. She'd assigned each of her wolves two or three of the Snowcrest soldiers to train, taking care to minimize the age difference and dominance levels between them. But nothing would stop the dominance conflicts that were sure to come with so many foreign unmated Weres challenging the Snowcrest Weres on their home territory.

Her opposite number in the Snowcrest ranks, Ash Cronin, was of *centuri* level, outranking her in the hierarchy, but their equal responsibilities had placed them on a more level stance. Considering that Ash's mate Jace was a Timberwolf and in ultimate command of Trent's temporary posting, she expected most of the skirmishes would be mild. But they would come. Besides, challenges would be welcome. Good grounds for lessons. Maybe a brisk challenge was what *she* needed, since tangling with any of the Snowcrest Weres or the less dominant Timberwolves under her command was out of the question. She needed something to settle the slow-building heat seething in her loins. She could find some unattached Were who wasn't part of the training group to blunt the edge of her need, but the call that kept her wolf prowling with agitation wouldn't be satisfied by a casual coupling with a willing stranger. She recognized the sharp bite of power that set her blood racing and knew she couldn't answer. Not unless invited, and she wouldn't be.

Not by the Alpha. Not when even a casual tangle could ignite an inter-Pack war.

If only the Snowcrest Alpha didn't lodge in the same building as her soldiers. In the much larger Timberwolf Compound, Alpha Mir and the Prima resided in their own den a distance from the main barracks, but here the Alpha—*Zora*—slept just one floor above her. Or rather, Zora didn't sleep. She paced, broadcasting her call on a wave of pheromones that grew stronger with each passing hour, her power a sweet nectar on Trent's tongue, rolling through her like the sharp edge of a claw, drawing blood.

An hour ago, Zora had finally abandoned her restless circling and escaped into the night. Rather than being relieved by the abrupt absence of Zora's scent, Trent was even more agitated. The moment Zora disappeared, Trent's wolf wanted to give chase. Zora was simmering with unanswered need, and now she was somewhere any Were might give her some release, if Zora relented and let any touch her.

With Zora's call burning through her, Trent snarled at the image of Zora skin-to-skin with another Were, sex-sheen gleaming over her taut, sleek form as she battled for release. *She* had heard Zora's call. *She* had felt Zora's need pounding in her blood. *She* should answer. No one else.

Limbs quivering and her wolf clawing at her insides, Trent shoved open the window above her bed, let her wolf ascend at last, and bounded out on four legs. The path Zora had taken around the Compound and out the eastern gate was as clear to her as if marked by signal flares, and she stubbornly swung westward and raced in the opposite direction. She trotted through the woodland gate, ignoring the Snowcrest sentries posted on either side, and struck off into the woods. The young guards did not offer challenge, and she gave them no more than a flicker of thought, her wolf too intent on capturing the scent of prey—any prey—to chase. Any prey to stir her blood and dispel the heat scorching her depths.

Trent raced through the unfamiliar forest, dense with pine and fir. Coming into fall, the air was crisp and cool and, at the higher latitude along the Canadian border, more biting than she was used to farther south in the Adirondack parkland. Huge boulders protruded like teeth from rocky escarpments bordering the faint game trail, providing natural stepping-stones for her wolf to bound onto and climb. She reached a ledge high above the forest floor, nearly level with the tops of the trees, and lifted her muzzle to the sky, her heart pounding, blood beating through her veins, a strange exultation streaming through her. Not so much freedom as anticipation. Her wolf waited, refusing to be caged by the warning signals buried deep in the part of her brain guided by reason. In pelt, her instincts prevailed, and her wolf ruled.

And her wolf knew why this path had called to her.

She caught the scent a second later, rich and vibrant, commanding and undeniable, stirring the heat in her loins to rise into her belly. She spun away from the edge of the drop-off and faced the sable wolf who studied her from across the clearing thirty feet away. Taller than Trent by a handsbreadth, Zora's sleek, muscular body heaved from the brisk run. Her head and muzzle jutted forward, and her ears perked upright. Gold sheeted her eyes, and a low, resonant rumble vibrated in the air.

A greeting. Or a warning.

Trent stood her ground but dipped her head, breathing softly. After a second, when Zora did not attack or growl a challenge, Trent yipped. Not the whine of a submissive wolf, but an offer. Her tone and posture said, *Do you want to play?*

The Alpha of the Snowcrest Pack trotted toward her, set her muzzle and powerful shoulders over Trent's, and the rumble turned into a growl.

Are all Timberwolves so insolent?

Trent quivered. The heat in her belly flared, scorching her every breath. She should not be able to hear the Alpha's mellow tones in her mind—they were not Pack. Her wolf accepted the unexpected connection, reveled in it. Trent took a deep breath and remained as she had been, motionless, allowing the Alpha the dominant position. She had no choice—to resist would be a challenge, and she was in Zora's territory. She acknowledged her supremacy there. Nothing more was necessary unless Zora wished to teach her a lesson in humility.

Trent's wolf was never humble, and because she wished Zora to know she would only submit so far, she answered with a mental shrug. *Not every Timberwolf is so bold. Only the brave ones.*

Zora made a chuffing sound that struck Trent as laughter. When Zora backed away, Trent shot upright, lifting her tail and dancing in place.

Will you chase me, Alpha?

Zora's eyes flashed and power rolled over the clearing, seizing Trent's blood and turning her sex to flame. *Do you think you can run from me?*

Let's find out. Trent shot a wolfie grin and yipped again. As she spun to bound down the far slope, a sharp bark followed by an ominous growl emanated from the dense cover on the far side of the clearing.

Snowcrest wolves.

Zora alerted, and Trent instantly bristled. Perhaps she would have a tussle yet. If she could not tangle, she could at least vent her disquiet with her canines and her claws.

Two large wolves bounded into the clearing, fur bristling and lips drawn back to show teeth. They circled Trent, flanking her even as they edged in front of Zora, shielding her. Trent recognized them—two of Zora's personal guards, Cybil and Ryan. Of course they would not let their Alpha run alone, even if Zora did not request—or welcome—the protection. Trent held her ground but offered no challenge. If they fought, she might lose—but worse, Zora would be duty bound to exile her if she attacked a Snowcrest Were. Or execute her.

Stand down, Zora commanded of her guards. Snarling, Cybil and Ryan backed away a few feet but never took their eyes off Trent.

Zora stepped into Trent's line of sight, drawing her attention as inexorably as the moon called to her blood. Impossible to resist.

Run with me.

Not an invitation. An order.

The answer was never in question.

As you will.

Trent barked sharply, eager and wild, as the Alpha spun and streaked away. Trent raced after her, aware of the guards falling in, just off her rear. Zora careened down the steep embankment, catapulting from one boulder to the next, her paws barely touching ground before she was airborne again. Trent was used to seeing Alpha Mir unleash her power with an unmatchable explosion of sheer strength and overwhelming force. Zora was no less powerful for her lithe, graceful agility and speed. Trent's wolf spirit soared with joy as she raced to keep pace.

Zora dodged into the dense forest, onto a narrow deer trail that threaded through pine-covered ground, and leapt into an icy stream, splashing through and up the other side without pausing. Sun shafted through the green canopy as dawn broke in a cloudless sky. Zora lifted her muzzle and howled, and Trent echoed her greeting. Ignoring the scent of rabbit and deer crossing their path, Trent streaked at Zora's side, unchallenged by the other Snowcrest wolves. Every scent, every *sense*, every beat of her heart sharp and swift and achingly perfect.

A herd of deer broke from the brush. The does and yearlings bounced away, their white tails upright, their lithe limbs clearing low shrubs and berry bushes with delicate grace. Zora howled again, and the Pack closed in behind her. They reached an upland meadow scattered with yellow and white fall blossoms where the tall grasses reached chest high on the deer. Zora slowed and the deer raced on, reaching the sanctuary of forest on the far side and disappearing into the undergrowth.

Today the wolves ran for the joy of the chase, not the thrill of a hunt. Trent slowed, her chest heaving, and drew alongside Zora until her shoulder nearly touched the Alpha's. Her body felt strong and vital, as if she could have run forever at Zora's side. She shouldered her lightly.

You let me catch you, Trent signaled. *Thank you.*

Zora swung her head to face her. Her eyes still blazed wolf-gold. *Not caught. Only joined on the run.*

Some other time then. Meeting Zora's gaze for the briefest of seconds, Trent trembled, aching to rub against her again, to feel Zora's heart beating against her chest.

Go back, Zora signaled. *There is work to be done.*

Zora spun away, barked sharply in the direction of her guards, and loped off, leaving Trent shivering and alone in the silent meadow.

CHAPTER TWO

In the Lost Realm

Francesca tapped her long, blood-red nails on the arms of the heartwood throne, eyeing the tall, ornately filigreed doors at the far end of the audience hall and waiting impatiently for them to open. Like the stained, dull wood of her throne, the gold panels on the doors—easily twice the height of the Elven sentinels who'd once stood guard eons before when this knowe had been an active part of Faerie—were tarnished and marred from neglect. No liveried soldiers or fawning servants graced the ancient halls now, and every day the remnants of the abandoned Faerie Mound seemed to shrink around her. Whatever spell had kept this knowe from disappearing altogether when its former inhabitants abandoned it, by choice or otherwise, was rapidly fading. Neither her Mage nor Fae allies could tell her why. Soon she would lose this last refuge, such as it was, and be forced once more into the human world or to make an entrance into greater Faerie itself. Either choice left her at the mercy of enemies who would see her true-dead unless her new allies were able to provide her with an army. An invincible army capable of defeating humans, Weres, and Fae.

Allies. The very word sat like acid on her tongue and burned sourly through her chest. She should be receiving this renegade Mage and outcast Fae as the servants they were while seated on her own throne, not as equals while she ruled an empty world and a handful of Vampires and blood servants. Being dependent on the skill and largesse of two lesser Praeterns for her survival filled her with a bitter taste for vengeance against all those who had betrayed her. Someone else sat on her throne now, someone she had if not precisely trusted, for she was far too experienced to trust anyone, at least relied on as her second-in-command and consort for centuries. Michel. Her *senechal* and lover, now ruling her domain while *she* was forced to scheme and scrape to reassemble her power, hiding in a lost land between the realms. Feeding her hunger with the ever-thinning blood of her human servants and the Fae prisoners who were smuggled to her all too infrequently.

Francesca hissed, fury obliterating the taste of defeat. She had lost battles before, but never a war, and she hadn't declared this war over yet. She would reclaim her throne, and those who had turned against her—Were and Vampire and human—would pay in blood. Still, the time for revenge had not yet come, and she could not afford to alienate her few allies, no matter how weak and inferior she might find them.

At last, the doors to the audience hall swung wide, and a human with shoulder length black hair, deep set black eyes, and a thin mouth framed by pale, bloodless lips slithered into the room. Wraithlike in black tailcoat, maroon pants, and calf-high, dusky black boots, he wore an array of silver rings set with crystal stones on each finger. The crystals glowed with power even when the Mage was not actively spell-casting.

"Tell me, Maester Finngar," Francesca purred before the Mage reached the foot of her pathetic throne, "how many of your creatures did we lose in this last assault on a group of Were *merchants*?"

"Not just merchants," the Mage said as if he was informing her of something she didn't already know or was too dense to grasp, "but a cadre of Timberwolf Were warriors and a Fae royal as well. Such a force was unanticipated."

"How many of our creatures remain," she repeated. She had agreed to the attack on the Snowcrest wolves when her initial raids to capture Were sentries for the Mage's experiments had been successful. The larger assault should have captured even more subjects that Finngar could turn into killing machines, but instead, their reanimated, magically enhanced beasts had all been destroyed, as had their portal into the Were territory. Worse, the Weres would be on guard now against further attacks.

"My Lady," he said, his unctuous tone just short of disdainful, "these *creatures*, as you call them, were fashioned for one purpose, and one purpose only. To do your bidding in battle." He shrugged one cadaveric shoulder. "We expect them to be destroyed. They're dispensable and replaceable. Happily, we have enough for another small foray."

"A small skirmish will not be enough," Francesca said. "I...*we*... need bargaining power if we are to force Sylvan Mir to side with us in reclaiming my territory. We need...leverage."

"And we will have that when our army of revenants takes control of the territory along Mir's northern border *and* we can unleash our *combined* power against any who resist."

The Mage seemed very sure that the renegade Fae Lords who sought to usurp the present Queen of Faerie would join Francesca's forces, but she had yet to be convinced. The Fae were clever creatures who always had ulterior motives, and they rarely included helping any non-Fae.

"What of Claudius?" she asked. "Has he delivered the Night Lord's support to our cause as he promised?"

"He assures me he has raised a sizable force of dark Fae to oppose Cecilia when the time comes to declare your return to power. Once the Night Lord deposes the Queen of Thorns, you will have all of Faerie at your back."

Francesca regarded him coolly. As if she would ever be fool enough to trust a Fae who turned on his Queen and conspired with a usurper. But for now, she needed Claudius to open the Gates into the human realm, and she needed his army of dark knights to defeat those who had stolen her throne.

"How long will it take you to replace the creatures we lost?" Francesca said.

"I will need more subjects before I can raise revenants in numbers."

"And if the next creatures of yours are as easily dispatched as the last army you set forth, what good are they?"

For an instant, flames sparked in the depths of his shadowed orbits. "Individually they might be vulnerable, but if unleashed in numbers, they will prevail."

"How many numbers?"

"The sortie against the Snowcrest wolves was a test, My Lady," he went on, his face composed and unconcerned. "One-on-one, the odds were not in our favor. Five to one, ten to one even better…we will be victorious."

"If I had such numbers at my disposal," Francesca said, "I wouldn't need you."

He bowed his head, but not before she saw the smug smile cross his features. "Of course, I understand. But circumstances as they are…" His voice drifted off, and once again he shrugged. "I can, with enough power, raise an army from more than just the Were dead. I can transform the birds and beasts of the Fae realm to swell our numbers."

"And how will we provide you with that power?"

"I believe you know." His gaunt features twisted in anticipation of pleasure. He was blood-addicted, just as any human blood junkie who hungered for the erotic pleasure unleashed by the chemicals injected during a Vampire's bite. Unlike ordinary humans, his spell-casting powers were magnified as well.

"My generosity is not endless, Maester Finngar. You would do well to remember that." She stretched out a hand. "Come then. Come taste the power."

His haughty expression turned to one of naked avarice as he rushed forward to kneel at her feet. His erection, long and thin and rigid, pressed against the laces of his trousers. Before he finished fumbling to withdraw himself, she jerked him upright between her thighs and buried her incisors in his neck. His head snapped back, and he finished instantaneously with a convulsive shudder, his eyes glazed and vacant. She sliced her wrist with one long scarlet nail and pressed it to his mouth. He drank, hardening instantly again against her thigh. His control was brief, and when he groaned and spilled a second time with a series of racking tremors, she left him slumped at the foot of her throne and went in search of her blood servants, hungry now for the taste of true pleasure.

She'd been forced to deny her own pleasure far too often after fleeing Nocturne the night Michel had attempted to destroy her and turned her dominion into a battlefield, lest she drain her few loyal servants to the point of death. She'd been able to teleport only a few of her human servants and a dozen Vampire soldiers with her through the passages to the portal into Faerie and the nebulous realm between the veils. Now she hid from those she had once ruled and feared discovery by the Faerie Queen, who would likely imprison her as Francesca hoped to do to her. Bitter irony burned in her breast. She would rise to power again, and those who had betrayed her, who had sought to destroy her, would become hers to rule.

She discovered David and Marguerite, her two favorite human servants, sleeping naked while awaiting her attentions in one of the rooms still inhabitable in the rapidly shrinking refuge. David, long and lithe of limb with curling brown locks that framed his face like a young Adonis, had been taken into her seethe when he was barely nineteen, almost a century ago. Her blood gave him longevity, just as his blood gave her erotic sustenance. The woman slumbering in the curve of his body was far younger, her skin still bearing the dusty hues of the sun's kiss. The taste of her youth and vitality raced through Francesca's blood more powerfully than the sweet ecstasy of orgasm.

Dropping her robe to the floor as she drew near, she stretched out between them, drawing one beneath each arm, stroking and murmuring and teasing them, already enthralling them as they slumbered. They would awaken aroused and desperate for her bite.

"Mistress," Marguerite gasped, her eyes opening wide, her lips already swollen with need. The delectable scent of her desire floated in the air, making Francesca's sex clench in slow voluptuous waves. "Please. Take me. Please."

"Soon, my sweet," Francesca whispered, pulling the young woman into her embrace. As Francesca kissed her, David caressed Marguerite's heavy breasts, gliding his distended cock between the curve of Francesca's hip and Marguerite's soft belly. He groaned and plunged faster in the warm cocoon of their flesh as Francesca took Marguerite's throat, swallowing languidly as her sex burst with power. Marguerite writhed in erotic ecstasy, her legs splayed wide, her hips rising and falling in wild abandon. Inarticulate cries tailed off to pathetic whimpers as her blood thinned and orgasm after orgasm drained her awareness.

Lifting her mouth from Marguerite's throat, Francesca turned to David and grasped his cock in her palm. His back arched, and his eyes glazed as she stroked. When she judged him close to erupting, she drew his rampant cock between Marguerite's thighs. When he entered her, Francesca raked her elongated incisors down his throat, waiting for the instant when he bucked and groaned, signaling his ejaculation. While he spasmed, Francesca struck deep into his flesh, devouring his blood, hot with pheromones, and the final surge of pleasure engulfed her. When she had filled herself, her own release rolling through her on twin wings of pain and ecstasy, she left them torporous and dazed. She needed them to regain their strength. She needed them to sustain her until she could return to her rightful place.

Not long now. She must bide her time, but not much longer.

Snowcrest territory

Zora doubled her pace as she raced through the forest toward Clan home. She abandoned the usual trails in favor of the untrampled forest floor, kicking up pine needles and bits of soft loam as she streaked between the close-set trunks of towering pines. Cybil and Ryan had been joined by Loris, her *imperator*, and Ash, the captain of her guard. Her wolves kept pace behind her but made no move to close the distance and join her. She had not invited them to run with her, although they were duty bound to protect her, and she would not admonish them for that.

She hadn't wanted company. She hadn't thought so, at least, until she'd picked up Trent's trail. She could have ignored it and avoided the Timberwolf completely, but she'd circled back, crept up on her downwind where she wouldn't be scented, and watched the black wolf bounding up the escarpment to the grassy plateau. The muscles playing in Trent's powerful shoulders and haunches were as sleek and powerful as Zora'd expected after watching her for hours in the training yard. Her pelt was dense and shimmering with ribbons of pure white in the midnight fur. She was larger than the average female in pelt, but agile and quick despite her heavy muscles.

Zora'd sensed Cybil and Ryan close by, waiting for her signal to confront the interloper, but she had not called them forward when she'd padded out from the cover of the low dense undergrowth and drawn Trent's attention. Trent had been just barely submissive, acknowledging Zora's position and her power with the slightest lowering of her gaze, but that had been enough to appease Zora's wolf. They were well matched in dominance, and that had not only been unexpected, but surprisingly exciting.

Zora broke from cover, dashed toward the stockade fence surrounding Clan home, and bounded over it, landing softly on the other side. She shed pelt from one step to the next. Loris and Ash followed her, taking a few seconds longer to shed pelt as well. Wordlessly, all three pulled plain olive-green pants and V-neck T-shirts from one of the many footlockers situated throughout the Compound. Ryan and Cybil veered off once they'd cleared the fence and retreated to headquarters now that Zora was safely back.

Zora pulled on the camos, grasped the shirt in her fist, and strode away. Her blood still surged and her skin shimmered with the lingering patina of sexual arousal.

"Alpha," Loris called after her, his deep voice still gruff from the change. "We have not given the Timberwolves leave to run unescorted."

Slowing, Zora glanced over her shoulder, not surprised that Loris took issue with Trent running alone. Loris was not happy to have a cadre of Timberwolf warriors foisted on him to have control over his soldiers, no matter how necessary the training might be. He had not resisted Zora's command, he wouldn't, but he was Zora's general, and Zora had no desire to undermine his authority, in private or in view of the Pack.

"We did not specifically restrict them, either," Zora said.

Loris huffed. Older by only a few years than Zora, his deep brown eyes, black hair, and tawny coloring hinted at his Native Alaskan heritage. He was built for combat, in skin or pelt, tight-bodied, compact, and ferocious. He had been in line to be Zora's father's *imperator*, and Zora had learned to fight alongside him as adolescents. When her father had been caught in an avalanche along with his *imperator* in the Canadian mountains bordering their territory, leaving the Clan without an Alpha, Loris had stood by her side as she took challenge after challenge for the right to lead, a right that was hers by birth. She trusted Loris and depended on his counsel, but still, he had never led Snowcrest Weres in battle, and only rarely fought in defense of Cresthome against the occasional rogues, renegades, or predators who threatened them.

Zora feared none of her forces were ready yet, and time was not on their side. She would not disclose her misgivings, not even to Loris. Her duty was to provide unyielding, unconquerable strength and security to all her Weres, including those closest to her. Her duty created the foundation of the wall that kept her always apart.

"I don't see any security risk in allowing the Timberwolves free rein to run," Zora said, glancing from Loris to Ash. Ash's mate Jace was Timberwolf, and no one in either Pack was quite sure how their mating would affect Pack dynamics or their personal positions in the hierarchy. Ash was the captain of Zora's guard and in charge of the new training program. Jace, one of Sylvan Mir's elite *centuri*, was her counterpart in the combat operation. Soon Zora and Sylvan would have to come to terms on the future of their wolves, but for now, the security of the Pack took precedence over private lives.

Loris grumbled but said nothing.

Ash spoke up. "By your leave, Alpha, I need to assemble our trainees for morning skirmishes."

Zora waved a hand as they walked toward the rear of the dormitory building. "Of course. Go."

Loris fell in at her side, the muscles in his powerful shoulders and back bunching and flexing beneath the tight cotton shirt. He growled. "You invited the Timberwolf to run with you this morning when you were alone."

"I did." That Loris should question Zora's attention to Trent irritated her, but her wolf instantly bristled as vehemently as if she'd been challenged. Zora waited a moment until the quick burst of battle rage faded. Loris was not challenging, only questioning. "And I was not alone. You and Ash were with me."

"She is unmated."

Zora stopped beneath the second story porch that adjoined her quarters. "You have a point, Loris?"

Ever vigilant to protocol, even when they were alone, Loris kept his eyes just below Zora's.

"Your call is powerful, Alpha," Loris said, his voice a hot rumble in his chest. "One any Snowcrest wolf would be honored to answer."

Zora sighed. Loris was her general, and she depended on his strength and wisdom and skill. Loris was also unmated, and his pheromones misted the air between them. There had been a time, when they were much younger, when Zora had tangled with Loris as she had with other adolescents—testing and searching and learning what her wolf craved. But she was not that Were any longer. She would not find the release she craved with him. She could not dampen her call, even had she wanted to, and Loris was not the only Were affected. Almost every wolf in the Pack would respond to her, welcoming the chance to tangle with her, but only the most daring would attempt to approach her.

She was careful to couple only with those who showed no sign of being vulnerable beyond the physical demands of her call. Only those who could tangle and remain untouched in its aftermath. Loris was not one of them.

"I did not extend that invitation to her today," Zora said, "or to any other. That is not your concern."

Loris nodded briskly. "Yes, Alpha."

Zora grasped Loris's nape and squeezed in a brief caress. "You know how important you are to me and the Pack, don't you?"

Shuddering, Loris leaned against Zora's shoulder, their bare arms touching. His skin was hot and slick and drenched in pheromones. "I would be more, if you desired."

Zora kissed his forehead. "I know that. Now I must go, and you have our soldiers to attend to."

"As you command, Alpha." Loris stepped back with visible effort. He would find someone to tangle with as soon as they parted.

Zora would not. She leapt to the landing above and bounded through the open window to her quarters.

The shower was cold and brisk and helped wash away some of the tension in her muscles but did nothing to quench the burning in her loins. She had long ago learned to control her need, discovering very quickly how willing others were to answer her call because she was powerful, because she was Alpha. But every instance of intimacy ran the risk of stirring a response she did not want. Once she tangled and a Were responded with more than just sex, they would suffer if she did not pursue a bond. She was not ready, although she did not know why she waited. Any number of Snowcrest Weres would make strong mates, and she was of the age when she was ready to mate and breed. The Pack needed a strong Alpha pair, and they needed strong pups. But still, she waited, and the hunger burned brighter every day.

When she stepped into the functional but stark room where she slept alone and walked naked to the open window overlooking the training yard, she sought out only one figure. At that instant, as if summoned by Zora's intent, Trent strode into view in khaki pants and a sleeveless tee, her body taut and tight, her presence sure and strong. Zora tensed as blood rushed to her core and her clitoris pulsed. Her sex readied, instantly full and demanding release. Her wolf clawed at the fabric of her control, ripping at the thin threads of resistance that kept her from broadcasting her call and allowing any Were nearby to ease her need.

Snarling, thwarted by her own will, she turned from the window. The Timberwolf was not for her, and she desired no one else to answer.

CHAPTER THREE

Trent made no attempt to follow Zora and the other Weres on the run back to Clan home. The Alpha had made it clear Trent was not invited. Trent's wolf clamored to follow, driven by instinct more powerful than reason. Trent had managed to hold on to her control despite the pressure in her chest and the burning in her belly that demanded she stay as close to Zora as she could. Trent was intrigued by Zora's call, a constant alluring undercurrent whenever Zora was near, but out in the wild, with Trent's wolf ascendant, she'd been captured by it on a primal level. The primitive impulse to respond was as unavoidable as breathing for any Were in the presence of an Alpha who was broadcasting their power.

Trent had run with Zora when Zora invited her, and if Zora had asked for more, she would have willingly tangled with her. But Zora had dismissed her.

Back in her solitary room, Trent shed pelt, and the trembling in her body subsided enough for her to recognize her response for what it was, instinct and biology, merely something she'd lived with all her life as part of a Pack. She tried not to ignore the other truth—that she'd never responded so intensely, so uncontrollably, to any other Were, not even her own Alpha.

Sitting on the edge of her narrow single cot, she breathed deeply, unable to stop searching for the singular scent that had dominated her consciousness for days. And there it was—a spicy, tantalizing bittersweet scent that danced over her tongue, twisted through her belly, and tingled along her spine.

Zora.

Trent's skin prickled, and a thin line of fine dark pelt shot down the center of her belly. Her sex tightened. Zora was somewhere nearby. The instant her body registered that unique constellation of hormones and erotochemicals, a terrible pressure mushroomed inside her. Her wolf pushed to the surface, demanding that she find Zora. Touch her. Demand Zora let her. The drive to be near her, to protect her, and to be protected by her was a physical pain. Trent wanted to be under her, and over her, and immersed in her.

And she could do none of those things.

She was here for one reason only, to fulfill *her* Alpha's command to aid their allies, and soon she would be back with her own Pack. Where she belonged. She had no place here, and for a Were, place and Pack were life itself.

With a shake of her head, Trent gritted her teeth, ignoring Zora's pervasive scent that assaulted her at every turn and teased her with every breath she took. After pulling on a tan T-shirt and camo BDUs, she headed outside to the training yard. Ash and the Snowcrest cadets waited on one side of the hard, packed-earth exercise square in a tight circle, bristling with barely concealed aggression. Twenty yards away, Jace—lithe, blond, and deadly—fronted the line of Timberwolf soldiers. Too many hormones clouded the air—sex, battle, lust—every Were in the Compound edgy, wary, and eager to prove their dominance, protect their territory, or release their aggression with a quick, hard tangle.

Trent nodded to Ash, who tipped her chin in greeting. Jace stepped into the space between the two groups and planted her hands on her slender hips. The power emanating from the *centuri* belied her age. Jace was part of the elite guard to the most powerful Alpha Were in the hemisphere, quite possibly in the world. She had earned her position in battle. She had nothing to prove. Now she was mated to a Snowcrest Were, something that hadn't happened in either Pack for decades.

"All right," Jace said, "listen up. Everyone pair off for close combat drills, Snowcrest and Timberwolf. Hand-to-hand only. Let's form up."

Trent's job was to supervise the sparring between the Timberwolf soldiers and the Snowcrest cadets to be sure the training was not only effective, but that the training pairs were equally matched. She walked the line, occasionally correcting form, and now and then switching partners. The Snowcrest cadets were not only eager to learn new skills, they had something to prove. They were facing off against out-Pack

Weres on their territory, and while they might be less experienced in combat, they were still as fierce as any other wolves claiming their territory. A particularly aggressive senior Snowcrest trainee, one of the guards Trent had seen posted on sentry duty the night before, slipped the front guard of a Timberwolf soldier and took him down with a particularly vicious leg sweep. The Timberwolf came up snarling, eyes glinting with rage. The blond Snowcrest Were snarled back in his face, her eyes instantly shimmering to gold. They'd be in pelt in a second.

"That's enough," Trent snapped, stepping in between them, planting a hand against each of their chests and shoving them back a step or two. The Timberwolf soldier grumbled but offered no challenge. The Snowcrest sentry bared her teeth, fangs already emerging.

"You don't want to do that," Trent said quietly.

"What makes you think I don't," she snarled back, meeting Trent's gaze in open challenge.

Trent sighed. All right, then.

"Make a space," she said to the surrounding trainees, who were all watching now. Everyone moved back to form a loose ring around them, Snowcrest in one half of the semicircle and Timberwolves in the other. Trent looked over at Ash, who nodded.

"Hand-to-hand," Trent said, "and keep your wolf leashed."

The blonde, with heavily muscled shoulders and long, lean thighs, curled her lip. "I don't need pelt to handle you."

Trent grinned, spread her arms. "I'm right here. *Cadet*."

The term, usually applied to adolescents in training, brought sneers and hoots from the Timberwolves.

The blonde charged, feinting with a punch and sweeping with her rear leg. If she connected with Trent's knee, she'd dislocate it.

But Trent expected the move, having seen it just a few seconds before. Lesson one—don't give the enemy a preview of your offense. She stepped in close to avoid the leg sweep, blocked the punch with a forearm, and hammered a fist into the blonde's inner thigh. As the blonde buckled from that blow, Trent caught her under the chin with an open-palm, upward thrust that snapped her head back. Her body followed, and the blonde landed on her back in the dirt with a whoosh of air exploding from her chest.

If this had been a demonstration of technique, that move alone would've been enough, but this confrontation was more than that. It was a test. One of the trainees had challenged Trent's authority, and that required more than a simple demonstration.

She leapt across the distance between them and grasped the blonde's arm as the Were vaulted upward. Pivoting behind her, Trent thrust a knee into the center of her back and took her facedown again, straddling her from behind. She let her wolf rise just enough so her pheromones danced in a heavy cloud that those crowding closer would scent. She wasn't interested in dominating this *particular* wolf, not sexually at least, but she wanted to send a clear signal to everyone around her that her power was more than enough to dominate any of them.

Still holding the Snowcrest's arm jammed up between her shoulder blades to immobilize her, Trent squeezed her thighs on either side of the blonde's hips, a taunting dominance move, and leaned down until her mouth was close to her ear. The blonde shivered, her wolf already close to submitting. If the Snowcrest Were turned belly-up and offered her throat, if she spent her essence in total submission to an out-Pack Were, she would lose status with the other Snowcrest Weres. She might lose her place in the Pack hierarchy. She would surely become an enemy.

"You're a good fighter," Trent whispered, her breath in the blonde's hair, "but you could be better. I can show you what you can be."

"I submit," the blonde whispered.

"I don't want you to. I want you to *fight*, just not with me. Do you understand?"

"Yes."

The blonde's face glistened, her pheromones pulsing below her sex-drenched skin, her trembling body on the verge of exploding in physical and sexual submission.

"Then we're done." Trent bounced to her feet and backed away.

The blonde lay with her eyes closed for a few seconds, her chest heaving, before she pushed herself to her knees, stood, and turned to face Trent. She kept her eyes just below Trent's gaze. Waiting.

"As you were, Sentry," Trent said, turning her back to the blonde.

The circle of onlookers slowly dissolved. The trainees moved back into position and resumed their practice exercises. The blonde shook herself, took one step in Trent's direction, and halted abruptly.

Zora Constantine stepped up beside Trent.

"Alpha," the blonde said, dropping her eyes.

"Freya," Zora said sharply to the blonde. "Don't you have training to complete?"

"Yes, Alpha," Freya said and turned away.

"That was quite a demonstration," Zora murmured, not looking at Trent.

Trent folded her arms and surveyed the trainees, forcing herself not to look at Zora. Her stomach cramped with the effort of ignoring her scent. "Your wolves are proud. Understandably. But discipline is as important to effective defense as the desire to fight."

"Desire," the Alpha said, still standing, hands on hips, watching the pairs of fighters working through their exercises. "Is that what you were trying to teach her?"

Trent smiled at the irritation in the Alpha's voice. She remembered the run of just a few hours before and the sensation of unbridled freedom she'd experienced. A wild, exhilarating rush that was different even from when she'd run with Alpha Mir. She remembered how the touch of her shoulder against Zora's, the scent of her wolf, and the power of her call had sent hunger pouring through her. She'd known desire, but nothing had devoured her like that. The blonde beneath her just now had stirred nothing, not even the primal urge to tangle.

"I was making an example of your Were," Trent said, "not sending an invitation."

Zora's head snapped around and she snarled, "Weren't you?"

Trent risked a direct gaze, one insolent and worthy of discipline. Zora's eyes were ringed in gold, her cheekbones sharp, a glint of fangs showing. Her wolf danced in her eyes. Trent caught her breath, her wolf instantly alert, her sex quickening as her clitoris hardened. Her skin burst with sex-sheen, and she trembled. "That was not an invitation."

Zora's nostrils flared and her jaw grew heavier. "Then be careful what you broadcast to my Weres. I could feel your call across the Compound."

"It was not an invitation to *her*." Trent's chest heaved, a thin line of pelt erupting down the center of her abdomen. Zora's fury stirred her wolf's need to meet her, body to body, passion for passion.

"But someone will answer." Zora's words ground out on a growl.

"Someone?" Trent dared. Quivering, she raised her chin to show her throat. If Zora took her now, right here on the earth in the center of Snowcrest land, she would welcome it. She was ready, urgent to spend.

Zora snarled again, pivoted, and vaulted away, leaving Trent trembling for the second time that day.

❖

The Adirondack Parkland, Timberwolf territory
Central NY State
First light

Sylvan burst from the underbrush, Drake running at her shoulder. Their two young, Kira and Kendra, raced after them. The prey shot ahead, darting off into the thick cover between the tall pines. Given a chance, the hare would go to ground, but even if it escaped, there was a lesson for the pups to learn. Today, Sylvan wanted to teach them the order of the hunt, the way to follow her as she stalked and flushed the prey, to hold their place until she signaled them to the flanks or the lead. Hunting, like life, was not a solitary pursuit.

They were Pack, always. Every Were lived, hunted, fought, and died as Pack.

Drake, her mate and the true source of all her power, easily kept pace, her breath flowing even and strong, her heart beating in time with Sylvan's. Sylvan was Alpha, destined to lead, to be the strongest and the surest, even when sometimes she was not. Drake's power matched hers, but her strength lay not just in muscle and bone, but in her willingness to give to Sylvan what she needed most—unbending, undying loyalty, trust, and love. Sylvan and Drake ruled the Pack by virtue of being the most dominant and the strongest, but they claimed the Pack's loyalty because they would die for any Timberwolf. This willingness to sacrifice for Pack was what her young needed to learn. To do that, they first needed to learn to be part of the Pack. The time would come when they would need to stand apart in order to lead, but not as long as she lived and ruled.

Sylvan slowed and Drake, so connected to her by heart and body, slowed with her.

Sylvan signaled her pup. *Kira, go!*

Kira, her silver pelt tinged with black on her ears and ruff, streaked past, pursuing the hare's scent deep into the forest, unmindful of obstacles in her path. She leapt with all the strength of youth, and the joy and vigor of invincibility. Sylvan chuckled, giving her exuberant young a chance to command. Over her left shoulder, she could feel Kendra's power building, recognizing it for what it was. Kendra was the alpha pup, and one day, she would lead. But for now, she must learn patience while others found their place in the Pack order.

The prey was clever and quick, and Sylvan sensed when it dove into its burrow, having escaped to live and run another day.

Kira circled the fallen tree and danced about the entrance to the hare's refuge, her nose to the ground, panting with enthusiasm.

Kendra, go, Sylvan commanded.

Kendra shot forward, arrowing directly to the opening of the burrow, nudging her sister aside with a rough shove to the shoulder. Annoyed to be pushed aside, Kira nipped at her, and Kendra nipped back. Within seconds, the twins had forgotten their elusive prey and were tumbling together on the ground in a cacophony of snarls and yips. Drake slowed and swung her head toward Sylvan, her expressive dark eyes filled with pride and wolfie amusement.

Sylvan settled on the ground to watch the pups with a huff. *So much for training.*

Drake dropped beside her, rested her muzzle on Sylvan's forelegs, and licked the corner of Sylvan's mouth. Sylvan lifted her head, letting Drake place her teeth gently around her throat—a position she would allow no other. Her vulnerability signaled both her trust and her devotion.

They did quite well, Drake signaled. *For a minute or so.*

Sylvan grumbled. *They have the concentration of ants.*

Kira caught the scent, Drake noted reasonably, *and Kendra showed remarkable control when you held her back. Patience, my love. They're young.*

You're too easy on them. Sylvan grumbled some more, but she didn't disagree. The pups were young and strong and full of themselves. Exactly as she would wish them to be. Her pride, though, would not keep them safe, or teach them to safeguard others. Only her example would do that.

Sylvan rose and called the twins with a sharp bark.

Drake bumped her shoulder as they headed back to the Compound. *You forget what it was like to be their age.*

Sylvan chuffed. *I remember being eager and full of myself and too quick to show my teeth.*

Not much has changed, I see. Drake jostled her shoulder again as they ran. *I suspect there was a bit more fueling your arrogance as well, but then—you were younger and in your prime.*

Sylvan snarled. *Is that a challenge?*

What do you think? Drake showed her teeth and sprinted ahead. A second later, Drake disappeared off trail into the forest, but Sylvan wasn't worried. She could track her mate anywhere, no matter the distance between them.

With a sharp yip, Sylvan summoned the *centuri* who'd been shadowing them since they left the Compound. Jonathan and Dasha loped out of the forest and fell in on either side of her and the young.

Take the pups back to the Compound to join the other juveniles.

Yes, Alpha, Jonathan replied and herded the two jostling young wolves onto the path leading to the main Timberwolf encampment.

Sylvan howled in answer to Drake's challenge and raced off in the direction her mate had taken. She caught Drake's scent, bounded off the trail, and cut through the dense forest. She knew where Drake was going. Her mate had a few seconds' head start, but Sylvan was a little larger and just a little bit faster, and she was first to reach the clearing surrounding their den, a single-story cabin a quarter mile of dense forest away from the Compound and several hundred other Weres. She sensed Drake a few seconds behind her, could feel her energy and scent her unique signature. Drake broadcast pheromones and sex, and Sylvan's clitoris filled in anticipation. The glands buried deep on either side of her sex pulsed with the hormones stimulated by Drake's call, and heat lightning flashed through her blood. She needed to take her mate, to couple and claim and empty for her. *Because* of her, and only her.

Panting, her body streaming with sex-sheen, Sylvan shed pelt and bounded naked up onto the broad plank porch just as Drake burst from the forest twenty yards away. The air around Drake shimmered as she shed pelt and leapt up beside Sylvan, wolf-gold still rimming her eyes.

"You cheated," Drake snarled, raking her canines down Sylvan's neck, leaving thin lines of burning need.

Sylvan caught Drake around the waist and dragged her close, her wolf still driving her instincts, the need to claim her mate thrumming through her blood and beating in the pulse between her thighs. She nipped at the soft skin at the base of Drake's throat, quick sharp bites in time with the blood beating beneath the silken surface.

Drake growled and plunged her hands into Sylvan's hair, the blunt tips of her fingers still lightly clawed.

The sharp pinpricks of pain incited a low rumble of pleasure in Sylvan's chest. She closed her jaws over the sensitive mark on Drake's shoulder, the spot she'd bitten to trigger the mate bond. She bore a similar mark on her chest that locked her body, mind, and spirit to Drake.

Drake shivered as Sylvan's slow bite sent showers of erotostimulants flooding her system. "You abandoned the chase."

"Oh no. You thought to leave me behind," Sylvan murmured, sweeping one hand over Drake's chest along the sensitive inner surface of her breast and down her abdomen to the delta between her thighs. She pushed her hand between Drake's legs and cupped her. The rumble in her chest became a growl as the heat of Drake's sex and the prominence of her clitoris filled her palm.

Drake nipped at her ear and kissed her. "I would never leave you, but I know how much you enjoy the chase."

"Well, I've caught you now." Sylvan circled Drake's waist and dragged her backward, nudging the door open with her shoulder. Once inside the main room, she pulled through another door into their bedroom. With a twist of her hips, she flipped Drake down onto the bed, climbed above her, and straddled her with one leg between Drake's thighs.

Laughing, Drake clasped Sylvan's thighs and pulled her upward until Sylvan's sex was above her mouth. "Caught me, have you?"

Sylvan shouted as Drake claimed her with her mouth. Sylvan's mind blurred as need speared through her, and her muscles clenched. Drake's mouth was hot, her tongue a swirl of teasing ecstasy around Sylvan's clitoris and a maddening pressure on the full-to-bursting mate glands on either side. Sylvan braced an arm against the wall, steadying herself to look down and watch Drake dominate her. She thrust her hips, pushing her distended clitoris deeper into the slick inferno, her stomach rigid as Drake's lips slid up and down her length. Burning pressure pounded in her sex and fire skirted down the inside of her thighs.

"Drake," she whispered urgently. She needed just a little more, harder and faster. She needed Drake to take everything she had. A whimper, nearly a whine, escaped her, and her claws erupted, gouging the timbered wall. The red haze of sex frenzy buried her in a wild storm of raging desperation. "*Now.*"

Her broken growl erupted into a roaring plea.

Drake reached up, dragged her short, blunt claws down the center of Sylvan's abdomen, and Sylvan released so suddenly the explosion snapped her head back and bowed her spine. Hips pumping wildly, she emptied, surrendering every drop of her being into her mate's demanding mouth. Finally finished, she dragged herself free of Drake's grip and pushed her way down the bed and wedged her hips between Drake's thighs. Pressing her still distended clitoris to Drake's cleft, she took her mouth in a hard, probing kiss. Drake's legs came around her and completed their joining.

"Mine," Drake gasped, gripping Sylvan's shoulders and urging her deeper.

"Yes." Panting, Sylvan unleashed her primal imperative to claim her mate, to take her, to own and be owned by her. She thrust, the aching pressure building again. Drake closed around her, hot and warm and ready, as full as she was. They released together, their *victus* blending, their unique hormonal signatures joining, creating the singular union that only mated pairs achieved.

Sylvan collapsed, drained, her face buried in Drake's neck. "I love you."

Drake stroked her back, holding her protectively, her embrace fierce and unyielding. "You're mine, Alpha."

"Always," Sylvan muttered. "You mean everything."

Drake kissed her. "That's because I want all of you."

"You have me."

"And you have me."

"You took me hard." Sylvan pushed herself up onto an elbow, studying Drake intently. "I didn't sense you were breeding."

Drake smiled. "I'm not. You know it's unpredictable for us. It may not happen again."

Sylvan kissed her. "We have two strong young. One is destined to be the next Alpha. If we have no more, we have Pack."

"Will you be disappointed?"

Sylvan barked a laugh. "How could I be? I have more now than I ever dreamed. I have you, I have our young. I have everything."

"Having young *does* change everything," Drake said quietly. "The Pack is ours to protect, but now I feel it even more than I ever did. The young are our future, not just yours and mine, but the Pack's. They are the lifeblood, and we can't let anything threaten them."

"What are you afraid of?" Sylvan said.

Drake pushed up on the pillows, and Sylvan rolled to her side, bracing on an arm to watch her as they spoke. Drake's eyes often told her even more than her words.

"What we saw out there in the Snowcrest territory—those abominations were sent to test our strength," Drake said. "That can't be the end of it."

Sylvan gritted her teeth. "I know. But right now, the enemy is faceless, and all we can do is prepare."

"The Snowcrest Pack is vulnerable," Drake said. "They might be safer if we annexed them."

"I thought of it, but Zora is a strong young Alpha and a capable leader. I know her and her *imperator*, Loris. He's not a wartime general, but he will become a strong tactician with good advisors. I would rather see Snowcrest stronger and keep them as independent allies. If we annex them, even for their own safety, we will create enmity between our Packs and possibly reprisals from other Pack leaders."

Drake sighed. "I agree with you, if we have time."

"You forget that our two Packs have already begun to form alliances." Sylvan smiled ruefully. "More than alliances. Ash and Jace are mated. One of them will have to choose."

"Jace will never renounce her ties to the Timberwolves," Drake said.

Sylvan's eyes flashed gold and her canines gleamed. "Nor would I want her to."

Drake leaned over and nipped at Sylvan's lower lip. "You are possessive, Alpha."

Sylvan grinned and ran her hand down the center of Drake's body, closing between her legs. She squeezed and Drake's eyes sparked, glittering silver and gold flecks dancing across the midnight. Drake readied again beneath Sylvan's hand as she stroked her. Drake closed her eyes and arched her back, firm and full beneath Sylvan's fingers.

"Again?" Sylvan whispered.

"Now," Drake ordered and Sylvan squeezed. Drake emptied into her hand, and Sylvan's belly tightened.

Drake turned swiftly and caught Sylvan by surprise, her bite on Sylvan's chest arrowing through her so forcefully, Sylvan roared. Then Drake was between her thighs, mouth on her again, pulling her deep.

Sylvan pushed herself up on her elbows and watched while Drake sucked her until she emptied with a helpless howl. She fell back, panting, the mate bite throbbing to the beat of the blood pounding through her clitoris.

Drake looked up, smiling. "I'm somewhat possessive myself."

Sylvan gasped, "I noticed."

A wave of alarm, broadcast from the Pack, rolled through the room, and Sylvan alerted. Drake sat up.

"The *centuri* are coming." Sylvan leapt from the bed and vaulted from the room.

Drake followed, pulling on pants and a T-shirt on the way outside. Jonathan and Dasha strode into the clearing.

"What is it?" Sylvan demanded.

"A portal opened outside our gates," Dasha said with unusual formality. "A contingent of royal Fae guards bearing the Queen's banner and a flag of peace requests an audience with the Alpha."

Chapter Four

Snowcrest Training Yard

When the exercises ended and the cadets slowly dispersed from the field, Trent lingered along with Ash and Jace.

"Our cadets handled themselves well," Ash said. "A few more weeks, and they'll be combat ready."

"We may not have weeks," Jace said quietly. "And we do not have enough warriors to withstand even a moderate assault."

"Then we'll escalate the training schedule," Ash said, her jaw tightening.

"We need to take them into the field," Trent said, "in order to truly test their battle worthiness. Simulated combat is not enough."

Ash folded her arms across her chest. "Are you suggesting simulated assaults on our Weres?"

Trent smiled, letting her canines show. Ash technically outranked her, but she had the advantage of being a veteran combat leader. She wouldn't let a little dominance difference prevent her from getting the Snowcrest soldiers battle-ready. Alpha Mir would be disappointed if that happened. Worse, so would Zora. "No, I was suggesting *actual* assaults. Ambushes, attacks on multiple fronts, overwhelming odds. Your soldiers need to be shocked, stressed, faced with things they've never encountered before. One-on-one, they're good fighters. Not yet as good as they need to be, but that's not enough in the face of experienced opposition. They'll break ranks and be overrun."

Glowering, Ash glanced at Jace. Jace lifted her shoulder and nodded.

"The lieutenant makes a point," Jace said. "Your soldiers are used to patrolling alone or in pairs on your frontier, or guarding your home territory. But they need to be able to work as cadres, in units, thinking and moving as one with a single leader in charge, and a clear chain of command. And not just that—they need to be confronted with challenges they've never faced before."

Ash grunted. "We're talking about Weres forced into situations where they will feel threatened and potentially dominated by strangers in their own territory. They're going to become aggressive. We're going to have challenges in the midst of battle fever."

"If being confronted in the field unbalances them, affects their ability to reason, all the better," Trent said. "Better it happens with us than with what we faced out there when the veil between the realms dissolved."

"I'll advise the Alpha." Ash's gravelly tone registered her unhappiness with the plan.

"Good." At the mention of Zora Constantine, Trent's gut tightened. Anticipation and an unexpected territorial surge of possessiveness burned through her like wildfire. Ash was the captain of Zora's guard, second only to the *imperator* in the chain of command. She was close to Zora, a trusted advisor and confidant. Ash would be alone with the Alpha, and the Alpha's call still rolled in the air. Trent growled, and Jace gave her a look.

Ignoring Trent's attitude, Ash ran a hand down the back of Jace's neck and squeezed lightly. "I'll catch up to you in a little while."

Jace stroked one hand down the center of Ash's torso with the certainty of ownership. "Good. I'll be waiting."

As Ash strode away, Jace's hungry gaze followed her.

Trent said, "I'll be inside, working on the training plans."

Still watching her mate, Jace said, "Whatever you're thinking, you should rethink it."

"I'm not thinking anything," Trent said.

Jace pivoted, her blue eyes, laser like, flickering with the lingering shades of her wolf. "That's my point. Your *wolf* is doing the thinking, and not much of that. Zora Constantine is the Alpha."

Trent's jaw ached as her canines throbbed, her wolf pushing to the surface, bristling at the challenge. "I know who she is."

"Do you know what the senior wolves in this Pack would do to you if you tried to answer her call?"

"I'm not afraid of any of them." Trent growled.

Jace rolled her eyes. "Of course you're not. You're a Timberwolf."

Trent grinned, and Jace laughed, shaking her head. "You can't take on half a dozen dominant wolves who aren't going to want you anywhere near their Alpha."

"That would be for her to say."

"Then you'll have to wait for an invitation. You know that, don't you?"

Trent's wolf bristled. She wasn't passive, and she wasn't fearful. "You don't have to worry."

Jace slung an arm around her shoulders. "I'm not worried, not about you. But Alpha Mir will not be happy if we start a diplomatic crisis in the midst of a coming war."

"I know my duty."

Jace jostled Trent with her shoulder as they walked. "I'm not questioning your duty. I'm questioning your judgment when you let your wolf lead you around by your glands."

Trent chuckled. "You should know."

"Believe me, I do."

"Don't you have somewhere to be?" Trent asked. "I think your mate was inviting you for a tangle."

"Oh, she was," Jace said, her voice dropping low. She paused in front of the dormitory. "And I plan to find her right now. Try not to get into any trouble."

"I wouldn't think of it." Trent waited as Jace turned and loped across the commons in the direction where Ash had disappeared. Once Jace was out of sight, she altered direction away from the dormitory and toward the one-story building where Zora could usually be found when she was within Cresthome. No guards stood at the door or on the porch that wrapped around the front and one side of the unassuming L-shaped headquarters. No one took notice of her approach. The commons was fairly empty in the late morning, with those who resided there either on patrol or traveling throughout the territory on Pack business. Trent took the three stairs up to the porch in one bound and entered through the main door. The short stone-floored hallway inside branched immediately on the right down the long, narrow L portion of the building where the infirmary and meeting area were located. Off to the left, an archway led into a large common area occupying the entire front of the building. A huge stone fireplace on the far wall held a simmering fire. Three sofas arranged at right angles in a square sat in front of it, all empty at the moment. A door in the rear led to Zora's office. Trent crossed the room and stepped into the doorway.

The Alpha was behind her desk, a stack of papers by her left hand and a computer on her right. She looked up, no hint of surprise in her face. She would have sensed Trent coming. She would have known anyone who approached by scent and sound.

"What is it?" Zora asked.

"Did Ash speak to you about field maneuvers?"

"No."

"Then I should wait until she does." Trent held as still as she was able under the barrage of pheromones battering her senses. Zora exuded so much power, Trent nearly choked on it. Her skin shimmered and her sex pounded painfully. She'd thought she was prepared for Zora's call, but she'd been wrong.

"That's not why you're here." Zora rose, circled the desk so quickly Trent didn't see her move, and then she was inches away. "Is it, Lieutenant?"

Zora traced a single blunt fingertip along the edge of Trent's jaw.

Shivering, Trent caught her breath. She'd never seen anyone except her own Alpha move that way. Faster than the eye could follow. Zora's heat washed over her and her skin prickled. Her sex tightened, and she readied instantly. Already so close. She tilted her chin and exposed her throat.

"You know what you offer?" Zora growled.

"I know," Trent said.

Zora reached past her, yanked the door closed, and pressed closer until Trent's back struck the rough wooden planks. Zora's thigh was between hers, Zora's hands pressed flat against the door on either side of her shoulders, her breasts a firm weight against Trent's. Trent panted, her instinct to clash and claim, to drag Zora down, to tear her clothes away and mark Zora as hers a white hot flame obliterating all thought. Zora's mouth was on her throat, the brush of canines so piercingly sweet, she whimpered. Zora didn't break the skin, didn't bite her. But Trent wanted her to.

"Answer me," Zora commanded. "Do you know what you're offering?"

"Anything," Trent murmured. "Everything."

"No." Zora slashed the button from Trent's fly and ripped her pants open. The button rolled across the floor, the sound like thunder. Trent stiffened and her head banged back against the door. Zora slid a hand down her belly and between her thighs. She cupped her, hard and demanding, and Trent's clitoris spasmed. Her hips bucked. Another tug of Zora's fingers around her clitoris, and she would spend. Her chest heaved with every breath. Her wolf clawed at her insides. Canines throbbing, she held her wolf back.

Zora stroked her mercilessly, each firm, expert stroke massaging her glands and forcing her pheromones to pour through her blood.

"Zora," Trent gasped. "I'm going to…"

"I know," Zora murmured, threading her fingers through the hair at the back of Trent's neck. Holding Trent's head with her throat exposed, Zora claimed Trent's mouth, her kiss deep and probing and powerful. Her breath was hot, her mouth a perfect fit as her canines grazed Trent's lower lip.

Trent's stomach turned to stone. Abruptly Zora relinquished her teasing grip on Trent's clitoris and slid inside her. Trent bucked against her hand, releasing in shattering bursts of unbearable pleasure. Her trembling legs buckled, and Zora clasped her shoulder with her free arm as Trent slumped to the floor.

Trent stared up, wild to touch her. Zora loomed above her, eyes slashed with gold and canines gleaming. The bold, stark line of Zora's jaw quivered as she strained for control. Trent wanted, *needed* to break Zora's iron grip on her reason. She grasped Zora's hips and jerked Zora tightly between her thighs. Her blood surged into her loins, every ounce of her essence rushing to fill her sex. All she needed was Zora's bite for the ultimate release.

Zora held herself away, apart, her body poised on rigid arms above Trent's, her face fierce and beautiful. Trent raked her blunt claws down Zora's back, dragged her shirt free of her pants, and found skin. Zora rumbled, a sound of pleasure and need. Trent slid a hand between them, groped for Zora's pants, and Zora pushed her hand away.

As quickly as Zora had taken her, she was gone. Trent scrambled to her feet and had to brace an arm against the wall when a wave of dizziness coursed through her. She was spent, emptied. And Zora had not finished.

"You can ride me until you release," Trent said. "I won't bite you."

"I wouldn't let you."

"I know. Then take…"

"I did. I took *you*. You may go now."

Trent bristled, pride and frustration warring with her instinctual need to obey an Alpha Were.

"As you will, Alpha." Trent bit off the words, spun on her heel, and yanked open the door. She caught herself at the last second and closed it without slamming it. She had known what she was offering, and Zora had taken only that and no more. Zora had taken her with a quick tangle—satisfying the most basic of needs—to release tension and aggression and blunt the powerful storm of threat hormones. Any Were would have sufficed. Trent just happened to be there.

And that's what burned in Trent's gut as she reached the porch and leapt down into the commons, her shirt loose and her pants open to an inch over her groin where Zora had slashed them open. She had been *convenient*. She had been willing, yes, but she'd wanted more. She'd wanted Zora to need the way she had needed. She'd wanted…Zora.

Zora let out a long breath. Trent had left. Slumped in her chair, the tightness in her gut made it hard to breathe and her sex throbbed around her painfully tense clitoris. She'd held back her release, fearing that at the moment when her passion overrode reason, she would take Trent completely. She'd been so close to burying her canines in Trent's throat, to tasting her, to filling her, sex to sex, and emptying over her again and again. She twisted a fist into her cramped stomach, trying to ease the coiled need that pounded through her loins. Body and blood burned with the relentless pressure in her glands until she dipped her hand inside her trousers and squeezed her sex. The instant agony of pleasure and pain shot down her thighs and forced her eyes closed. Grunting harshly, she massaged her sex, her stomach a tight board, her chest a vise preventing a full breath until her head was light. Relentlessly, she squeezed and stroked until with a swift jolt that wracked her body and brought a snarl to her lips, her clitoris spasmed. The series of tremors in her sex was a weak substitute for what she really needed, but the engorgement subsided enough that she could breathe again. Her wolf rebelled, slashing her with tooth and claw until sweat broke out on her neck and torso. Her wolf wanted more. *She* wanted more. Needed more. But that need would pass. Like always.

Sensing Ash approaching the door, she quickly straightened. "Come."

"Alpha," Ash said apologetically as she entered, stopping before Zora's desk. "Sorry to interrupt."

"You're not," Zora said, ignoring the swift probing glance Ash cast over her face before looking to one side to avoid meeting her gaze directly. She'd known Ash since they were adolescents, testing their skills and strength against all comers, including each other. When Zora had stood challenge against the handful of Weres who did not accept her as her father's heir, Ash had been the first to voice allegiance, even before Loris. Ash was the closest Were she had to a friend. But friendship was secondary to the needs of the Pack, to the order of rule, and Ash knew that. "What is it?"

Ash grimaced. "The Timberwolf lieutenant thinks our soldiers will panic in an actual firefight."

Zora bristled. "Trent said that?"

"Not in so many words, but her meaning was clear." Ash sucked in a breath. "Jace pointed out that our soldiers are not trained to defend against an organized assault. She agreed that our teams may fracture if challenged with overwhelming odds or if the kind of...*things*...we fought from the Otherworld appear again."

Rising, Zora strode to the window and shoved it wide, letting the cool air quell some of the heat of her temper along with her lingering arousal. No Alpha wanted to hear an outsider like Trent—an emissary of a stronger, more powerful Pack—deem their Pack weak. Trent's assessment was a threat to Snowcrest sovereignty, and by rights she should be expelled from Snowcrest territory. Loris would surely demand it.

"Who else heard the conversation?"

"No one."

Zora faced her. "Your opinion."

Ash hesitated.

"Captain?" Zora snapped.

"We haven't had to develop the combat teams we need to fight the kind of enemies we faced recently. Our soldiers will fight valiantly, and they *won't* panic." Ash straightened her shoulders. "But we may incur unnecessary losses unless we prepare them."

"Then that's what we will do," Zora said. "What did the Timberwolf suggest?"

Ash recited Trent's recommendations, and calmer now, the lust and need tempered by her responsibilities, Zora listened. Trent was too arrogant for her own safety in suggesting that the Snowcrest Weres would fail in battle, but she was also right. They needed every advantage more experience could give them.

"Take the plan to Loris, and advise him it came from me."

"And Trent?"

Zora growled at the thought of her senior soldiers or her *imperator* challenging the reckless Were who questioned their strength. If anyone disciplined Trent, it would be her. "I'll deal with the Timberwolf."

CHAPTER FIVE

Timberwolf Compound

Sylvan strode out of the forest into the clearing in front of the Compound's main gate, Drake at her shoulder and the *centuri* arrowing out at their sides. Her *imperator*, Niki, flanked by Max and the rest of the *centuri*, plus Callan, the captain of Sylvan's warriors, formed an impenetrable cordon before the barricades. *Sentries* lined the battlements, armed with crossbows loaded with iron bolts, a far deadlier weapon against the Fae than bullets. If Sylvan gave the word, two dozen lethal projectiles would neutralize the Fae royal guards arrayed in formation at the edge of the clearing, deep in the heart of Timberwolf territory.

Despite the weapons trained on them, the dozen tall, sylphlike Fae, with the pale, nearly translucent glow of their otherworldly physical manifestations, stood at attention in two rows behind their leader without moving. Their shimmering silver armor bore blue star-shaped emblems on the chest, and weapon belts of the same sky blue held ornate scabbards and longswords with elaborate bejeweled hilts. A slender blond, clearly the leader from his position and stature, stood half a head taller than the rest of the retinue, his shoulder-length, nearly white hair wafting in the breeze, his silver-blue eyes, deep and shadowless. His long, delicate fingers clasped a gold and silver-emblazoned pike upright by his side, the point glittering in the sunlight. Just behind him, another Fae held a banner atop a similar pike, the blue and silver shield against a field of pure white symbolizing Cecilia's court fluttering from the top.

Sylvan scanned the surrounding forest and saw no evidence of a portal opening into her world from Faerie. The sky overhead was clear and blue. No black void marked a tear in the veil between realms like the one that had spewed forth the revenant Weres and other reanimated creatures they'd fought on Snowcrest land. Still, the presence of potential enemies literally at her gate was tantamount to a declaration of war. That the Fae trespassed was undeniable. She would be within her rights to summarily execute them. Niki undoubtedly would have already done so, if the choice were hers. Sylvan delayed the order to fire for one reason—these Fae must know what they risked by appearing unannounced and without warning like this, but still they had come.

Pride before reason often exacted a high price, and as Alpha, Sylvan could not afford to let instinct alone dictate her decisions. Only in the heat of battle did she give her wolf the freedom to rule. She could never completely suppress her instincts, nor did she want to. This land and all who dwelt there were hers to protect. She dropped the restraints on her wolf and morphed into warrior half-form, a foot taller than her normal skin form, heavier in the chest and thighs, her jaw broader, her canines exposed, and her fingers tipped with full-length claws. Most Weres never achieved the warrior form, and none could hold it as effortlessly as Sylvan.

"I am Sylvan Mir, Alpha of the Timberwolf Pack." Her power rolled through the Compound, setting off a chorus of howls from her Pack. "You are in violation of our borders. Why?"

The leader lowered the tip of his pike, and the twelve members of the envoy saluted as one, bladed hands over their hearts.

"Alpha Mir," the leader said, his melodic voice drifting like music on the air, "I am Antulli Ever Born. I bring you glad tidings from Cecilia, Queen of Thorns and All of Faerie, Ruler of Dark and Light, and Mistress of All Seasons."

As he finished, he lifted his pike back into the upright position and remained at attention, his gaze fixed straight ahead, his expression as calm and cool as if he had been carved from a block of ice. Twelve pikes snapped upright as the rest of the retinue finished their salute.

Sylvan regarded him with arms crossed. "What prompts you to disregard all rules of sovereignty and trespass without invitation?"

"I bear a message from my Queen," Antulli said.

Niki snarled. "What kind of message requires a dozen armed Fae to deliver? And how, exactly, did you *get* here?"

"My *imperator* is right," Sylvan said. "Cecilia could go through diplomatic channels to reach me. Why the secrecy?"

"We come with more than a message," Antulli said. "My Queen desires an audience with the Alpha of the Timberwolf Pack. We have been sent to guide you into Faerie."

Drake pressed her hand to the center of Sylvan's back. "The Alpha is not leaving our territory. If your Queen wishes an audience, she can *request* a meeting here."

"My Queen cannot make the journey." Antulli kept his attention fixed on Sylvan. "She reminds you of your past alliance and formally requests that you honor your pledge of allegiance."

Niki pushed forward. "Where was Cecilia when the Timberwolves faced our enemies at Nocturne? Where were the Fae when we fought for the Snowcrest Weres against *something* sent from Faerie? The Alpha is here. Let your Queen join us if she has words for us to hear. Or are you afraid you will not be able to protect your Queen if she comes out of hiding?"

Midnight rolled through Antulli's silver eyes, and for an instant, his fragile beauty shimmered. Beneath it, curved horns circled a heavy head with flared nostrils and curving tusks, and a massive four-legged body akin to a mountain caprine. The air crackled with light and color and faded an instant later.

Niki growled and positioned her body between the Fae and Sylvan.

"Hold." Sylvan gripped Niki's shoulder and said calmly, "Tell your Queen I pledge her safety and await her presence here in my territory."

Sylvan spun on her heel, and her *centuri* fell in behind her.

"Alpha," Antulli said, his words carrying even though he hadn't raised his voice, "there are more creatures like the ones that assailed the Snowcrest wolves massing for another strike."

Sylvan slowed and spun, a growl rolling from her chest. Her warrior form gained mass, her eyes wild and ferocious, and her growl reverberated through the clearing. "You would threaten me on my own land?"

Antulli's royal guards shuddered, but *he* did not lower his gaze despite the power that buffeted him like a hurricane. "I bring no threat,

Alpha. Only the offer of information that might be of value to you and your Pack. Cecilia extends this gift as a sign of her goodwill."

"Neutral ground," Sylvan said. "I will not journey to Cecilia's court, but I will meet with her on neutral ground, chosen by Lord Torren, who will secure the Gate by which I enter. Torren must be guaranteed safe passage in and out of Faerie, along with me and my *centuri*. Those are my terms."

Antulli nodded once. "I will relay the message to my Queen." The air shimmered, as if a rainbow had shattered upon touching the ground. The colors coalesced into a solid sheet of brilliant light, spun off into the air, and were gone.

"Alpha," Nikki said urgently, "you can't—"

Sylvan held up a hand. "I have decided. Summon the war council and Lord Torren to headquarters as soon as possible."

"As you command." Niki, broadcasting battle lust with every breath, saluted and signaled to Callan and his warriors to follow her. The gates swung open, Sylvan and Drake entered along with the *centuri*, and the gates closed once more.

Sylvan headed directly to the two-story building that centered the Compound to await the leaders of her Vampire and Fae allies. As soon as they were alone, Drake gripped Sylvan's arm. "You can't mean to go."

"I have to," Sylvan said. "If Cecilia has made the first move, it's only because she feels threatened by something she can't fight alone. If that's the case, our enemy is far more powerful than I imagined. We need to know what we're facing."

"It's a trap," Drake said, her voice heavy with scorn. "You know it. *I* know it. Why would you risk yourself, now, on the verge of war?"

Sylvan cupped her cheek. "Because I must. And I'll have Torren, who has thwarted Cecilia's power more than once. Cecilia fears Torren more than me."

"Torren is not my mate," Drake said, "nor is she the Alpha of our Pack. Without you, we—"

Sylvan slid a hand behind around Drake's nape and jerked her close. Her kiss was hot and fierce. "I will not leave you or the Pack. By my oath, I will return."

Drake spread both hands over Sylvan's chest, tracing the curve of her collarbones with her fingertips and the hard muscles beneath with her palms. She lingered over the mate bite at the junction of Sylvan's shoulder and neck, that spot warmer than the surrounding flesh. This was the mark of their union, the place where she had claimed Sylvan as hers. Sylvan shuddered. Drake caught Sylvan's mouth in another kiss and bit her lower lip, hard enough to pull a growl from Sylvan's throat. "Niki and I will accompany you to the Faerie Gate. One hour Earth time, and if you're not back, we will come through for you. I will not be concerned about allegiances."

Sylvan grinned. "I didn't expect you to give me that long."

Drake growled. "Don't test my patience, Alpha."

"As soon as the war council is over and I have you alone, we'll see just how patient you can be."

Snowcrest Clan Home

Enraged by Zora's rejection, Trent bounded out of the building and over the porch railing to the hard-packed ground of the training yard. Lust and battle frenzy flamed her vision red. Zora had dismissed her again, as if what had passed between them had meant nothing. Less than nothing. Trent rumbled, a slow steadily rising growl she didn't bother to hide. She'd welcome a tussle right now—a chance to show pelt and use her teeth and claws on a worthy opponent might bleed off the rage crushing her every breath. Pain might blur the arousal pounding in her loins.

She shouldn't have any trouble finding someone to goad into a quick, hard tussle. Most of the Snowcrest soldiers would be on guard duty or in the broad training grounds adjacent to the dormitory. Cutting down the narrow alley between the barracks and the mess hall, she quickened her pace. Her skin tightened with the urge to let her wolf emerge. As she rounded the corner onto the field, an arm snaked out and grasped her around the neck, jerking her back into the shadows cast by the two buildings.

Snarling, she twisted, preparing to strike. Before her canines could find flesh, the grip on her neck loosened and she was free. Jace glared at her, hands on hips and face riddled with fury.

"What the hell?" Trent's battle lust cooled, and she restrained her wolf. Jace was not her enemy.

"What did I tell you!" Jace shoved a hand against Trent's shoulder, pushing her back against the rough-hewn log wall. Splinters pierced her shirt in bright pinpoints of pain. From anyone else, the act would have been one of challenge, but this was Jace, and they had tussled their entire lives. Now that Jace carried the rank of *centuri*, Trent owed her the respect her position demanded, and she did not strike back.

"I don't know what you're talking about." Trent fumed.

"How long did it take you to search out Zora after I walked away," Jace snarled. "Five minutes?"

Trent grinned. "Two."

Jace prodded her again. "I should send you back to the Compound right now."

Trent's wolf surged, Jace's rank be damned. She wasn't going anywhere, even if Jace commanded it. *Zora* was here. She wasn't leaving. "This is not your concern."

"Oh, but it is. I'm in charge here, by the Alpha's command."

"And I am fulfilling my duty," Trent said. "You have no cause to discipline me."

Trent's resistance bordered on issuing a challenge, but she didn't care. Jace threatened to come between her and Zora, and nothing mattered more than that. If she had to fight Jace to prove she would not be ordered out of Cresthome, she would. Even if it meant she must leave the Pack. She'd go nomad before she'd let anyone, even the Alpha, keep her from her—

"You're not mated," Jace said as if she'd been reading Trent's mind, puncturing the air in front of Trent's face with a claw-tipped finger. "And you're not going to be, no matter what you think you're doing."

"You have no idea what I'm doing," Trent snapped, taking a step forward. Her canines punched down, and she didn't try to hide them.

Jace's lip curled, revealing her gleaming canines, but she made no move to attack. "What you're *doing* is creating an incident that could destroy the relationship between our Packs. Snowcrest might not survive without our help. Are you willing to be responsible for that?"

Trent stiffened. "I've done nothing—"

"Do you call tangling with the Snowcrest Alpha nothing?"

Trent couldn't deny it. They'd coupled, even if Zora had refused to let Trent satisfy her need.

"Trent," Jace said, the anger in her voice replaced now by honest concern. "Think past your hormones. Don't you think I understand what you're feeling? But you are a Timberwolf, and Zora is the Alpha of this Pack. None of her wolves will accept you touching her."

"Zora did," Trent snapped.

"I know that. Don't you think I can scent her on you? Don't you think any Snowcrest wolf will be able to as well?"

Trent blew out a breath. "My wolf wants her. If she wants me, I can't deny her."

"You mean you don't *want* to." Jace ran a hand through her hair. "Stay away from her if you're unable to resist answering her call. If Loris or even one of Zora's guards challenges you, our Weres will retaliate. We'll precipitate a dominance skirmish, and this entire mission will be compromised. Do you really think Zora wants us here in her territory? Dominant wolves from a larger pack that nearly surrounds her territory? Think. She has no choice but to accept us until she has an army strong enough to stand on its own. She's already compromised in the eyes of some of her Weres. You could force a challenge to her rule."

Trent's gut clenched. "I don't want to be the cause of endangering her Pack...or her."

"Then ignore her call. Let someone else answer her need."

Imagining Zora with another Were, of her taking them the way she'd taken Trent—wild with lust and craving release—shattered Trent's slender control. She trembled, and her wolf cut scathing tracks through her vitals. "I'm not sure I can."

"If you can't, I'll have to send you down. I can't risk having the operation disintegrate and our alliance fracture." Jace clasped Trent's neck and dragged her close. "And I don't want to do that. I need you here—remember who you are, Trent."

Jace's power rolled over her, and Trent snapped to attention with a thundering salute. "I understand, *Centuri.*"

Jace's gaze cooled. "See that you do, Lieutenant."

Trent spun on her heel and vaulted away. Jace was Pack, but she might no longer be a friend.

Chapter Six

Trent.

The command shot through Trent like a touch, setting her afire. The call came from the forest, clear and sharp and undeniable. Before reason could prevail and she could remind herself of the pledge she'd just made to Jace, the *order* she had vowed to obey, Trent pelted and dropped to all fours. Racing toward the far reaches of the sanctuary, she avoided the gates where Snowcrest sentries might question her as well as the training grounds where Jace might compel her to stop. Propelled by the urgency of her wolf to claim the one she deemed hers, and the wild rush of anticipation seething in her loins, she vaulted the fence in one long leap. Landing with her limbs already in motion, she tore through the underbrush, heedless of obstacles, forging her own path, unerringly drawn to the echoes of Zora's command pulsing in her veins.

She ran for close to a mile, deeper and deeper into unmarked, old-growth forest, until she suddenly broke through dense brambles beneath thickly grouped towering evergreens into a clearing the width of a small pond carved out of the mountainside. Meadow grass, topped with golden chaff and small white and purple flowers, carpeted the ground around the water. A rocky overhang curved around the bowl of green, and a rushing stream pockmarked with boulders bordered the downhill side. Another time she might have stalked the tall grass for a hare to startle into running in order to give chase, or stretched out by the cold, clear water for a drink, but not today. Today all her attention was riveted to the wolf who'd already staked claim to the clearing.

Zora, muzzle resting on her forepaws, eyes alert and upright ears flickering, rested on one of the huge fingers of rock extending from the piney ridge overhead down to the water's edge.

Gaze fixed on Zora, Trent settled back onto her haunches and waited.

Zora had called her. Trent would not move first.

Zora's wolf chuffed, stretched, and in the time it took Trent to draw another breath, Zora shed pelt. She sat looking down at Trent, brilliant and beautiful in her nakedness.

Trent's heart pounded as she pushed past her wolf to shed pelt and stand on two legs. Cocking her head, she grinned up at Zora. "You called?"

"You'll find a niche under the rocks over there," Zora called, reaching behind her and coming out with a pair of plain black cotton pants. She stood and pulled on the pants. "You can dress."

"Your private cache?" Trent called as she reached into the shadows and pulled out a waterproof nylon go bag. Inside were several pairs of T-shirts and pants and two pairs of short leather boots. She left the boots. She'd return to Cresthome the way she'd come, in pelt. Taking her time, she crossed the clearing and stopped beneath Zora's perch, the clothes in her hand. Zora was watching her, and the intent way her gaze moved over Trent's skin fanned the simmering coals deep in Trent's belly. The inferno quickly spread lower, and her clitoris grew pronounced and firm. She grinned, knowing Zora would be able to tell just exactly what had happened. Why hide her arousal? Zora had instigated it.

With Zora tracking her every move, she stepped into the pants, pulled them up, and zipped the fly halfway, leaving the top open over her belly. She held the shirt in her fist and, registering the invitation in Zora's appraisal, climbed up the rocks to stand next to the Alpha. Zora's eyes dropped to Trent's breasts, and a low rumble percolated in her chest.

The growl sent a jolt to Trent's sex—swift and sharp. A spasm twitched down her thighs and coiled in the heated space between her legs.

Zora scraped a blunt claw down the center of Trent's bare abdomen. "Your wolf needs a leash."

Trent sucked in a breath, the muscles in her abdomen tightening and a thin line of pelt streaking down the muscular divide beneath her navel and into the open V of her pants. Zora's claws lightly scratched lower on her belly, and Trent closed her eyes. Her glands pulsed, full and ready. So soon. So ready. "Not usually. You rile me up."

"Put your shirt on," Zora murmured.

"Why?"

"Because I said so."

Trent quivered. Zora's command had not been that of an Alpha, but of another dominant Were, toying with her. Testing her. Would she yield? Would she submit? Would she let Zora command her?

"And if I refuse?"

Zora pressed her claws deep enough to draw pinpricks of blood on Trent's belly. Putting her canines against the beating pulse in Trent's neck, she pressed *almost* hard enough to break skin. Almost. "You won't."

Trent's skin ran with sex-sheen, hot and slick. Zora licked her neck.

"I need…" Trent gasped.

"I know," Zora said with satisfaction and stepped back. "Put your shirt on."

This time, the command came from the Alpha, and Trent jerked, opening her eyes. Zora regarded her with calm, utter control, as if she'd never touched her. As if Trent wasn't on the verge of exploding. Fury warred with lust. "Why?"

"Because I said so."

Trent bared her teeth. "What is it you want, *Alpha*?"

"I want you to learn your place, *Lieutenant.*"

"And what would that be?"

"You are a guest in Snowcrest territory. By order of your Alpha, your duty is to assist my *imperator* and the captain of my guard in training our soldiers for war."

Trent snarled. "I've been doing that."

"My captain informed me that you consider my soldiers unworthy for battle." Zora's canines flashed. "You insulted my Pack, and you threatened me."

"That was not my intention." Trent dipped her chin, ever so slightly. Zora was Pack Alpha. Zora had won her place, and Trent yielded to her dominance. "My apologies, Alpha Constantine."

"I don't want your apology. I want your obedience. You could have forced my Weres to issue challenge if they'd heard you. Loris has never been happy to have so many Timberwolves within our borders, and you would have given him all the justification he needed to evict. You're arrogant and reckless, and you overstep."

Trent growled and made a show of *stepping* forward until her body touched Zora's along every surface. Her bare breasts pressed into the tight cotton shirt where Zora's nipples stood out like small, hard stones. She swept her fingers through the dark waves of Zora's hair, her mouth a fraction from Zora's. "Do I?"

Zora's power burst from every pore, bombarding Trent as if a thousand fists struck her at once. Her knees buckled, and she would have fallen were it not for the arm that came around her waist. Zora spun her around and down until her back landed on the hard rock. Trent barely noticed the jolt of pain coursing through her tense muscles, a swift shock just as quickly gone. All she felt was the desperate need for more. More of Zora everywhere.

Zora poised above her, thighs on either side of Trent's hips, canines glinting just above Trent's face. "Foolish and arrogant."

"Don't forget reckless," Trent taunted, pumping her hips hard enough to tease Zora's clitoris through her cotton pants.

"I haven't forgotten." Zora's kiss struck like a lightning bolt exploding between Trent's thighs.

Trent's back bowed off the rock, and she drove her pelvis into Zora's. The pressure-pain and pleasure blended into one massive burst of excitement, scorching her nerve endings and leaving her blind. Blind with lust and need and the brilliantly clear desire in Zora's gold-rimmed eyes. Grasping Zora's shoulders, Trent opened for her kiss, pulling her deep and drenching her with pheromones.

"Wild and fearless," Zora gasped, yanking Trent's zipper the rest of the way down and thrusting a hand between her legs.

Trent shredded Zora's T-shirt, baring her torso, and slid her hand over the rigid planes of Zora's abdomen to cup the fullness of her breast. Zora's nipple hardened against her palm, and Trent flicked it with a claw.

Zora threw her head back, a rumble of pleasure slipping between her gritted teeth. She was holding back a torrent of need. Pheromones thick with sex chemicals and Zora's unique scent misted Trent's skin. Zora was frenzied, and so very, very controlled.

Trent hungered to crush that control, yearned to bring the Alpha to her knees the way *she* had been. She wanted, needed, *ached* to claim Zora as she had been claimed. Lust turned to imperative—she *had* to bite her. Mating frenzy clouded her mind, driving her beyond caution.

Zora was wiry and quick, but Trent was more heavily muscled, and Zora hadn't anticipated Trent's quickly shifting her weight and twisting Zora under her. Zora stared up in shock when she landed on her back, no longer in control.

"You've never been beneath anyone, have you?" Trent growled and wedged her hips between Zora's thighs. Her clitoris pulsed against Zora's, hot and hard, despite the layers of clothing separating them. Trent palmed Zora's breast beneath the tattered shirt and rubbed a claw over her nipple.

"Arrogant and dangerous." Zora raked her fingers down Trent's shoulder, leaving faint tracks that made Trent's clitoris pound faster. "And careless with your life. You're toying with death right now."

"I don't see your guards anywhere."

Zora growled. "You know they are not here."

Trent grinned and dragged her canines down Zora's throat. "Tell me to get off you."

"Would you heed my command?" Zora's eyes held more than that question.

Was she asking Trent to submit? To acknowledge her as Alpha? Or something else?

"I want you." Trent gave Zora an instant to protest, to remind her she had no right to touch her, to want her, to take her. But Zora met her gaze and said nothing.

Desperate to immerse herself in Zora's essence, to drown in her scent, Trent took Zora's nipple into her mouth and taunted it with her teeth. Zora bucked beneath her, claws scraping down her back. Trent straddled Zora's thigh and worked her center up and down the hard muscle, her cotton pants a thin barrier between her rigid clitoris and Zora's. Aggravated, frustrated, she pushed her pants down to midthigh.

"This time," Trent gasped, "I won't release alone."

Licking, biting, teasing her way down the middle of Zora's torso, she traced the soft pelt line with her tongue until it disappeared under Zora's pants. She didn't bother with the zipper but hooked her claws on either side and tore the fabric open. Zora's scent, wild and rich and bright as sunlight, enveloped her. Her glands throbbed and *victus* coated her thighs and Zora. She dipped lower and licked Zora's clitoris.

Zora gripped Trent's shoulders and heaved her upward with strength she hadn't anticipated.

"No."

Staring directly into the Snowcrest Alpha's eyes, Trent snarled, "Why not?"

Zora's pupils were huge, ringed in gold, her wolf straining to ascend. "You know why not."

Trent pushed up on both arms, her clitoris throbbing against Zora's belly. "Why do you call me then?"

Zora gripped Trent's hips and drew her up and down over the tight muscles of her belly. The downy softness of her faintly pelted skin caressed the sensitive undersurface of Trent's clitoris, edging her to the brink of emission. Zora dug claws into Trent's ass and her glands swelled against Zora's middle. "This is why—*you* ready for *me*."

Trent gritted her teeth, still locked to Zora's gaze. The pounding in her loins spread through her belly to her spine. Her vision dimmed until there was nothing but Zora, and she exploded. Coating Zora's abdomen with her essence, Trent whimpered with pleasure and need. Zora growled, her canines pressed to Trent's breast. But she did not bite.

"Please," Trent begged. "Please."

"No," Zora said, her mouth against the bounding pulse in Trent's throat. "This is the last time this will happen. Remove your warriors from my Compound—"

"Zora—"

"*Alpha*," Zora snarled.

Trent shuddered. "Alpha—please. Your soldiers need further training—"

"You will set up your base at the outpost beyond this ridge and conduct your maneuvers from there."

Trent gasped, hollowed out and still so hungry. "As you command, Alpha Constantine."

Zora pushed Trent aside and stood. Stripping off the remnants of her tattered clothing, she shifted. Her wolf, powerful and untouched, shook her thick black pelt and launched from the rocks into the clearing below. With a howl that drew answering howls in the distance, she broke into a run and disappeared into the forest.

Drained, Trent sat up and lowered her head to her bent knees, her breath ragged, her soul in tatters. Jace had told her to stay away from Zora, from *Alpha* Constantine, and she hadn't listened. She couldn't. She couldn't take a breath without wanting her. She couldn't fight the raging fury of her wolf to mate.

Zora was right to tell her to go.

CHAPTER SEVEN

Timberwolf Compound
War council gathering

Jody Gates, the Vampire Liege and heir to the Northeastern US Vampire seethe, shook her head. "Bad idea."

Sylvan snorted. "Eloquent as always, Liege Gates."

Jody's dark eyes, slashed now with the crimson marker of the most powerful Risen, blazed for an instant with humor rarely seen. Beside her, her consort, Becca Land, stroked her arm.

"Really, darling," Becca said with her customary calm, "you're usually far more succinct."

Jody, her pale face made paler in the flickering firelight, smiled, another rare occurrence and something she apparently only reserved for her consort. Cloaked in shimmering black leather pants and a midnight silk shirt open down the center of her torso, her slenderness belied the strength that matched even Sylvan's. She sighed. "*Cecilia* is known for subtlety, and this is anything but—or so she would want you to believe. She wants you to think she is desperate, that you have the upper hand in any negotiations. But that's the lie. Her appearance of vulnerability is just another of her manipulations. It's a trap. Once you cross over into Faerie, she can cloak you from your allies. We won't be able to follow."

"You forget," Torren de Brinna pointed out, "I will be with Sylvan. Cecilia cannot keep me from any path in Faerie I wish to travel. I *choose* to remain earthbound for the sake of peace."

What Torren, an ancient royal Fae, did not need to say was that she remained earthbound to prevent a power struggle that would reignite ancient Fae rivalries and drag her mate, one of Sylvan's Weres, and all the Praetern nations into a war.

Misha, draped across Torren's lap in her customary seductively possessive position, one hand beneath Torren's silken shirt, shook her head. "Both you *and* the Alpha will be in danger." At Torren's smirk, Misha snarled. "Oh, I know you believe you're invincible, but Cecilia will have all of Faerie at her command."

Torren raised a midnight brow, the air around her glimmering for an instant, as if shattered with rainbows. She murmured something in Misha's ear.

Misha growled low in her chest and her canines gleamed.

With a self-satisfied shrug, Torren said, "I have all the reason I need to return to your realm. In Faerie I am at my full power, and Cecilia knows it."

"We all know nothing will keep the Lord Torren from returning," Drake said, her eyes on Sylvan. "Nor you either. But Jody is right. A handful of you, no matter how powerful, will be no match for Cecilia and all her forces."

"Cecilia will not risk open war against the combined strength of the Weres and Vampires," Sylvan said. "She's too smart for that."

Max, the highest ranking among her *centuri* and married to a human, added, "Our allies among the humans increase every day. While they are frail, their numbers are mighty, and they will come to our aid if needed."

Sylvan scanned the gathering. "I appreciate your counsel. All of you may be affected by the outcome of this journey, especially if war ensues. But as Alpha, as the leader of all Weres in the northern continent, I have a responsibility to ensure their safety. If Cecilia is planning war, I…we…need to know. If something is threatening Cecilia to the point that she wants a parlay, I need to know that as well. I have no choice."

"And Cecilia knows that," Drake said quietly.

"Cecilia made an overt invitation," Sylvan said. "If she wanted war, she would not announce it. She knows if she breaches the rules of parlay and threatens us, she *will* have war. That makes no sense."

"And what if Cecilia is not the only enemy within Faerie?" Jody said. "If Cecilia's rule is threatened, you may be facing other enemies who will not care about the etiquette of parlay."

Drake said, "We already know there are other dangers in Faerie. Whatever…whoever…is behind the assaults on the Snowcrest Weres came from Faerie. How do we know Cecilia did not send them?"

Torren shook her head. "No, those are not Cecilia's creations. If they were, she would not be seeking an audience with Sylvan. Those creatures were ensorcelled. Cecilia, like most Fae, has no love for Mages."

"Cecilia does not need to love something…or someone…to use them," Drake pointed out. "Forgive me, Lord Torren, but Cecilia is Fae, and all Fae play a long game."

Torren nodded, the tilt of her head and the faint smile regal. "That's true. We have little else to do with endless time." She glanced to Misha and stroked a hand along the angle of her jaw. Misha's eyes flared, and her wolf, called by her mate's power, strained to emerge. Torren smiled. "That is, unless we find something better than games."

"Niki," Sylvan said, turning to her *imperator*, "your opinion?"

Niki stood with legs spread and her arms crossed over her chest between Sylvan and Torren, her small tight body tense, a muscle bunched along the angle of her jaw. "I agree with Liege Gates that this smells like a trap. And the Prima makes a good argument regarding Cecilia's motives." She took a slow breath. "But I support your decision to accept the parlay, under one condition."

Sylvan's brow rose, and she growled a warning. She was Alpha, and no one set conditions. "What condition do you presume to make, *Imperator*?"

Niki shuddered under the Alpha's hard gaze, but to her credit she held her eyes just below Sylvan's. "That I be allowed to lead your guard."

"You are my second," Sylvan said. "We cannot leave the Pack undefended."

"I am also your general." Niki glanced at Drake. "The Prima does not need me here. Max is your third and can stand in my place."

Max squared his shoulders. "The *imperator* is correct. I know what must be done to secure our borders in your absence, Alpha."

Sylvan didn't like it. She wanted her most powerful Weres to remain behind with her Prima, her young, and the vulnerable members of the Pack. But she wasn't reckless. She trusted Max and, more than that, trusted her mate. Drake would see that no harm came to their Pack.

She also appreciated that a show of power was essential within the walls of Faerie. She would arrive with her general, the Master of the Hunt, and the strongest members of her guard.

"Very well," Sylvan said.

"If you're set on this," Jody said, "then you will also take a member of my guard to remind Cecilia that she deals not only with the Timberwolves, but the Vampires."

"Agreed." Sylvan glanced at Drake. She would never show what some would consider weakness by consulting her mate except in front of those in this room. But these were her most trusted allies, her most valuable friends, and Drake was her Prima. She was proud of all they shared. "Agreed?"

"As your mate, no," Drake said softly, but loud enough for everyone in the room to hear. "But as your Prima, I agree." She leaned across the distance between them, gripped Sylvan by the shoulder, and pulled her forward. She kissed her, the low growl in her throat a show of ownership.

Sylvan's wolf silently howled in delight. Nothing excited her more than being claimed by her mate. Sylvan's power surged, encompassing everyone in the room. Max and Niki shuddered, their wolves instantly alerting. Misha whined softly and shivered into Torren's lap. Laughing, Torren threaded an arm around her waist and kissed her. Becca gripped Jody's hand, lifted it to her lips, and kissed her fingers.

Crimson eclipsed the endless black of Jody's irises. "We shall leave soon, my love."

"Hurry then," Becca whispered.

Sylvan stood, pulling Drake with her. She clasped her nape and held her close. "We are decided then."

"How will you get a message to Cecilia?" Jody asked, straightening the sleeves on her suit jacket that was without a single wrinkle to begin with.

Torren spoke up. "We won't." For an instant, another burst of power rolled through the air, this jolt carrying the sensuous edge of the Otherworld. "We'll arrived unannounced, as did her guards."

Laughing, Sylvan dragged Drake toward the door and called over her shoulder, "At dawn, then."

"At dawn." Torren lifted Misha into her arms and kissed her before disappearing in a shower of crystal light.

❖

"You're not happy with me, are you," Sylvan said when they reached their den.

Drake sighed. "I meant what I said in there. You are my heart. I trust you, and I respect your strength." She caught Sylvan's jaw, her claws unsheathed, and Sylvan stilled. "But that does not mean I don't fear for you every time you leave me. And you always leave me when there is danger to be faced."

Sylvan pulled Drake down on the bed beside her. "*And* most of the time you insist on coming with me, no matter how hard I try to protect you."

Drake dragged Sylvan's shirt from her pants and stroked the places on her chest and abdomen that set Sylvan aflame. "True. You wanted a mate. You didn't want a mate who wouldn't challenge you, did you?"

Smiling, Sylvan kissed her. "Until you, I didn't want a mate at all."

"Well, now you have one, and I will never stop loving you, and wanting you, and wanting to protect you…as you protect me."

Sylvan rested her brow against Drake's. "I will always return to you. You have my promise."

"I know." Drake pulled her shirt off, opened her pants, and pushed them down. She smiled, watching Sylvan's eyes flash gold. Her clitoris strained at the emergence of Sylvan's gleaming canines, hungry for her. "Now I want something else besides the promise. I want you."

With a snarl, Sylvan shed her clothes and pulled Drake down on top of her. "I am yours, always."

Drake sat astride Sylvan's abdomen, running her hands over Sylvan's chest, circling her breasts, tracing the etched lines in her abdomen with her claws. She kissed her, smoothing her palm down the pelt line in the center of Sylvan's abdomen until she reached the cleft between her thighs. Deepening her kiss, catching flesh with her teeth, she gripped her sex and squeezed.

Sylvan's neck arched and she hissed, the bones in her jaws angling, harsh and stark and wild.

Drake nipped her throat. "Remember, you said I could have you."

"Be careful, mate," Sylvan said through gritted teeth. "It is dangerous to tease an Alpha."

"Is it now?" Drake nipped her lower lip again, hard enough to produce another growl. "I'm afraid I'm not intimidated." To punctuate her words, she stroked the length of Sylvan's clitoris, pressing against the glands buried deep beneath, forcing Sylvan's hips to buck beneath her hand.

Sylvan tensed. Her instinct was to assert her dominance, to take her mate in swift, hard claiming thrusts, but her passion for Drake was not only instinct. Drake was her heart, her equal, and her love. She would let Drake take her in any way she wanted. But her wolf knew Drake loved a challenge as much she did.

Sylvan clenched her jaws and shoved upward, unseating Drake and flipping her onto her back in one powerful surge. Before Drake could reassert herself, Sylvan straddled her torso and clasped her nape. Pushing her hips forward, she pressed her clitoris to Drake's mouth, heedless of the glint of canines. A bite would only make her release harder.

"Take me."

On a snarl, Drake gripped Sylvan's ass, her clawed fingertips piercing skin, and closed her lips around Sylvan's clitoris.

Lust hammered at Sylvan's sanity. Her pelt shimmered beneath her skin, sex-sheen running in rivulets down her bare chest onto her etched abdominals. She pumped into Drake's hot mouth and her glands pulsed.

Drake sucked and Sylvan emptied. Her stomach contracted, her clitoris spasmed, and her essence filled Drake's mouth. Groaning, she fell beside Drake, her cheek on Drake's chest.

"I'll always come back," Sylvan murmured.

Drake took Sylvan's hand and pressed it to her swollen sex. "I know."

CHAPTER EIGHT

Cresthome
Midday

Zora felt Loris land on her balcony, pushed aside the report from Ash on their combat readiness she'd been trying to read, and moved to the open door. In casual battle dress—black combat pants and tee—Loris leaned against the railing, his arms crossed over his chest, his legs extended in front of him. He'd look relaxed to anyone else but her. She recognized the pose as his relaxed but wholly alert position. She'd never seen him under any circumstances be less than ready to jump into battle.

"What is it?" she asked.

"The Timberwolves are gone."

Zora's stomach tightened. Of course they were gone. She'd told Trent to take her soldiers into the forest. That had to be the reason. "All of them?"

Loris nodded. "Including Jace. Ash is not happy."

"No, I imagine she isn't."

"If I may speak," Loris said.

"When have you not?"

He almost grinned, but his dark eyes remained serious. "Something will need to be done about that."

"*That*? You mean Ash, the captain of my guard?"

"Forgive me, Alpha, but Ash is now mated to a high-ranking Timberwolf, and"—he shrugged—"we can't make room for Jace without substantial challenge from within our ranks. Nor should we."

"If I appoint Jace to a position within our Pack, there will be no need for a challenge. I am Alpha here, and I choose who serves, and where."

He was quiet for a moment before he slowly shook his head again. "That's never been done."

"There are many things that have not been done, Loris," Zora said quietly. "We've never been attacked by creatures like the ones we saw, and we've never been in an alliance like this with another Pack in all the history of our time in this territory."

"I understand. But Pack is Pack, and hierarchy is hierarchy. It can't be…" He appeared to be searching for a word.

"Appointed?" Zora said helpfully.

"Exactly. Position must be won and held through strength and power. Even yours."

"Believe me, I am well aware of that." Zora grimaced. "And I don't disagree with you. For now, we have more important things to consider. I will deal with this at the first reasonable opportunity."

He nodded. "I think that's all our Pack needs to know. They trust you."

"And you, General? Do you?"

"Yes," he said instantly.

But his scent was wary. "Something still troubles you."

"Besides our new enemies?"

"Beside that."

"Trent."

Zora's skin heated at the aggression in Loris's tone. "What about her?"

"She won't be accepted in our ranks, challenge or not."

In a single leap, Zora crossed the fifteen foot span of deck, stopping mere millimeters from Loris's suddenly tense body. She growled, low and steady, until Loris dipped his head and exposed his throat. Zora fixed her descended canines against the pulse beating in his carotid artery until he shivered, sweat trickling down his throat. Only then did she step back. "Do not presume that your position gives you leave to tell me what my Pack will or will not accept, or what commands they will follow. I respect your experience and value your counsel when it comes to war, General, but do not ever forget who rules here."

"Forgive me, Alpha. I have not forgotten."

"And I expect you to set an example for the others and obey, unless you wish to challenge my command." Zora loosed the rein on her wolf and power rolled.

Loris gasped. "I understand. You are and ever will be my Alpha."

"Then tell me, General, what are my soldiers prepared to do in response to this new approach from our allies?"

Returned to Zora's graces, Loris grinned. "I have them ready to march within the hour, Alpha. The Timberwolves have only been gone a short time, and they won't expect us to follow so quickly. They'll be making camp and preparing their own ambush, but *we* will be in place well before nightfall."

She nodded. "I want you to strike first. We will show the Timberwolves that our Weres have ruled in these forests far longer than any visitor, and that we know how to defend our territory."

"Yes, Alpha." Loris showed his canines in a satisfied smile.

"I will rendezvous with you for a briefing to review the plans," Zora said. "You have scouts out already?"

"Sent out as soon as I was informed of the proposed maneuvers."

"Very well. But remember, the Timberwolves are not our enemies, and you *will* control your soldiers. Overpower them, submit them if need be, but avoid outright challenge. These are maneuvers, not Pack wars."

"As you will, Alpha."

She nodded in dismissal, and bracing an arm on the top of the railing, he jumped over the side.

Zora returned to her quarters to prepare for her return to the forest. She planned to oversee the skirmishes herself and, most importantly, lead the first assault on Trent's forces. Trent thought to distance herself after Zora's rejection of her advances by demonstrating the weakness of Zora's soldiers. An image of Trent on her knees, proud and aroused and begging to touch her, sent a shiver of exquisite pleasure through Zora's sex. Trent had much to learn about Snowcrest power, and her wolf rejoiced at the opportunity to teach her.

Chapter Nine

Timberwolf Compound
Dawnbreak

Sylvan stopped at the gate, slung an arm around Drake's shoulders, and dragged her close. "I will return as soon as I can."

Drake pressed a hand to Sylvan's chest. "In one piece, and uninjured."

Sylvan grinned, her eyes sparking. "As you wish, Prima."

Drake kissed her again. "I wish you many things, and when you return, I'll make sure you know what they are."

"I'll be ready. I'll see you soon, Prima." Sylvan stepped away and nodded to Torren, who stood nearby, Misha's hand in the curve of her elbow. At the edge of the forest, Niki pulled Sophia, her mate and the Pack's Omega, against her body and kissed her. Rafe, a senior member of Jody's personal guard and the last of Sylvan's retinue, waited a few feet away by the side of Jody's black limo, apparently unperturbed by the approaching dawn. Rafe was old and powerful and could tolerate a few moments of sunlight, but even had she been concerned, her marble-like, sharply curved façade would not have revealed it. Her wide, full lips lifted, a glint of incisor showing when she caught Sylvan's gaze. Sylvan rumbled, amused at the arrogance and what, from any Were, would've been considered a challenge. The Vampires had long been their allies and had just as often been their enemies, but under Jody's command, their allegiances had grown stronger.

Sylvan signaled the others to join her with Torren. "Ready?"

Torren pressed a kiss to Misha's temple. "Until I return, stay safe, My Lady."

Misha stroked a hand on Torren's shimmering countenance. "As My Lord wishes. And remember what I said."

Torren chuckled, a lilting, sensuous sound Sylvan had rarely ever heard. "As I value all my body parts, I shall be certain to heed My Lady's warning."

"See that you do, My Lord."

Misha moved away to stand next to Sophia and Drake, her gaze fixed on Torren, who waved a hand amidst a shower of light.

The brilliance winked out, and Sylvan experienced nightfall again—a darkness without stars so dense it eclipsed the coming dawn. A shuddering breath later and the sun rose in an instant, dazzling enough to make her blink, gorgeous enough to make her heart lift. Such light—so pure and bright her wolf wanted to howl with joy.

She glanced at Rafe, concerned. "You are well?"

"I had not thought to see this moment again." Rafe gazed at the sky, at the *magenta* sky, breaking into pale pinks and oranges and, in its center, a blood-red sun.

A sharp cry, birdlike, but with the eerie echo of a Pack at night, heralded the graceful flight of a four-winged creature overhead, its long tail swishing, its scaled snout on a long, narrow head streaming tendrils of flame. Dragon.

Torren watched the flight of the enormous monster, unperturbed. "Cecilia has marked our arrival, and her Herald greets us."

"Does it speak to you?" Sylvan asked.

Torren's smile reminded Sylvan of a lethal predator. "Ixtal sends a warning. Cecilia reminds us we have arrived unannounced, which could be taken as an act of war."

"Tell Cecilia," Sylvan said as the dragon spiraled closer, its jaws opening wide to reveal double rows of daggerlike teeth, "that we arrive as we had been visited, unannounced, but ready for her parlay."

The great howling cry, sharp and piercing, came again, and the dragon swept majestically sunward until its form winked out as if swallowed by the sun.

Sylvan glanced at Torren and raised a brow.

"A royal pathway, direct to Cecilia's throne room in the royal Faerie Mound."

"Are we close to that, then?" Sylvan said.

"In distance, no. If we follow the royal pathway, mere seconds."

"And if we do that, what will we find on the other end?" Rafe inquired.

"That," Torren said softly, "I do not know."

Niki growled. "It seems we are at the disadvantage here."

"Not if we have something Cecilia wants," Sylvan reminded her.

"Besides us," Niki rejoined with a disgusted grunt.

"That is true." Sylvan motioned to Torren. "Let's be on our way then."

"Report," Zora said as Loris returned from conferring with her scouts. She'd been waiting impatiently for a sighting of the Timberwolves' position since nightfall, when the Snowcrest forces had moved under cover of darkness into the forest. The Timberwolves had covered their tracks as much as possible, fording creeks and traveling along rocky paths, but this was her land, and no one could hide from her here. She'd led her advance guard rapidly along the trail and now was only a few hours and a shorter distance behind Trent's warriors.

"It is as we expected," Loris said. "The Timberwolves are encamped a mile away, beneath the bluff beside the river. They have good cover from above and will be able to see any attempt to cross the river in a frontal assault."

"Are all of them there?"

"That we cannot tell, Alpha. We can see their campfires and movements, but not clearly enough to accurately count. There may be others sequestered in the forest on the near side of the water."

Zora nodded. Trent would not be foolish enough to put all her forces in one place. "They will have sentries posted, and Trent will have divided her forces enough to protect her flanks."

"Yes, but we expect they will be moving into position to ambush us."

Zora smiled. "Well, where they *think* we will be."

Loris grinned.

Zora gestured to Ash. "Captain, choose six of your most experienced, and we will form the head of the spear."

Ash moved off and Zora turned to Loris. "Assemble four other cadres, on our flanks. We will be in position as they move down to circle Trent's right and left platoons. At my command, we will close the pincer and force them to the banks of the river. Once there, they will have no place to retreat that will not leave their rear guard vulnerable. The bluff will become their prison, not their protection."

Loris nodded. "If I may, Alpha?"

"Go ahead," Zora said.

"I would lead the first cadre at the point of the spear, Alpha, to protect you from—"

"No," Zora said.

Loris's jaw bunched, but he made no argument. Instead, he saluted and followed Ash back to the encampment where their soldiers were secluded downwind of the Timberwolves.

Zora carried no weapons. She would fight this day as wolf. Once the Timberwolves acknowledged the sovereignty of the Snowcrest Weres in their own territory, and her Pack was assured that they were under no threat from them, their alliance would be more secure. There would be no call for challenge.

And Trent would be safe.

CHAPTER TEN

Sylvan glanced at Torren uneasily. She sensed they had moved, but the glade seemed the same—only different. The trees were taller, the sun in a different position in the sky. Had they somehow been transported to a new destination, or another time altogether? Time kaleidoscoped and the very fabric of reality warped in Faerie. Sylvan couldn't tell if she'd been standing in the glade for a few minutes or even days. Cecilia was toying with them, a maneuver Sylvan understood well, although not one she cared for herself. When she hunted prey, she respected them and gave them the opportunity to outsmart her if they could. Outrun her, outlast her, or, like the clever hare that took to the underbrush and foiled her pups, outwit her through sheer force of will. But this foreignness, even while she understood the purpose, unsettled her. And of course, that's exactly what Cecilia intended. Knowing the Faerie Queen wanted her off-balance and disoriented, Sylvan shook off the disquiet. Beside her, Niki stood at rigid attention while internally her wolf paced, a far less controlled reflection of Sylvan's wolf, unhappy and itching for a fight. Niki was her general and always ready for a fight. That battle lust made Niki the great warrior she was and also, at times, the one Sylvan needed to control with teeth at her throat.

Don't give her what she wants. Sylvan spoke wolf to wolf.

Niki's lip lifted in a snarl, her elongated canines the only sign that her wolf was prowling close to the surface.

Cecilia seeks to tease you, to put you off-balance.

I am not concerned by Fae games, Niki replied.

Laughter like the sound of birdsong in flight, undercut with the predatory warning call of the hawk, floated through Sylvan's mind. *Tell your general she should be concerned with* this *Fae.*

Sylvan stared at Torren. *My Lord Torren. I did not realize you could participate in Pack communication.*

Ordinarily I would not be able to.

Like all Fae, friend or foe, Torren often spoke in riddles and half thoughts. Sylvan tamped down her irritation. *And Cecilia? Can she too share our thoughts?*

Torren shook her head. *I don't think so. I am bonded to Misha, and Misha to you. Through you, I am linked to your Pack. Here in Faerie, those bonds are entwined with the magic of the land. That merging has strengthened our link in unexpected ways.*

Sylvan had no time or reason to question Torren's assessment. Many things had changed as members of her Pack had mated outside their borders with other Weres, humans, and even Fae. A new world order was emerging, one Sylvan needed to understand so as to protect those who were hers. She had left her mate, her young, and her Pack behind when she'd stepped through the Faerie Gate, just so she could begin to understand what forces might be arrayed against her. Torren was a friend of the Pack, and she trusted her. *You are welcome then, Lord Torren. Do you know where we are? Or* when *we are?*

Time is meaningless here. Torren's full melodic voice reverberated through Sylvan's mind. *What may feel like hours or even days to you is mere illusion. We are creatures with endless time, and therefore time has no significance.*

And when we return to our own world, Sylvan queried, a pang of fear roiling in her belly, *will my young be adults, will my Prima have gone years without me?*

Only if Cecilia bends the dimensions, and that might require even more power than she possesses. Torren held her gaze, something no other being dared do without challenge. Sylvan showed her canines in warning, though she smiled inwardly, adding Torren to the small circle of her equals, her *friends*, in the ongoing fight for Praetern survival. Time was changing, despite its irrelevance here in Faerie.

You are not here voluntarily—nor bespelled as most earthlings are when they arrive. I do not believe Cecilia would be foolish enough to perpetrate what would be considered an act of war. If you do not return...soon, Torren smiled, and for an instant rainbow colors slashed through her eyes, *Drake and Misha and I suspect a legion of Vampires will find their way through the Gate. As I am connected to Pack, Misha is connected to Faerie, more strongly than she realizes.*

Sylvan frowned. *If that's true, can she open...* She shook her head and closed her mind. Whatever Misha's emerging powers might be, Cecilia did not need to know of them. Beside her, Niki growled.

"Yes," Sylvan said aloud, "I feel it too." Power, pressing against her chest, attempting to choke her. Her skin prickled and pelt rolled beneath her skin. Her wolf alerted, signaling danger, ready to do battle.

Attillus, the Fae warrior, stepped into the glade as if he'd merely opened a door and walked through. Behind him, twelve Fae guards bedecked in Cecilia's livery, standards held high and spears in hand, stood at placid attention. Attillus's gaze swept over Sylvan and came to rest on Torren. His eyebrow arched, the only expression on his transcendent, perfectly etched features.

"Torren," he said coolly, eschewing Torren's title.

Torren smiled. "Attillus. We are here to see Your Lady."

If possible, Attillus's features cooled even further. "The *Queen*," he said, emphasizing the word, "is aware."

"If Cecilia has changed her mind..."

"*You* will address the Queen as she deserves to be addressed."

"I shall?" Torren shrugged. "And you? How shall you address me?"

The royal guard behind Attillus remained as immovable as statues. Sylvan, attuned to the nearest movement of prey in the deepest shadows, sensed Attillus's tension.

"Lord Torren, Master of the Hunt," Attillus said, as if the words were acid pouring over his tongue, "Cecilia, Queen of Thorns and All of Faerie, Ruler of Dark and Light, and Mistress of All Seasons, welcomes you to Faerie and invites you to her royal presence."

"Consort," Torren said evenly, "I come with Sylvan Mir, Alpha of the Timberwolf Pack, and Rafe, Emissary of Liege Jody Gates of the Northeastern US Vampire seethe, for audience with Cecilia, Queen of Thorns and All of Faerie, Ruler of Dark and Light, and Mistress of All Seasons."

Attillus swept an arm in a glittering semicircle, and Sylvan found herself on a marble path as wide as many highways. At the horizon, a pair of golden arches fronted a gold-domed mound that rose in the midst of an ephemeral glade, circled by tall trees with bright orange leaves and delicate green and turquoise fruits dangling in bunches from vines as thin as hairs. In a crystal magenta sky, the blood-red sun shimmered within a golden halo. Beyond the golden arches, Cecilia no doubt awaited. Along the length of the marble colonnade, more guards as still as statues held the Queen's standard with its fluttering blue pennant adorned with Cecilia's crest of roses and thorns, while another dozen flanked two towering ornate doors cast in what might be pure gold. The grandeur was a show of power, so like Cecilia.

Without waiting for an invitation, which would only underscore the advantage Cecilia held in her own territory, Sylvan took a step onto the marble walk, shoulder to shoulder with Torren and Niki. Rafe and the Vampire guards fell in behind her. Time to see exactly what Cecilia had planned.

CHAPTER ELEVEN

Trent drew Jace aside as the first glimmer of dawn broke above the tree line in the east. She'd stood guard all night, too restless to sleep, her wolf agitated and pacing. The Snowcrest Weres would be on the move now. The engagement might commence at any moment. And still, she scented nothing. Where were the Snowcrest wolves? More importantly, where was Zora? Trent shuddered at the memory of Zora's hands and mouth on her, and still, the air carried no scent of their opponents.

She asked Jace, "Does it bother you how quiet it is out there?"

"I was thinking the same thing myself." Jace glanced around the clearing, checking their warriors' positions. Most were secluded under cover in the surrounding forest or on *sentrie* duty along their perimeter. "None of our runners have reported sign of them yet."

"I don't like it," Trent said. "It's not like Loris or Ash to let us have the high ground."

Jace smiled, the satisfied look she got whenever Ash crossed her mind fused with a warrior's hunger. "This is a perfect encampment for defense," Jace said, "and Ash would know that. So would Loris."

"Which means they may suspect our location."

"They still have to approach us," Jace said, "and by the time they draw close enough to engage, we will have the advantage of location."

"We should have the advantage of time on our side too," Trent said. "We left quickly."

"True," Jace said slowly, "but this is their territory, and they know the ground."

Trent scented again—still nothing, but the wind was coming from behind them. If the Snowcrest were foolish enough to launch a frontal assault, she wouldn't know until she sighted them. The Snowcrest Alpha and her general were not warrior trained, but they were wolves. They would not be foolish. "We need to send out an advance guard—I don't want any surprises."

Jace nodded. "Take the point with six of your best warriors, cross the stream, and occupy the bluff above the trail. You'll see any movement from the direction of Snowcrest from there, even if they try to circle around behind us."

"As you command, *Centuri*."

"And Trent," Jace said quietly, "remember, they are our allies."

Trent showed her teeth, but she did not argue with her commander. She wasn't so certain exactly how much of an ally Loris and some of the other dominants really were. Even Ash, mated to a Timberwolf or not, was Snowcrest, and she led the Snowcrest soldiers today.

Trent saluted. "Good hunting, *Centuri*."

"And you," Jace said, shifting into pelt and loping to join her cadre.

Trent gave her wolf leave to ascend, her pelt swiftly rolling over skin. She dropped to all fours, signaled with a quick bark, and trotted off into the forest, her warriors at her flanks. The bluff from which she would command the hunting ground was a quarter mile away. They should be well ensconced before Snowcrest moved in for a counterattack. She expected them to advance in groups along the line, sweeping outward fanlike from their Clan home, protecting their flanks while driving forward in the center. A sound defense, but not always the best offense. But then, that's what she and her warriors were here to demonstrate.

Her heart thundered as battle hormones and the simple joy of running filled her blood. That, and, knowing Zora was coming. The Alpha would not let this battle pass her by. No Alpha would, and Zora, above all else, was Alpha. Were she not, Trent would've pushed her claim on Zora's wolf by now. Would have let *her* wolf show all her power, would have let Zora know her desire, and would have answered the pull of instinct and primal need that could not be denied even if they should want to.

But Zora was not for her.

Had Zora merely been Snowcrest, as Ash was, then Trent might have chosen as Jace had chosen, to move into the uncertain ground between the two Packs to claim her mate. No *might've been* about it. She would not have hesitated. Sometimes, the wolf in them understood far better the rightness of an action than their reasoning mind. But she was not *all* wolf, and Zora had made it plain what she wanted, and that did not include anything more with Trent than the one-sided tangles they'd shared. Trent was duty bound and heart bound to follow Zora's command. The ache in her chest never relented despite her focus on the coming engagement.

At the crest of the bluff, she signaled with a low growl for her warriors to follow her off the path and into the forest. Perhaps if she hadn't taken that route, and the wind hadn't shifted in just that instant, she would not have scented the dark, oily, foreign scent of the enemy.

They were not alone in the forest. She could turn back and warn Jace, but then the enemy would be behind her, and she and her wolves would be vulnerable in retreat. At the very least, she needed to know what they faced.

Benjamin, she signaled to another lieutenant. *Take three, scout left. Dara, two on the right.*

She sent the last Were back to warn Jace. Silently, her wolves melted into the undergrowth. She went forward alone, slipping through shadows, climbing ever upward toward the scent of *wrongness*, of death and the metallic stench of sorcery. If the Snowcrest wolves were spread out in an advancing line as she suspected, they would be at risk for attack from whatever held this bluff. They needed to be warned.

Zora needed to be warned. If she could not warn them, she would have to search out the enemy and attack before the enemy could make the first move.

"Ah, Sylvan, so good to see you again. And you brought your friends!" Cecilia's voice shimmered through Sylvan's mind, a sound like the tinkling of bells and the rustle of the wind through the trees, mixed with the scent of spring blossoms bursting with life. And underneath it all, the sharp, bloodied edge of thorns.

Cecilia sat ensconced on a surprisingly modest throne that only with close inspection revealed its construction of precious metals and even more precious jewels studding the curving surface that wrapped around Cecilia as if it was a living beast. For all Sylvan knew, it might be. The Faerie Queen seemed to emerge from the glittering gems and swirling gold and silver filigree as if she herself was a precious jewel, her skin the pure translucency that marked the high Fae, her hair a gleaming shimmer falling around her breasts to her slender waist in golden ripples, and her green eyes, the rarest of all emeralds. She was beauty personified, and Sylvan often wondered what lay beneath her glamour. Perhaps she was even more beautiful, or something more terrifying to match her power. Sylvan never forgot that nothing in Faerie or of the Fae was as simple or true as it appeared.

"Cecilia," Sylvan said, intentionally eschewing all her many titles, "I think you know my *allies*."

Sylvan emphasized allies ever so slightly. Friends, they were indeed, but they had come with one intent—to do battle if needed. "My *imperator*, Niki Kroff and Rafe, of Liege Gates's guard, and of course—"

"Torren de Brinna," Cecilia said, sex and censure rolling through her throaty caress. "It's been far too long since you've graced my court, my love."

"Only a century or so, my Queen," Torren said, the sarcasm imperceptible to those who didn't know her well.

Sylvan knew her well enough to know she'd spent a century in an earthbound prison, stripped of her powers at Cecilia's hand. But as well as she knew her, Torren was still Fae. Immortal, centuries-old, a power without reckoning and motives far more complicated than what might appear on the surface. If Torren and Cecilia were involved in some ancient Fae game, Sylvan didn't care, as long as it didn't impact those she was sworn to protect.

"We could have made you comfortable at the Compound," Sylvan said, "or met with you somewhere of our joint choosing. But considering your invitation, I assumed there was some urgency to this meeting."

Cecilia swept her gaze over Attillus and his guards, coming to rest on Attillus. Her expression was far cooler than it had been when she'd first greeted Torren. Torren had called him *Consort*, but as the Fae did not take partners, or mates, Cecilia undoubtedly had many lovers. Nothing showed on her face when she said, "Leave us, Attillus, and take the others."

Attillus's displeasure, a swirling breeze heavy with anger and surprise, raised the hair on Sylvan's nape. Her wolf tensed, and pelt prickled her skin.

"My Queen—" Attillus protested.

"It's quite all right," Cecilia said, her smooth tone doing nothing to hide the steel in her voice. "Go now."

Every Fae in the spacious chamber snapped to attention and saluted as her power flooded the air like an ocean wave. Within seconds, the audience chamber was empty. Cecilia drifted down from her throne. To say she stepped or walked would be to do an injustice to her motion. She was as ephemeral as the wind, as beautiful as a ray of sunlight slanting through the evergreens. Sylvan wondered what the others saw, if what they perceived as beautiful would be how Cecilia appeared to them. Sylvan blinked, but the glamour remained. And then, Cecilia was within touching distance of her, and Niki growled.

"Stand," Sylvan murmured.

Cecilia leaned in and kissed Sylvan's cheek. "It's been far too long."

Sylvan sighed. Cecilia's glamour slid along her skin like a soft touch, teasing and provocative. Even had she not been mated, she would not have been tempted. Now, she was barely amused. "As I recall, at our last meeting, we didn't exactly agree as to much of anything."

Cecilia laughed again, the peal of the bells dancing through Sylvan's consciousness, and her wolf perked up. Her wolf recognized the ploy too, the seduction that was second nature to the Fae. She huffed, annoyed, and settled back into wary watching.

"You needn't have brought so much power with you." Cecilia stepped up to Sylvan and slipped her arm through Sylvan's, as if they were about to promenade. She turned, ignoring the others in Sylvan's party, and Sylvan followed her down the length of the audience hall and through the arches. Instead of the marble colonnade she'd entered through, she stepped out into a verdant meadow, surrounded by more of the trees with the orange leaves and delicate fruit. A rainbow-haloed stream cascaded into a shallow pool the color of morning glories. Niki, Torren, and Rafe followed as Sylvan accompanied Cecilia along the path lined with polished opalescent stones.

"It appears," Cecilia said, "we have a common enemy."

"Do we," Sylvan said.

"I'm afraid so." Cecilia stopped beside a marble bench and settled down on it, gesturing for Sylvan to join her. She tucked her diaphanous skirts around her legs, and when she finished, her hand came to rest on Sylvan's thigh.

Sylvan shifted just enough to break the contact, and Cecilia laughed. "Still not one to be tempted."

"You spoke of enemies?" Sylvan said.

Celia glanced up at Torren. "You remember the Dark Lord of the South?"

"Of course," Torren said. "The last time I saw Cethinrod, he commanded a small army and coveted your throne."

"Not much has changed," Cecilia said conversationally, "although now, apparently, his army includes a Sorcerer and a Master Vampire."

Rafe hissed. "Francesca."

Celia nodded. "They're cloistered somewhere in a peripheral realm, one of the old Fae knowes that's been long abandoned and slowly disappearing. They won't be able to stay there for long but…" She sighed, and frustration and anger tingled in the air so thickly Sylvan could taste it. "I cannot find her. The Mage—Sorcerer—whatever they are, has managed to mask them."

"And they're using this place," Sylvan said carefully, "as their headquarters while they regroup and move back into the human world."

"I think so, yes."

Sylvan narrowed her eyes. "Why call on us with this news? What they might do in the human world doubtlessly gives you no pause."

Cecilia smiled, a smile that offered so much more. "And that's why you're here, because not only are you honest and trustworthy, and oh so handsome, you're also intelligent. They're not just interested in what is in the human realm. They are—"

Torren interjected, "Interested in your throne."

"As are so many," Cecilia said, as if to throw off the threat as of little importance. But they would not be there if she wasn't worried.

"My Queen," Torren said, respectfully, "I would think you would be able to find them."

"I would, under ordinary circumstances," Cecilia said, "but my situation is unusual."

Torren barely registered surprise with a flicker of her eyebrows. "Unusual."

"My power has been…diverted somewhat by a greater demand."

Torren stiffened. "There hasn't been a royal Fae birth in millennia."

"Apparently that is about to change." Cecilia smiled, and a flight of doves broke from the trees above them, spiraling into the sunlight like diamonds. "So you see, now is not the time I want to go to war."

"What is it you want from us?" Sylvan said.

"An alliance. I want the Weres and their allies to fight for me, if my throne is threatened."

Chapter Twelve

Zora led her soldiers along the winding deer trail toward the high bluff above the creek. From that vantage point, she would be able to see the most likely positions where the Timberwolves lay in wait for her and her wolves to walk into their trap. She chuffed. As if they were so naïve. They were wolves, hunters, and among the largest predators in the forest, but not so arrogant or inexperienced that they would allow themselves to be seduced into a trap.

She was halfway up the bluff when she scented Trent and the other Timberwolves. Four—no, six wolves, close but rapidly scattering into the forest. She slowed, scented again, and Trent's power stirred her wolf. A pulse of danger followed the wash of heat that stirred her as only Trent's essence could do. Something threatened Trent's wolf.

Zora reached out to her soldiers. *Spread out, form a line, be ready for an attack.*

She couldn't risk her small force being surrounded, although separating them might be just as risky. Still, if faced with an overpowering enemy, some of them would escape to warn the others.

Pressing low to the ground, stalking forward through the thinning scrub, she sent a warning through the Pack bonds to the rest of her Snowcrest wolves, alerting them to danger and calling her lieutenants for reinforcements. Well out ahead of her own small troop, she bounded the final yards to the bluff, homing in on Trent's scent. Trent was close, her battle lust a potent tang on Zora's tongue, emboldening her wolf with the joy of the hunt. Zora covered the ground with long bounding strides, heart pounding, blood simmering, her only goal to reach Trent. To stand beside her and fight whatever danger she faced.

Soaring up and over the rocky ledge, she landed on a barren shelf of rock in the midst of a nightmare. Trent battled half a dozen of the creatures Zora had seen before, wolves but not wolves, their skeletons twisted and deformed, their elongated muzzles dripping saliva from fangs too long to be contained within their muzzles, eyes a fiery red, their coats mangy patches of fur interspersed with leathery skin, as if their pelts had been burned away. At the center of the ring of reanimated wolves, Trent charged and snapped, spinning with power and grace to drive back first one, then another of the creatures that lunged at her, attempting to clamp their jaws on her limbs or her neck. Blood darkened Trent's pelt in a dozen places from bites and tears, but she fought with relentless fury.

Zora's wolf growled and vaulted over the nearest creature, landing at Trent's side.

Go back, Trent demanded.

On your left, Zora warned, ignoring the foolish wolf. As if she would leave her to fight alone. Trent spun away, and Zora drove beneath the snapping jaws of the nearest creature. Catching its throat in her jaws, she clamped down hard and twisted her shoulders with a sharp snap, tearing out its throat and severing its spine. The head lolled, and the creature collapsed, oily smoke seeping out of its disintegrating body. Nothing with any spark of life would do that.

A second creature joined the first as Trent tore into its skull.

Now they were two against four. Zora howled, wild with unbridled power.

The creatures were twice the size of even an Alpha Were, but their battle prowess was fragmented and fractured. Had they fought as a Pack, Trent and Zora might've been overcome, but these creatures had no Pack sense, perhaps had no free will.

Trent took down another, and Zora dispatched a fourth. One-on-one now, and in the distance, Zora felt her Pack nearing. She circled the last creature, dashing in to pull it away from Trent. Above her, lightning flashed and the sky tore open.

A beast the size and distorted shape of a bull moose dropped to the ground a few feet in front of her. What would have been a rack of antlers appeared like rows of gleaming, two-foot long silver-tipped spikes. A wound from one of those might kill even an Alpha Were. The maw pulled back to expose double rows of canines, longer than her forelimbs, and talons tipped the cloven feet at the end of limbs resembling human legs. The massive chest heaved, and the beast bellowed a sound like demented thunder, lowered its head, and charged. Zora twisted, and a silver spike glanced across her shoulder, opening her flesh. The silver burned, her muscle froze, and she stumbled. Ignoring the pain, she caught her balance and swirled to face the beast again as it rammed forward, head down, lethal spikes aimed at her chest.

Trent streaked in from Zora's side, slammed into the beast, and latched onto its throat. Blood, black and thick as pitch, poured from the wound. With a roaring bellow, the beast vaulted skyward and, in an instant, was swallowed by the darkness that closed as if a giant eye had winked shut.

Three Timberwolves raced into the clearing, and a dozen Snowcrest soldiers cleared the bluff. Within an instant, the two remaining creatures were torn asunder. Zora searched frantically for Trent's scent, for the connection that had settled in her chest the moment she'd seen her, and that she could no longer find.

With a howl, she threw back her head and raged.

❖

Trent landed on her back, the weight of the beast pinning her to an uneven stony surface. The scent of blood and rot choked her. She thrashed, kicking and twisting until she broke free. Backing away on weakened limbs from the feebly writhing creature, she panted as pain cut through the battle lust. Shaking off the torpor that threatened to immobilize her, she spun about in search of more enemy. She was alone except for the thing that had dragged her to this place.

Some kind of cave, dim and dank and smelling of death. Not far away, a glimmer of light called to her. The beast thrashed weakly, blood, or something that might've been blood had it been alive, seeping from its neck, black and odorous. Leaving it to whatever end existed after death, Trent trotted cautiously toward the light and emerged on a ledge beneath a hazy greenish sky. Moss the color of orange blossoms covered the hillside below her. She sniffed, scented the waning signature of the creatures she'd fought in the clearing. If those creatures had a way into her world from this, she needed to find it and make her way home.

Zora was somewhere beyond the veil, and Trent's imperative was to find her. Nothing else mattered. Stepping onto the strange moss, she padded downhill, searching whatever cover she could find behind shining obsidian boulders and short clumps of brush that tugged at her pelt as she passed. The forest, or what she assumed was one, loomed ahead, the trees twining their branches together in a filigree pattern of yellows and white, like an impenetrable latticework, dense and ominous. Following the lingering scent of death, Trent slipped into the shadows underneath the arching branches and padded on.

CHAPTER THIRTEEN

"Did you invite us here to drive these intruders from Faerie?" Torren asked.

"You doubt my ability to protect my realm, Hunt Master?"

"I would never underestimate your power, my Queen," Torren replied, neatly sidestepping the question, Sylvan thought.

Cecilia sent Torren a chiding smile, clearly recognizing the dissembling reply. "If I knew their location, I would do that myself." She paused as if listening to a distant melody, her gaze darkening like storm clouds boiling down a mountainside, threatening to drown anything in their paths. "Forces are gathering, testing our will. Some foreign magic hides the intruders from our sight."

"What is it you need of us then?" Sylvan said.

"I need your power," Cecilia said, her voice deepening, blinding white light radiating from her glowing form and encompassing them in a shimmering cloud. "Open to me that I might see."

Sylvan shuddered as electricity coursed over her skin, speared beneath her flesh and bone, and struck at her wolf deep inside. A seductive heat built in her loins, forcing the blood in her sex to pulse and pound. She snarled and drew on her ties to Drake, to her Pack, to counter Cecilia's assault. An answering surge of strength and magic flowed into her depths, and she grew taller, gritting her teeth as her bones and body shifted into her half-form. Massive chest heaving, her claws erupted from her forelimbs, her face and jaws elongated into her lethal warrior shape. She towered above the Faerie Queen. "Do not attempt to steal what is not yours."

Beside her, Torren laughed, her body incandescent, a circle of power enclosing and shielding her from Cecilia's reach. "My Queen, you have a strange way of welcoming those you would want as allies."

The shimmering cloud of pulsating force surrounding Cecilia dissipated, and she resumed her usual shape with a playful smile. "You've both grown in power."

Sylvan refused to relax her guard and ground out, "You have broken the parlay. We are leaving."

"They have one of yours," Cecilia said conversationally. "Would you leave that one behind too?"

Sylvan snarled. "What are you talking about?"

"I can't reach them, but I can sense where they are, and I sense something else too. A wolf." She cocked her head. "Take my hand and see for yourself, *Alpha*."

"*No!*" Niki pushed in front of Sylvan and grasped Cecilia's hand. With a high, keening whine, she shuddered and fell to her knees.

Sylvan growled and lunged, but Torren intercepted her.

"Wait," Torren said.

"Move aside," Sylvan growled, torn between attacking her ally and rescuing her wolf.

Cecilia stepped back, and Niki dropped to her hands and knees, panting. Sweat dripped from her forehead onto the gleaming marble floor. She gasped. "Trent."

"You saw her?" Sylvan knelt by Niki's side and wrapped an arm around her, let her power and Pack magic flow into her. Niki leaned hard against her, her breath rasping in and out.

"Not saw," she finally said. With each passing second, she grew stronger until she pushed upright. "I sensed her. Alone, wounded. Somewhere…" She shivered violently. "Somewhere not this world, not ours."

Sylvan jerked around, baring her teeth at Cecilia. "*Where* is my wolf?"

"I told you," Cecilia said with exaggerated patience, "some lost knowe. Of Faerie, but not *in* Faerie."

Sylvan bolted to her feet, slipping back into her normal form. "How do we get there?"

Cecilia regarded Torren. "Are you willing, Hunt Master?"

"If I open my power to yours," Torren said calmly, "will you abide by the terms of parlay?"

"No harm will come to you."

Torren smiled thinly. "No harm will come to *us or ours*."

"Until you leave this realm," Cecilia said, "no harm will come to you or yours."

Torren glanced at Sylvan. "She makes no promises about the future."

Sylvan glared at Cecilia. "Nor do I."

Bowing regally to Cecilia, Torren held out her hand as if inviting her to dance. "My Queen."

"It has been far too long." Cecilia's smile was self-satisfied and sensual as she took Torren's hand.

Weres in pelt poured out of the forest onto the bluff, the Snowcrests and Timberwolves facing off on opposites sides of the clearing, the air clouding with battle pheromones. In the center of them all, Zora raged, her power and fury blasting into their bones and their blood. Wolves snarled and bared their teeth in challenge, pelt bristling, ears pulled back and heads low to the ground. Loris raced to Zora's side, blocking her flank from the slowly encroaching Timberwolves. Ash joined her, and the two most dominant Weres in Zora's Pack readied to protect their Alpha.

Jace burst out of the mass of Timberwolf warriors, shoulders bunched, eyes gone wolf, and confronted her mate and Loris.

"Hold your soldiers," Jace growled at Loris.

Loris swung to face her, quivering with rage, dripping saliva from gleaming canines.

"Back away from the Alpha," Loris demanded.

"Control your wolves," Jace repeated and glanced at her mate. "Ash, help me."

Shuddering, torn between Pack bonds and mate, Ash reached out to Loris. *General, there is no challenge here. Our enemy...* Chest heaving, Ash fought the primal urge to charge the foreign wolves in the heart of her territory. Her mate waited, proud and strong and trusting. *Our enemy is not these wolves.*

Zora, mad with fury and battle lust, howled again, straining at the

Pack bonds for more power, pulling everything—anything—she could in her need to find Trent. The Pack bonds strained, and one by one her wolves fell, writhing and panting on the ground as she took their strength. Their agony finally broke through her fury, and a thread of sanity glimmered. Pack above all else, and she was their Alpha.

Hold, she ordered and shed pelt. The Snowcrest wolves slowly relented, and the Timberwolves backed away.

"What happened?" Jace asked.

"Another attack," Zora said. "They have Trent."

The Timberwolves snarled and snapped.

"Stand *down*," Jace commanded, overriding their wild energy with her own power. Turning to her warriors, she added, "Captains, secure the perimeter."

Loris repeated the order and the two Packs formed a defensive perimeter around the clearing. Satisfied the immediate threat was over, Jace trotted over to Ash, who stood with Loris and the Alpha.

"Where did they take her?" she asked.

"Through another Gate, like before," Zora said, struggling for reason with every cell in her body, fighting her wolf's demand that she find Trent.

"Are there other enemies still here?" Jace asked.

"Not that I can scent," Zora said.

"Clan home?" Ash queried.

Zora reached out along the Pack bonds, sensed no disturbance. "All is quiet, but we must fortify our defenses there."

Loris said, "Should I send our soldiers back, Alpha?"

"Do it." Zora spun, her eyes fierce, and fixed on Jace. "I need your warriors. We *will* find Trent."

"Alpha." Jace lowered her gaze. "Let me contact my Alpha. Another attack may be coming. We are not ready."

Zora didn't hesitate. Calling on the Timberwolf Pack's superior strength was a risk, but Trent was missing and her Clan home was endangered. She would not invite a slaughter for the sake of pride. She had trusted Sylvan Mir thus far. She would continue.

"Do it."

❖

Drake paced restlessly behind the stockade barricades. Sylvan had been gone only a few hours, but her wolf bristled with an uneasy sense of danger. The Pack bonds vibrated and tugged at her depths when Sylvan pulled power and shifted into her warrior form. Some kind of danger. Her need to be at her mate's side clawed at her body and her will.

Max trotted up beside her. *I've doubled the* sentries, *Prima.*

You feel it? Drake queried.

Yes, Prima.

Secure the maternals and all the young, Drake ordered.

I shall see to it.

Max leapt away and Drake bounded onto the top of the fortifications. Surveying the forest, she lifted her muzzle to the sky and breathed deeply. She could not capture Sylvan's scent—that had disappeared with her through the Gate that had opened like an impenetrable black mirror, winking out when Sylvan and the others stepped through it. But her mate bond remained strong. Still, something, somewhere had alerted her wolf. Sylvan would call on her if she needed, but something else, some other threat, was close.

Anya burst out of headquarters and raced across the Compound to Drake.

"Prima," Anya said. "Jace on the sat radio. Something's happened at Snowcrest. An attack."

Drake spun around, shedding pelt as she followed Anya back to headquarters. She jumped onto the porch, pausing only long enough to grab pants from a stack by the door, and took the stairs to the comm room two at a time. Once she'd pulled on her camos, Anya handed her the radio.

"Jace," Drake said, "what's the situation?"

"A raid in the forest near Cresthome, Prima. Only a few invaders, but Trent was taken."

"No other evidence of an invasion?" Drake asked.

"Not yet, Prima. The Snowcrest soldiers and our warriors are securing Cresthome. Alpha Constantine requests additional soldiers."

"We'll send two more teams," Drake said instantly. She had no doubt that would be Sylvan's decision. They could not allow the Snowcrest territory to be invaded or their allies to be destroyed. "What about Trent? Can you follow her trail?"

"No, Prima," Jace said. "She was taken through the veil. There are no Gates."

"I'll try to reach the Alpha," Drake said. "Misha may be able to contact Torren, also."

"Yes, Prima."

"Reinforcements will be there as quickly as we can mobilize them. Do not let Cresthome fall."

"As you will," Jace responded.

Drake disconnected and reached through her mate bond to Sylvan. *We need you to return.*

The mate bond burned deep in her chest, Sylvan pulling power— first from Drake, then through her from the Pack. Wherever she was, whatever she was doing, Sylvan could not help them now.

Chapter Fourteen

Sylvan landed on all fours on a slope covered with musty smelling orange moss. Torren's massive Hound shook itself beside her, the rumbling in its chest like thunder. Niki's wolf drew close, rubbed its shoulder against hers.

Where are we, Niki asked.

Somewhere other, Sylvan replied, instantly on guard. She hadn't expected to be pulled into her change when Torren's power and that of the Faerie Queen catapulted them through a Gate, and the swift involuntary change left her momentarily disoriented. Wherever they were, the magic was old and, surprisingly, not completely unwelcoming. Remnants of broken song and sweet breeze tugged at her mind, but the ruff on her back bristled a warning. When she reached out for any sign of Trent, she hit a barrier as substantial as if she'd awakened in a cage of silver. She growled. *This place holds danger.*

"This place is very, very old," Rafe said, twin iron-forged short swords in either hand. "Old enough to have a mind and will of its own. And we are strangers to it."

She lowered but did not sheathe her swords in a show of nonaggression.

How is it the Queen did not sense your weapons? Sylvan asked, iron being one of the few substances that could counter or even destroy Fae power.

"We have shields as well," was Rafe's simple and no doubt truthful answer. She smiled, magenta shards slashing through her obsidian pupils. She was far older than Sylvan had realized, a well-kept secret, apparently. Rafe was Risen, a Vampire in full possession of her powers and strong enough to lead her own seethe. Yet she served Jody Gates. The new Liege Lord was amassing power of her own, it seemed.

Sylvan chuffed. *Jody chose well sending you.*

"My Liege is wise."

Hunt Master, Sylvan asked, leaving the always tangled mesh of Vampire politics aside, *do you know where we are?*

The Hound lifted its massive muzzle to the sky and drew deeply. Air rushed into its bellows-like lungs with a tornado's force. After a moment, her answer filled Sylvan's mind. "This was once a minor realm. When the Faerie Queen came to power, those who resided here remained loyal to the old Queen and closed their Gates, choosing to remain until their power waned and they slowly faded."

Yet it is not empty. Or dead, Sylvan said, scenting a dark and pungent force, like roiling death, on the air.

"No, not any longer. Whatever powers hide here, they have not restored the knowe to life. We have little time before all the exits disappear." The Hound swung her head toward Sylvan, fiery eyes glowing hot. "Can you sense your wolf?"

No, Sylvan said. *Something is blocking my connection to my Prima and my Pack—to everyone except Niki.*

Rafe gave a dark laugh. "Sorcery. Powerful, but not unbreakable."

If you can open a path for us, Vampire, Sylvan said, her wolf snapping at her restraints, *do it.*

Rafe slipped in front of them, and the three formed a shield at her back. Extending both iron blades in a cross at arm's length, she opened her arms wide in a sweeping circle, spoke a few words in an ancient tongue, and what had appeared to be only a thick, heavy miasma of rot clouding the air parted before her blades.

Enchanted iron? Sylvan didn't ask what she knew would not be answered. She shuddered as her mate bond blossomed within her along with her connection to Pack and the resurgence of her power. The rush of air through the rent in the foul magic brought a plethora of scents, some living, some dead. And *there*, a thin filament she recognized.

Trent.

I have her, Sylvan said.

"Then take us there, Alpha," the Hound growled.

Sylvan reached for Trent and bounded into the Gate.

Her wolf was injured and surrounded by danger.

❖

Trent stood her ground, forelegs planted, head lowered, haunches bunched and preparing to spring. The thing in her path hissed and waved two distorted limbs from its leathery chest, pincer-like claws opening and closing. Once, it had been a big cat. Now, it was a horror, the sinuous and graceful body of a mountain lion deformed into something that stood on two short, jointless rear legs, beneath a torso covered with mottled fur, a cavernous midsection, and a bulging chest stripped of everything except bone and swaths of decaying muscle. The head was earless, with yellow, slitted eyes, a long, misshapen jaw with upper canines that hung down below the hinged and gaping maw.

Trent hoped it was dead and not something that knew what an abomination it had become. The claws snapped out, faster than she'd anticipated, and fire ignited in her shoulder. She landed hard on her back twenty feet away.

Too slow, too weak.

The wound in her rear leg, still leaking blood, had sapped her strength, and she struggled to rise. She was no match for the size and speed of the cat-thing, but she would not die on her back. Struggling against the pain and slowly encroaching darkness, she managed to get up and face the thing again.

Readying for the blow, she growled her challenge. *Come, try me.*

She drew a breath and prepared to leap with the last ounce of her strength. An infusion of strength struck her like a fresh wind blowing down from the mountainside. The Alpha had come! Trent howled, leaping at the same time as the cat-thing pounced, and managed to rake her claws across its belly as she flew past. Being smaller had its advantages now. With some of her strength regained, she pivoted as she landed and jumped clear as the creature screamed in frustration, pulled its oversized overbalanced body around, and crouched for another attack.

Sylvan soared into the clearing and landed on its back. The massive wolf, twice Trent's size, clamped down on the creature's spine, her powerful shoulders and jaws wrenching at it. The creature reared up, and Sylvan's body whipped from side to side. Niki struck at its hindquarters, and the Hound tore into its exposed underbelly. Entrails and foul ichor spewed from the gaping wounds.

The flame in Trent's shoulder spread into her chest, and she dropped to the ground, dizzy and weak. Her breath was tight, her heart pounding. Through her dimming vision, she caught flashes of steel and a shadow circling the creature, too quickly for her to make out, cutting and slashing.

The creature fell with a long, keening cry, and Trent closed her eyes. She hoped her Alpha could hear her thoughts.

Tell Zora I died like a wolf, fighting.

CHAPTER FIFTEEN

Shadows fell across the clearing, the sky turning an oily black and swirling above their heads like grasping fingers, blocking out the sun. The air grew dense with a suffocating presence, stealing the breath from Zora's chest. She stood on the spot where Trent had disappeared, ringed by Ash, Jace, and a phalanx of Timberwolf warriors.

"*Stand,*" Zora ordered, broadcasting her power with primal force. Whatever came through the next tear in the veil between realms, they would face, and they would defeat. This was her territory, her Weres to protect, and she would not fail.

Several of the less dominant warriors dropped to all fours, compelled to give rein to their wolves in the presence of an Alpha. Jace steadied herself, confident in the strength and will of her warriors. A slash of black lightning tore through the suffocating barrier above them, and in a flash, as if sucked into a whirlwind, the oily mass disappeared, leaving clear sky behind.

Jace gave a cry of exultation. *Her* Alpha knelt in the center of the clearing a few feet from Zora, with Trent's wolf in her arms. Torren and Niki dropped at her side, and a Vampire ghosted away into the cover of the surrounding forest, almost too quickly to be seen.

Zora leapt forward, landed in front of Sylvan, and reached for Trent. "Give her to me."

"No," Sylvan said in a snarl, rising to her full height, Trent cradled against her chest. Power rolled through the clearing, and the rest of the Timberwolf Weres shifted into pelt. "She is mine."

Zora's canines gleamed and a growl burst from her chest. "She is *mine.*"

Sylvan's eyes glowed gold and pelt rolled beneath her skin. "You would challenge me now?"

"I would have her," Zora thundered.

Niki eased forward at the same time as Ash stepped to Zora's side. "Alpha," Niki murmured, "Zora seeks her mate."

"The wolf needs a healer," Ash murmured gently to Zora, "and we have none here. Her Alpha might be able to save her."

Zora shuddered, warring with her frantic, enraged wolf who knew only that a strange wolf kept her from her mate. "Can you heal her?"

"There is poison," Sylvan said. "Something unknown to me—but she is strong. If we have time—"

Torren slipped into Zora's view, her gaze drawing Zora into a deep well of seductive power. "I can counter the poison, but the process will tax her body. By your leave, Alpha Constantine, I will tend to your mate."

Sylvan stiffened. "Trent is bonded to me. I can feel her."

"Reach in, then, Alpha," Torren said, "and search her bonds. See what her wolf has done."

With a snarl, Sylvan centered her power, connected to Trent's wolf—injured and furious—and read the tangled bonds mired in dark magic in Trent's spirit. She met Zora's gaze, held it. "Her wolf has chosen, but you have not yet claimed her, nor allowed her to claim you."

"She knows I am hers," Zora said. "As do I."

"Then help me protect her." Sylvan knelt and gently placed the unconscious wolf on the ground. Tarry fluid oozed from a row of ragged tears in her shoulder, the flesh puckered and inflamed.

"Give her your power, both of you," Torren said.

Sylvan reached out to Jace and her warriors, drawing them closer and amplifying their strength. She buried her fist in the ruff on Trent's neck. Zora knelt on the opposite side of Trent's still form and pressed her hand over Trent's heart.

Torren crouched between them, her magic glowing like an incandescent prism. She placed her spread fingers directly over the wound, and then her hand disappeared inside the wolf. Trent twitched and whined, and Zora snarled.

"Hold," Sylvan murmured.

Pelt burst down Zora's chest and over her arms, her wolf riding hard beneath the surface. She trembled, forcing her power into Trent, reaching for the connections that she'd never been able to ignore and that now only her ties to the Pack could equal.

Torren whispered on the wind, more music than words, a slowly rising symphony of sound that drowned out the scent of rot and the putrefaction destroying Trent's shoulder. Slowly the festering flesh receded until a raw, red wound remained, free of the oozing black death.

Torren withdrew her hand, and the light around her dimmed. Trent's wolf sighed and settled into an easy sleep.

"We are in your debt once more, Lord Torren," Sylvan murmured.

"As am I," Zora said.

Torren, paler even than usual, rose and stepped back. "She will need time to heal, and all the strength you can give her."

"And you," Sylvan said, "need to recover what you have given her. Go now, and take Rafe to safety too."

"I will find my Lady and await you at your Compound, Alpha." Torren bowed and was gone.

Zora, her hand still on Trent's chest over the steady beat of her heart, felt some of her fury drain away as the fear slowly settled. She met Sylvan's gaze. "I would have her now."

"If she so chose," Sylvan said, leaning back, "then it shall be so."

Zora lifted Trent's wolf into her arms. "I must return to Clan home and ensure the safety of my Pack."

"My wolves are coming," Sylvan said. "Once we secure this area, I will meet you there."

Zora looked to the sky. "And what of those in the beyond? Are they coming also?"

"We saw no others where we found Trent," Sylvan said. "The enemy may have departed, for now."

"For now," Zora said.

CHAPTER SIXTEEN

The fire searing through Trent's chest seeped away into the fading blackness. With the first glimmer of light, warmth, like the embers of the fire pit in the center of the Compound, flared deep within her, bringing a sense of peace and safety that burned away the agony and quieted the terror. She basked in the light and basked in the connections that bound her to Pack. She clung to cords of silk and steel that whispered of strength and power, tenderness and compassion, lust and need. Cords that were new and wild, yet somehow familiar. Her wolf rose within her, stretched, breathed freely, growing stronger with each passing second. The light eclipsed the last dark slivers of pain, and she opened her eyes to fingers of dawn sliding through the window high above her head.

"Good morning, Wolf," a husky voice murmured in her ear.

Trent laughed, feeling the silken cords tighten around her heart with joy and expectation. "Good morning, Wolf."

Zora kissed the angle of her jaw and nuzzled her neck. "How is my wolf this morning?"

My wolf. Trent's heart leapt, and her wolf howled in answering joy. "Yours, as always."

"And the pain?" Zora asked gently, skimming a hand down Trent's bare flank.

The touch, both possessive and claiming, ignited Trent's core. "I am healed, Zora. How long?"

"Almost a day." Zora nuzzled Trent's neck, a low rumble of invitation vibrating against Trent's throat. "You are a stubborn wolf. You refused to give up." Zora kissed her, her grip on Trent's hip tightening, the press of claws the only sign of her wolf prowling close to the surface. "I would rather you did not risk another wound like that again."

"Stubborn," Trent teased, seeking to ease Zora's worry, "but yours."

Zora shifted her naked thigh over Trent's hips, her center pressed to Trent's flesh. She was hot and open. "Not yet mine, though, are you?"

Trent grasped Zora's shoulders and drew Zora atop her until Zora straddled her, sex to sex. The need that had simmered deep inside Trent for weeks flared into mating lust, and desire raced through her. She growled and, claws bursting free, raked them down Zora's back. "I have been yours for the taking always, Alpha."

Growling as the faint slivers of pain stoked her sex frenzy, Zora's eyes blazed gold and her canines gleamed. She rubbed her clitoris, hard and proud and hot, over Trent's. "You know, if I take you, you will be mine, and I will not let you go."

Trent lifted her hips, urged Zora deeper. "I am yours already, and I do not want to go anywhere you are not."

"And if I must challenge your Alpha for you?" Zora panted, her skin shimmering with sex-sheen, her abdomen etched in muscle and quivering with the pressure to complete the mate bond. Her sex pulsed, full and flushed with hormones and ready to explode. "Answer quickly, Wolf. I cannot wait any longer."

"I would submit to any punishment to prevent that," Trent said.

"That I will not allow. Do you trust me?"

"I love you," Trent said, "with all that I am. I trust you, Zora, but I would not see you hurt."

Zora grinned, an Alpha predator's grin. "I would not lose a fight that I fought for you."

Trent lifted her chin, exposed her throat. "I am yours, as I've ever been."

"I would not have you submit, but I would have you accept my claim." Every muscle taut, Zora softly pressed her canines against Trent's throat, barely piercing the skin. "Choose *now*."

"My wolf already has." Trent pushed her fingers through Zora's hair, clenched tightly, and drew Zora's head to her chest. "I am yours. Take me."

With a lash of power, Zora settled her hips deeper between Trent's and locked her sex to Trent's with her clitoris riding Trent's cleft. Joining them body-to-body and heart-to-heart, she pierced Trent's flesh just above her breast. Trent arched, the rush of power rocketing into her loins and exploding from her sex. Her clitoris pounded with each pulse of her heart as she emptied over Zora's sex. Zora drenched her as she released, their *victus* fusing, their unique body chemicals joining, reconfiguring, and linking them heart, body, and soul.

Zora's head snapped back, a snarl of passion and possession rolling from her chest, bombarding Trent with fury and need. Trent arched from the bed, clamped her jaws down at the angle of Zora's neck and shoulder above the pounding lifeline, and buried her canines, claiming as she had been claimed. Zora pumped between her thighs, sending her into a shower of racking pleasure as their sexes fused again.

Zora collapsed upon her. "The next time we're in a battle, you fight by my side, *not* in front of me."

Trent chuckled. "You are mated to a warrior, Alpha. My wolf will always fight for you."

Zora pushed herself up on both arms, glared down at her mate. "You will fight for me and our Pack, Prima. But never alone again."

Trent answered with a growl and a kiss.

❖

When Trent emerged from Zora's quarters, the first Were she saw was Loris, standing guard at the end of the hall. She'd sensed him outside Zora's room, just as she'd sensed all the Snowcrest Weres from the instant Zora's bite had joined her to Zora and, through the commingling of their very atoms, to the Pack. The Snowcrests, her Pack now, would have felt her bond join theirs as well, and some would not be happy.

Some would think to challenge. She wouldn't mind a fight, but she would not destabilize Zora's Pack now, in the midst of a war. And Zora would see any challenge to her mate as a sign of disloyalty.

Trent moved quickly, before Zora could do what needed doing for her. If she was to lead at Zora's side, she must claim her place and hold it on her own. With her own power. She leapt the length of the hall and landed a few inches from Loris. His eyes held tinges of gold, his wolf on the brink of challenge.

"Don't," Trent warned, putting every ounce of new power into her tone. "We are on the brink of war, and the Alpha will need her general."

Loris quivered, a cascade of fine dark pelt dusting his throat and upper chest. He breathed deeply, nostrils flaring as he drew in Trent's changed scent. Now she carried the scent of Zora and their mate bond.

Trent held his gaze, letting her wolf rise, and growled softly. *Do not test me.*

Loris's eyes widened at the unspoken command.

Softly, lethally, Trent whispered, "Yield, Wolf, or you will die."

Gasping, Loris lowered his gaze as he lifted his chin.

Trent pressed close, her chest to his, her groin to his. She could make him submit, sex and soul, but she clamped down on his throat without drawing blood. She held him in her grip until he whined softly and relaxed against her.

"Prima," he murmured.

"*Imperator*," Trent replied and, with a final roll of power, released him.

Zora appeared at Trent's side and slid an arm around her waist. "Are you done, mate?"

Trent's sex readied again at the first scent of her mate, and she slid her hand beneath Zora's shirt to caress her abdomen. "Not yet."

"I should hope not." Laughing for a heart-stopping instant, Zora sobered and nodded to Loris. "We need to see to our soldiers. Join us."

Loris saluted. "Yes, Alpha."

When Trent and Zora stepped outside together, Loris on Zora's left in his usual position, Zora paused and surveyed the training yard. Snowcrest soldiers and Timberwolf warriors milled about. Sylvan Mir stood with her *centuri* in the very middle of the yard, as if she'd been waiting there the whole time Trent had been healing.

"Wait for me here," Zora said to Trent.

"Zora," Trent murmured, "this is *our* fight."

"This is for me to do. Trust me." Zora vaulted the distance to Sylvan in one leap. Meeting Sylvan's glacial gaze, she said formally, "Alpha Mir, the Snowcrest Weres thank you for your aid and welcome you to Clan home. Forgive my absence. My *mate* required my attention."

Sylvan glanced past Zora to Trent. "She is still bonded to me and mine."

"I know."

"She cannot give her allegiance to both."

"She doesn't have to," Zora said. "She is my mate, and she will lead my Weres with me. But we are your allies, and we will both honor your call, should you have need of us."

Sylvan huffed and cut her gaze to Jace and her Snowcrest mate. "And Ash?"

Zora sent a silent question to her captain. *How do you choose, Ash?*

Ash straightened, her hand moving to Jace's back. *By your leave, Alpha, I would join my mate.*

"It seems," Zora said, motioning Trent to her side, "our Packs will share more than one bond."

Sylvan nodded. "We may find ourselves united in war *and* peace in the days ahead."

Zora took Trent's hand. "Together we will fight, and together we will triumph."

About the Author

Radclyffe has written over sixty romance and romantic intrigue novels as well as a paranormal romance series, The Midnight Hunters, as L.L. Raand.

She is a three-time Lambda Literary Award winner in romance and erotica and received the Dr. James Duggins Outstanding Mid-Career Novelist Award by the Lambda Literary Foundation. A member of the Saints and Sinners Literary Hall of Fame, she is also an RWA/FF&P Prism Award winner for *Secrets in the Stone*, an RWA FTHRW Lories and RWA HODRW winner for *Firestorm*, an RWA Bean Pot winner for *Crossroads*, an RWA Laurel Wreath winner for *Blood Hunt*, and a Book Buyers Best award winner for *Price of Honor* and *Secret Hearts*. She is also a featured author in the 2015 documentary film *Love Between the Covers*, from Blueberry Hill Productions. In 2019 she was recognized as a "Trailblazer of Romance" by the Romance Writers of America.

In 2004 she founded Bold Strokes Books, one of the world's largest independent LGBTQ publishing companies, and is the current president and publisher.

Find her at facebook.com/Radclyffe.BSB, follow her on Twitter @RadclyffeBSB, and visit her website at Radfic.com.

Books Available From Bold Strokes Books

Best Practice by Carsen Taite. When attorney Grace Maldonado agrees to mentor her best friend's little sister, she's prepared to confront Perry's rebellious nature, but she isn't prepared to fall in love. Legal Affairs: one law firm, three best friends, three chances to fall in love. (978-1-63555-361-1)

Home by Kris Bryant. Natalie and Sarah discover that anything is possible when love takes the long way home. (978-1-63555-853-1)

Keeper by Sydney Quinne. With a new charge under her reluctant wing—feisty, highly intelligent math wizard Isabelle Templeton—Keeper Andy Bouchard has to prevent a murder or die trying. (978-1-63555-852-4)

One More Chance by Ali Vali. Harry Bastantes planned a future with Desi Thompson until the day Desi disappeared without a word, only to walk back into her life sixteen years later. (978-1-63555-536-3)

Renegade's War by Gun Brooke. Freedom fighter Aurelia DeCallum regrets saving the woman called Blue. She fears it will jeopardize her mission, and secretly, Blue might end up breaking Aurelia's heart. (978-1-63555-484-7)

The Other Women by Erin Zak. What happens in Vegas should stay in Vegas, but what do you do when the love you find in Vegas changes your life forever? (978-1-63555-741-1)

The Sea Within by Missouri Vaun. Time is running out for Dr. Elle Graham to convince Captain Jackson Drake that the only thing that can save future Earth resides in the past, and rescue her broken heart in the process. (978-1-63555-568-4)

To Sleep With Reindeer Justine Saracen. In Norway under Nazi occupation, Marrit, an Indigenous woman, and Kirsten, a Norwegian resister, join forces to stop the development of an atomic weapon. (978-1-63555-735-0)

Twice Shy by Aurora Rey. Having an ex with benefits isn't all it's cracked up to be. Will Amanda Russo learn that lesson in time to take a chance on love with Quinn Sullivan? (978-1-63555-737-4)

Z-Town by Eden Darry. Forced to work together to stay alive, Meg and Lane must find the centuries-old treasure before the zombies find them first. (978-1-63555-743-5)

Bet Against Me by Fiona Riley. In the high-stakes luxury real estate market, everything has a price, and as rival Realtors Trina Lee and Kendall Yates find out, that means their hearts and souls, too. (978-1-63555-729-9)

Broken Reign by Sam Ledel. Together on an epic journey in search of a mysterious cure, a princess and a village outcast must overcome life-threatening challenges and their own prejudice if they want to survive. (978-1-63555-739-8)

Just One Taste by CJ Birch. For Lauren, it only took one taste to start trusting in love again. (978-1-63555-772-5)

Lady of Stone by Barbara Ann Wright. Sparks fly as a magical emergency forces a noble embarrassed by her ability to submit to a low-born teacher who resents everything about her. (978-1-63555-607-0)

Last Resort by Angie Williams. Katie and Rhys are about to find out what happens when you meet the girl of your dreams but you aren't looking for a happily ever after. (978-1-63555-774-9)

Longing for You by Jenny Frame. When Debrek housekeeper Katie Brekman is attacked amid a burgeoning vampire-witch war, Alexis Villiers must go against everything her clan believes in to save her. (978-1-63555-658-2)

Money Creek by Anne Laughlin. Clare Lehane is a troubled lawyer from Chicago who tries to make her way in a rural town full of secrets and deceptions. (978-1-63555-795-4)

Passion's Sweet Surrender by Ronica Black. Cam and Blake are unable to deny their passion for each other, but surrendering to love is a whole different matter. (978-1-63555-703-9)

The Holiday Detour by Jane Kolven. It will take everything going wrong to make Dana and Charlie see how right they are for each other. (978-1-63555-720-6)

CPSIA information can be obtained
at www.ICGtesting.com
Printed in the USA
BVHW032312080920
588418BV00001B/12